Praise for *A Serpentine Affair*

"This is a well written, confident novel. Tina Seskis has managed to weave together both a strong story and a web of characters, intricately related to each other, with convincing histories. The structure is ambitious, but she pulls it off – she builds up our expectation and some suspense, but we don't feel let down by the resolution. Excellent."

The Literary Consultancy

"A Serpentine Affair: 25 years of friendship, several jealous clashes, doubt, mistrust, anguish. All wrapped up in the pages of this 'must read,' 'impossible to put down' work of creative genius." *Maurice Coldicott, Northamptonshire*

"I just could not put it down! I really liked the slow build as I got to know each woman. And those men!! The delicious shivers of finding out the details about each one's past and also their perspectives on situations and each other!!! Another fun and twisted novel with interesting characters... old friends indeed!" *Denise Crawford, Missouri, US*

"Seskis weaves together the stories of these seven women skillfully. She brings her characters alive and excels at giving them deep-seated flaws and vulnerabilities. I also loved the way she touched on a number of social issues without bogging down the narrative or coming across as preachy or judgemental. Seskis proves that she is an author to look out for." ...Delhi, India

"Clever clever lady! Again, despite the fact that Seskis switches time, place, person, she still manages to hold it all together and keep me intent on finishing. It was a credible story with interesting storylines which was twisty, convoluted and intense... It actually does take a lot to surprise me – so well done!"   *musingmaddie.com*

"It was fabulous, I enjoyed it just as much as *One Step Too Far* and finished it as quickly. The author has a real knack of creating suspense, she seems to know just the right time to leave a scenario so the reader is frustrated... but in a really good way. That's the 'unputdownable' factor. Superb."
                                        Maxine Leech, Hertfordshire

"I felt great empathy with the central character and really felt I 'got' her. What I loved most of all was that although the characters could have fallen into caricature none of them did. Each had their own idiosyncrasies and unique story. A fantastic and intelligent read."   *Jennifer Johnson, Teddington*

"Tina Seskis's books are so easy to get into and I read the whole thing in a day. The author did a great job of knitting all of the strands together and keeping them intertwined and believable. There are parts of this book which are very dark and I genuinely felt for the characters affected. An enthralling read."
                                        Natalie Minto, Leeds

"It's the follow-up to the hit *One Step Too Far*, and Seskis again weaves a tale of suspense and mystery... there are many hidden dramas that happened over the years, driving invisible wedges between the characters. Intriguing." *allisonwrites.com*

"It has a lot of characters and the plot jumps from one time frame to the next. Sound confusing? It's not. Tina does a marvellous job of keeping you in the moment and making the plot easy to follow and understand. The descriptions of the area are so beautifully written that you will feel like you're right there, living with the characters. This is a must-read and a book you're not likely to forget."

Dawn Cummings, Texas, US

"A Serpentine Affair is amazingly brilliant. Tina Seskis writes with an extraordinary flair. Her descriptions are vivid and make the pages come to life. Seven people meet for their annual picnic and six leave. Aren't you wondering what happened now? Put this on your reading list..."

Mattie Piela, Massachussets, US

"Tina Seskis has a gift for creating a world full of sights, sounds and emotions with her vivid descriptions and attention to detail. She brings her characters to life, gives them deep-seated flaws, but remembers to give them their 'public persona' to hide behind. Her character dialogue is often brutally frank with dark undertones that match the turmoil each woman feels. And her ability to 'bring the ending home' with a flourish? Genius!"   *Dii at Tome Tender*

"Once this story gets going, MY does it get going. The author leaves little hints at mysteries and lies with the truths coming out later in the story. It has an intriguing effect which only makes you want to read more. Very well written and will definitely be on my list of best books of 2013!"

Debbie Krenzer, Texas, US

"I really liked the way the various layers of the story untangled over the second half of the novel and how they developed in part and from different perspectives weaving across time and in various threads, it really kept me engaged in the story. An amazing book." *John Belchamber, Cambridge*

"These revelations are the sucker-punch that I remember Seskis landing on me with One Step Too Far and I couldn't help but think 'Damn! Tina's got me again.' Overall, I loved A Serpentine Affair. It's about friendships, relationships, guilt, forgiveness, and redemption. What I've learned is to get what needs to be said out of the way in order to move on. There's not always that chance to make it right in the future." *Patrice Hoffman, Illinois, US*

"You need to keep your wits about you when reading this book... it is the way the author has put the plot together and revealed it a little at a time that makes for a story that you HAVE to get to the end of to see how it all pans out. As always this author's excellent use of the English language clearly paints each scene."

Christopher French, Tauranga, New Zealand

"The author effortlessly weaves together seven separate lives, creating a powerful web of deceits, lies, and misdeeds. The descriptive writing was incredible – done in vivid detail – and the last chapter (which I loved) leaves you with a crescendo of suspense." *Wanda Beaver, Philadelphia, US*

Tina Seskis

Tina Seskis grew up in Hampshire and after graduating from Bath University spent over 20 years working in marketing and advertising. She is the author of two novels, *A Serpentine Affair* and *One Step Too Far*. She lives in North London with her husband and son, and is part of a group of seven best friends from university who do still like each other.

Also by Tina Seskis

One Step Too Far

Collision
(DUE FOR RELEASE 2014)

A Serpentine Affair

Tina Seskis

KIRK PAROLLES
LONDON

First published in Great Britain in 2013 by Kirk Parolles.

A CIP catalogue for this book
is available from the British Library.

ISBN 978 0 9575443 7 6

Typeset by Ellipsis Digital Limited, Glasgow

Printed and bound in Great Britain by
Clays Ltd, St Ives plc

Kirk Parolles' policy is to use papers that are
natural, renewable and recyclable products made from wood
grown in sustainable forests. The logging and manufacturing
processes are expected to conform to the environmental
regulations of the country of origin.

www.kirkparolles.com

For Alex, Annabelle, Brigette, Jackie, Lisa and Rachel

Part One

1

Fulham, West London

The evening was set to be balmy, perfect for a picnic, even one destined to end in disaster. Light was dappling in the sloping back garden, enormous for London, and it had rarely looked so lovely. A glass of white wine stood gleaming on the window-ledge, chasing shadows across its surface. A squirrel hot-footed it across the lawn.

Juliette stood at her beautiful white sink looking out the window fuming, ignoring the too-loud sounds of children misbehaving. Her husband had just called, and he would be home late again, although he'd *promised* he'd be back by six. He knew she was going out with her friends, and she really didn't want to be late for a change. Her children were sat at the table behind her, throwing their food around like hand grenades, and she just didn't have the energy to stop them anymore. She'd been effectively a single mother (apart from the nanny of course) for the entire week, as usual, and she was tired of it now. She trusted Stephen, there were no problems on that front, he was way too obsessed with his job to have time for affairs, but she was thoroughly sick of taking place to his career. He was only editor of a newspaper, e always used to remind him when they still had that kind of relationship (you know, the one where people talk, really properly talk). No-one died, she'd joke, but then he would remind her that people did, that the stories he told could wreck or make a life, depending on his whim (or perhaps savagery, she'd thought) at the time. She often wondered how she could have married such a man – maybe it was because she'd met him when they were both students at university, before she'd had time to grow into who she wanted to be, instead of who *he* wanted her to be. He'd been behind her at the queue for the pay phones and they'd just got chatting, and she'd thought he was quite nice, but not like *that* at the time, he'd been wearing a Chelsea shirt for a start. And after that they'd said hello to each other around the campus, in that polite way where you don't really know someone, until eventually one night he'd come and chatted to her in the student bar, and they'd both known when they finally got it together that he was doing well for himself – and although he was keener than she was, before she knew it they were seeing each other *every* day. Somehow by the final year they were even living together in a shared house, and despite a brief split when he'd gone to America after they graduated (she'd put her foot down for once) when he came back he'd pursued her until she changed her mind. And when they both moved to London he'd thought they may as well get a place together, they could just about afford a studio if they both pitched in, he'd said, and somehow she found herself agreeing, and then she'd never quite got around to dumping him again. And so here they were now, married with three children and happy,

4

apparently. Juliette couldn't complain from a material point of view – the rented studio was long gone, their house was done up and beautiful, the kids were in private school, they had a place in Italy, and Stephen was making loads from having become a quasi-celebrity, appearing on late night game shows and being asked to present televised awards events. It was odd how other people always found him funnier than she ever had, they'd never shared much of a sense of humour.

Juliette kept her back to her children and thought about the evening ahead. She was meeting up with six of her oldest friends from her university days – every year they got together at some point over the summer, and although they had all been such great friends once, that was a long time ago now. Privately she thought that these occasions felt a bit forced these days, there were far too many conversational no-go zones for a start, and she still found it hard to see JoAnne especially – but she wanted to go, for Sissy mainly, although she wasn't even sure if Sissy would be happy to see her, not after what had happened. This year they were having a picnic in Hyde Park, and it wouldn't be some half-hearted affair, but a traditional picnic, with old-fashioned dishes like coronation chicken and home-made potato salad served in handmade Italian bowls on real china plates with knives and forks, no plastic rubbish. It was all too heavy to carry really, but her friend Camilla was posh and liked to do these things properly, and everyone indulged her of course. Even when they'd been students a few bought pork pies and a family bag of Twiglets would never do in Camilla's book. It was all such a lot of work, but Juliette had acquiesced as usual, she didn't want to upset Camilla. And it wasn't cold or raining for a change, so hopefully they'd all enjoy it.

Juliette turned wearily from the sink, exhausted suddenly by the thought of seeing everyone, cross again with her husband for letting her down, and as she looked across to the table she felt her back stiffen, although she did her best to contain herself.

"Noah, put that bowl down, darling." Her tone was pleasant, cajoling. Her middle son pretended not to hear her.

"Noah, I said put it down please." He lifted it off the table and, ignoring her still, took aim.

"NOAH! Will you put that bowl down NOW," she yelled, as he prepared to fling the yoghurt at his little brother, who was racing screaming out of the kitchen to avoid it.

Noah looked at Juliette and his expression was one of reciprocal hostility, a look she was becoming used to. He hesitated, went to put it down as requested, and then just as it touched the solid oak table, he changed his mind and flung it anyway.

Juliette stared into her wine glass as she counted to ten. Then she walked without speaking over to the spattered yoghurt, its garish patterns perversely making her think of the markings on some type of cow (*Friesian she thought, or was it Piebald?*), and she picked the melamine bowl out of the pink bovine-shaped mess as if it were contaminated, and took it to the sink and put it down, too calmly now. The two children still in the kitchen (Jack had escaped unmarked and hadn't reappeared) sat at the table motionless, watching their mother – the magenta violence of the incident had shocked

6

them all, and none of them was sure which way this would go. Finally she turned to Noah and said wearily, "Go to your room," before she pushed her tumble of hair behind her ears, went down on her delightful knees and got busy with the dish cloth – they'd run out of kitchen roll, and Mrs Redfern had left for the day.

2

Chelsea, West London

Camilla fiddled with a strand of her mid-length, mid-brown Alice-banded hair as she ended the call with a forced, "OK then, see you later, bye bye," and frowned at her mobile. Really, there was no need for Juliette to be so stroppy, she hardly knew her these days. She used to have the sweetest nature, but over the years seemed to have transformed into the archetypal fiery red head. Perhaps she'd just been married to Stephen for too long – or maybe she'd still not got over all that business with her mother, she seemed to get more bitter about her as the years passed somehow, instead of letting it go like she should do. We all have our crosses to bear, thought Camilla, and although she wasn't prone to self-pity she thought that hers was probably greater than most, and *she* didn't go round taking it out on everyone else.

Camilla tried so hard to keep the seven of them together, and sometimes she wondered whether she was wasting her time, whether she should finally let them all drift off their separate ways – after all just because they'd in effect saved her life once, that was over 25 years ago now, maybe the bonds simply weren't there anymore, perhaps she was kidding herself that she could recreate what they'd once had. But then she remembered the hell that Sissy was going through, and she was still worried about Juliette, despite her occasional obnoxiousness, and poor Siobhan's life seemed to be as disastrous as ever, and she thought, no, they did all still need each other, and besides, it would be lovely to see everyone. She always had been an optimist.

Camilla put down her mobile and checked the oven – she pulled out the wire rack and admired the way the frangipani had risen around each individual raspberry, cushioning each one like a precious jewel. She pushed her finger gently into the torte, and the sponge sank under the pressure. Never mind – five more minutes, she thought, and it will hardly notice. She closed the oven door and picked up her phone again, tried to call Natasha to confirm that she was definitely making a tabouli as well as a potato salad, but Natasha didn't pick up, so instead she sent a group text to everyone, saying how much she was looking forward to the evening and reminding them all to bring chairs.

3

Soho, Central London

Siobhan stared at the brown smear down the left thigh of her coral pink skinny jeans, the broken cake stand, the torn carrier bag on the ground, and felt like wailing. At least the wine hadn't broken, instead was rolling drunkenly towards the gutter, and she managed to catch it just before it dropped off the pavement into Broadwick Street. A young man in indigo jeans and a dark shirt, thin white tie arranged just so, black glossy hair swept asymmetrically across one eye, sidestepped the Tupperware as he walked past, studiously ignoring the catastrophe that had befallen her, as if stopping to help or interact with this tall slightly deranged looking woman would be bad for his image.

Shit! Why was it always when she was meeting her university friends that disaster befell her? She was a successful career woman these days: a million miles from the girl at college they'd known, the one who was always losing her keys, stealing her flatmates' food, forgetting her library card, going to the wrong lectures, mangling her washing. She'd wanted to turn up in Hyde Park looking cool, happy, confident, successful – a shining example of how you don't need marriage and kids to be a complete, fulfilled person. Her hair was long, honey-coloured, her outfit glamorous – until two minutes ago she'd been perfectly happy with how she looked. She'd even been fine with Camilla's picnic instructions, pleased with her profiteroles – they'd risen really well for a change – and now they were strewn half across the pavement and the rest were down her trousers. She wished Matt were here to help her, but he was miles away, and anyway when she'd tried to ring him earlier his phone had gone straight to voicemail, again. She remembered the last time she'd spoken to him, nearly a week before, how although she'd tried not to be, she'd been silent and sulky, and she wondered with a pang whether he'd deliberately turned his phone off, was maybe about to even dump her. She wouldn't blame him if he did – she'd been such a nightmare lately, her fixation on their future, or otherwise, utterly joy-sapping. What was wrong with her? Why did she always manage to push men away, especially the nicest ones, the ones she liked the most?

Siobhan felt even more miserable now, and wondered whether she should just ring Sissy and cancel – Sissy wouldn't give her a hard time, out of all of her friends she'd be the one to understand. She felt so inadequate turning up like this, plus she didn't really know where she was going and it would take ages to get there on the tube. She wanted to go home, get into her pyjamas and watch something slushy on the telly that she could have a good cry to, that always helped. Work had been so stressful today – although she was pleased she'd been promoted again she wondered whether she could cope with her new job, and she found the high-octane aggressiveness of her boss exhausting sometimes. Advertising sales was a tough business, no matter that anyone else said it was just talking.

In the end Siobhan bent down and rescued what profiteroles she could, which was only about half of them, thank goodness she'd made so many. The rest she kicked into the gutter. She picked up the broken pieces of the cake stand and grimaced as she threw them in the bin. She put the lid back onto the Tupperware, retrieved the wine and rammed it into the depths of her handbag, placed the box of profiteroles back in the carrier bag, and slung the fold-up stool over her shoulder. She was sure the evening would go well still, it was such lovely weather, and it would be great to see everyone – hopefully they'd all be nice to her, not tease her too much for a change, she wasn't in the mood for it today. She was also a little worried about how Juliette and JoAnne would be with each other – normally one or other of them made some excuse, but according to Camilla they were both coming this year. Siobhan checked her phone one last time – just in case Matt had called after all – and then she tottered in her cream-smeared heels towards the tube station, positioning the carrier bag carefully in front of the stain on her jeans, hoping no-one would notice.

4

Hyde Park, Central London

Sissy was the first to arrive, as usual. She had never succeeded in quite shaking off her need to be not a minute late, although she knew all the others would be definitely at least another 15 minutes: seven meant sevenish to most of them. Camilla was the only other one of the group who was normally punctual, and she had texted to say the traffic on the King's Road was even more terrible than usual.

Sissy felt anxious on her own – where should she lay out the rug, which was the nicest spot, which way was the sun going? It was odd how much she worried about it, as if it really mattered, but she didn't want to upset anyone, particularly Siobhan – she was the one who got het up about these things, none of the others were that bothered, not even Camilla (as long as there was a tablecloth), and Sissy *hated* it when Siobhan had a strop. Siobhan was one of those people who could turn the whole tone of a social situation, depending on her mood, on whether she'd had a bad day at work or had just split up with someone. Sissy knew some of the others found Siobhan more than a little tiresome these days, and Sissy had to admit she seemed to be getting worse as she got older – but she had a heart of gold, Sissy was certain of that. It was just a shame the others couldn't see it: a couple of them seemed to treat Siobhan almost with contempt now, which she definitely did not deserve. After all, it was Siobhan out of all of them who'd been there for her when Nigel had died, unlike some of the others Sissy could mention, and she had completely stepped in to help Sissy cope, a widow at not much past 40, with a new house to do up and two little children still in primary school.

Sissy looked at the grey granite circuit that had been designed to be smooth, water-worn, but if you looked closely had had little crinkle-cut gouges added as a safety afterthought, and as she watched the gushing water she felt sure that Diana would have preferred it all to be a bit prettier, more playful somehow. Sissy admired the sentiment of the memorial, thought it was nearly right, but it lacked something visually, maybe some flower borders to soften the stark of the grey next to the plain green grass. It all seemed a bit industrial to Sissy – she could see why the early comments had been that it looked like some kind of drainage system. Sissy wondered how the artist must have felt, to take that much criticism over something so personal, something she had created; and then what about when that child had fallen and banged her head, and everyone was up in arms about the fountain's suitability as a children's playground, and they had even closed it for a while, and when they reopened it they'd installed No Fun patrols to stop children walking in the water, it was quite ridiculous really. *Let the parents take responsibility for their children, that's their job, life is full of risk after all.* And then that thought made Sissy think about Nigel and she almost felt like crying here on her own with her stupid picnic that she'd humped all the way from Balham, and she thought maybe she should get up and leave right now – she wasn't sure she could cope with any drama tonight, the unspoken rivalries and resentments that had built up over the years. Why didn't people say what they meant anymore? Sissy often wondered why she got so upset about things, she should try to think less, be like other people who never seemed to notice if there was tension in the air, or care how anyone else was, not how they really were anyway.

In the end Sissy made her decision on where to sit, she couldn't stand there dithering for ever, and she plumped for an area on the south-east side of the fountain, where the water ran belligerently, with no thought for tiny unstable children, fast and relentless and cold. She could always move again if the others weren't happy, and here she could keep a watch on whether they were coming – she thought they were most likely to approach along the path that ran next to The Serpentine from the bridge. She spread out her picnic rug, a wedding present from her Auntie Shirley, made of tartan Scottish wool with a waterproof backing, which despite being years old was still good as new. You couldn't beat quality, it was always worth paying the extra, she thought absently as she shook it out and the year-old creases smoothed away as if the evening sunshine had ironed it. And that thought made her sad again, made her think of her poor dead husband, and she really definitely wanted to go home now, there was a group of young tourists – students probably – looking at her, she was sure they were, alone with her blue and green rug and pathetic pasta salad, and she felt conscious of her short sensible haircut and floral summer dress that really wasn't her, made her look mumsy, out of place somehow, and her eyes pricked and swam, she just couldn't help herself. Why was it *still* happening, when would she ever get better?

As she was fishing in her handbag for a tissue (amongst half open make-up, old receipts, a hairy brush, her purse full of nothing but coppers, a battered copy of Zola's Debacle, her mobile phone, a hair pin that went up her nail and shot a pain straight to her heart) she heard somebody call her name and she startled, wiped quickly at her eyes. It was her friend JoAnne, approaching from the northern gate, and she was looking tanned and gorgeous and Sissy felt that familiar pang of envy that had never quite gone away, not since they'd been 21 and had travelled round the Greek Islands together and Sissy may as well have been invisible on that trip. She couldn't help having a tiny, buried feeling of triumph when in their final year Nigel had asked her, Sissy, out although JoAnne was convinced that he was always calling around and staying for *ages* because he fancied her. JoAnne would never have been interested in someone like Nigel of course, but she adored the power she wielded over men, and Sissy hadn't had the heart to disavow her, tell her it hadn't worked on this one.

"Hi darling, knew you'd be here first," said JoAnne, dropping down beside her and crossing her legs, the skirt of her khaki shirt-dress bunched between her thighs, just the right side of decent. A tiny skull tattoo was inked inside her ankle. "Where are the others?"

"Late as usual," Sissy smiled, the threat of tears receding

now. It was always good to see JoAnne, although she could be infuriating at times.

"Love the rug," said JoAnne. "Very *Five go mad in Dorset*."

"Wedding present," said Sissy.

"Oh. Sorry, Siss," said JoAnne. She changed the subject as she opened a bottle of Prosecco. "Is Katie coming? Has her Neanderthal husband let her out for a change?"

"Apparently so," said Sissy with a half-smile. "But please *promise* not to slag him off in front of everyone, you know how upset Katie gets. She's the only one who's allowed to be rude about him." She stopped and looked guilty, remembering herself.

"Yeah, and isn't she?" said JoAnne, mildly. "And then when everyone agrees with her she gets all annoyed. Silly bitch."

"Ssshh," said Sissy, looking around nervously, as though the students ten feet from them knew Katie, or even worse Darren, her husband.

"Don't worry, Siss, he's not behind that bush. Or – hang on, maybe he is! He's so paranoid I wouldn't put it past him to spy on her."

"Don't be mean," said Sissy. "He's OK really." Sissy nearly always tried to see the good in people.

"I'm only joking," said JoAnne blithely. "You really need to lighten up sometimes." She grinned and shoved a glass of sparkling wine into Sissy's hand. "Cheers, darling."

Sissy put down the glass carefully, untouched, and as she looked up she saw Juliette and Katie walking – no not walking, *staggering* – along the path, holding one handle each of a colossal picnic basket, she had never seen one so big, and although Juliette had a couple of those fold-up chairs slung across her back, her posture still managed to be graceful, like a dancer's. She's still so beautiful, thought Sissy, is she ever going to look older?

"Hi both, sorry we're late," called Juliette across the fountain, plonking her half of the basket down with a dangerous-sounding clank and readjusting the canvas chairs that had slipped off her shoulder.

Sissy went to help, trying her best to be normal with Juliette, to not recoil as she was hugged by her friend – after all *Juliette* wasn't to blame for anything. By the time they'd carted everything over to Sissy's chosen spot JoAnne was lying down on her own rug (which was blood-red and satiny, more porn film than picnic), dark hair fanning out like a dried-up stain, legs bent into perfect flesh triangles, silky knickers shamelessly on show – and instead of sitting up she just smiled and vaguely waved hello, and Sissy wasn't sure whether it was deliberate rudeness or JoAnne being typically louche. Juliette seemed equally awkward, and Sissy wondered if something new had happened for them to fall out over – they usually made a bit more of an effort to pretend to get along – or whether it was just the same old feud that had been going on for years. Sissy put down the chairs and sat back on her rug, twisting her wedding ring, wishing she could go home, to Nigel – and then she remembered all over again that he was dead.

"Thanks, Sissy. My God, getting here was a nightmare," said Juliette. "First Stephen was late home, and then our taxi didn't turn up, so we had to call some dodgy minicab and it stank of car freshener. Thought it was going to contaminate the picnic, ha ha." Juliette kicked off her silver sequinned flip-flops and sank onto Sissy's rug, her back to JoAnne, her extraordinary hair glowing in the amber sunshine. "Is that Prosecco? Pour me a glass will you, Sissy, I'm gasping."

There were only a few people left at the fountain now, it was getting late: one other picnicking group who were drinking wine from white plastic cups and eating out of carrier bags; a couple, tourists surely, with backpacks and zip off shorts and matching sensible walking sandals, those velcro ones, who were sat on the wall eating supermarket sandwiches; a family of noisy, very wet children (the mother had wrung out her little boy's shorts and was attempting to put them back on him again); and a lone man in a business suit who was dangling his bare feet in the fountain and reading a book on the Franco Prussian War. He had a gently unremarkable face, familiar somehow, but he looked melancholy, Sissy thought, and she wondered why he wasn't on his way home – he didn't look the type to take off his socks in public, or to read history books for that matter.

Sissy, Katie and Juliette sat down and chatted happily enough about their children as JoAnne continued to lie insouciantly on her back, her eyes closed, catching the last of the summer sun. It was only when they heard a screeching noise that even JoAnne sat up to see what the fuss was. It was Siobhan of course, stumbling through the gate, with what appeared to be a folding chair over her shoulder and a wrecked-looking carrier bag in her hand. The bag's handle had broken, and she seemed to have made another hole in the plastic, cutting off the blood and making her wrist look angry. Sissy noticed she was wearing heels that were far too high for her, as usual, and her skinny jeans had a dark stain down the left thigh, maybe she'd spilled her coffee earlier.

"Oh, there you are!" she squealed, too loudly, so everyone in the fountain's enclosure turned to look at her, everyone except the businessman who carried on reading his book determinedly. "I couldn't bloody find this place, I thought you said it was by the Serpentine Gallery, Sissy!" Her tone was accusing, but Sissy didn't rise to it, was just as polite as ever.

"Sorry Siobhan, I'm sure I said it was by the Serpentine *cafe,* near the Lido, but maybe I got it wrong. How are you?"

"Hot. Fed up. Dropped my profiteroles, had a row with my boss, he's such an arsehole sometimes. Anyway, whose idea was it to meet here, it's a bloody nightmare to get to on public transport."

The others sighed inside themselves. *Here we go,* thought Sissy with dread, as she continued helping Juliette sort out the food. No-one bothered correcting Siobhan, that in fact it had been her suggestion to have the picnic here – Siobhan was one of those people who managed to fit history to suit her version of the truth.

Siobhan plonked her things down and looked around. "Don't you think over there's better?" she said. "It's a bit higher up, so it's got a nicer view of the river."

JoAnne gave Sissy a distinctly unsubtle *told you so* look, and Sissy looked down, embarrassed, but she needn't have worried, Siobhan seemed oblivious. They were about to start packing up, to move to where Siobhan suggested, when the usually demure Katie spoke.

"I think we're all right here, Siobhan. It's too much palaver to move everything now."

Siobhan stared at Katie, aghast, like maybe she had a rat around her neck, just below her perfectly bobbed hair. "But it's better over there," she said eventually, and the whine in her voice was like that of a little child.

"Yeah well, you shouldn't have been late," said Katie, in her flat Basingstoke monotone, and she sounded even more assertive now, as though her initial outburst had fired her up, given her courage. "The others will be here soon, let's just get on with it instead of fussing about nothing."

"Oh," said Siobhan, huffily. "There's no need to be rude."

"Sorry," muttered Katie, instantly contrite.

"Don't worry, we're fine here, aren't we Siobhan?" asked Sissy, and she sounded almost desperate for Siobhan to agree.

Before Siobhan had time to reply, they heard a loud, horsey "Helloooo," and as they turned they saw the final two women approaching along the path from the other direction. Natasha was thread-thin and stressed-looking, aggressively blonde, in a scarlet dress suit that was too hot for the day, too dated for the year, and she walked in her heels like she wished they were running shoes. Camilla was short, immaculately pastel, in white jeans that made her legs stumpy like iced buns, and a pink stripy shirt with the collar turned up under a string of pearls. A pale blue jumper was slung nonchalantly over her shoulders. Sissy caught JoAnne looking at them and hoped she wouldn't say anything. She was always threatening to take them both clothes shopping, but Sissy could tell already that Natasha wasn't in the mood for any dress sense jokes. Sissy wondered what was wrong; it was unlike Natasha to be miserable, or to show it anyway.

Sissy observed JoAnne continue to lie on her back (rather

than sit up, she just murmured hi and closed her eyes), and Juliette hunch into the apparent effort of unfolding the chairs (were they still not up?) instead of turning and saying hello properly, which seemed odd to Sissy, and Siobhan was looking moody still for a whole host of reasons – and as she watched them, Sissy knew with the certainty of someone primed to spot trouble these days that she had been right all along, that she shouldn't have come.

5

Bristol

The room was high-ceilinged and elegant, despite the ancient furniture, the two unmade single beds tucked away under the sash windows, the clothes horse full of damp faded washing in the corner, the Morrissey poster pinned up over the mantelpiece. It was as if the size of the room made up for the student chaos it contained, enabled it to rise above it somehow.

Juliette and JoAnne were curled up on the couch, under a blanket, watching Blind Date on the crackly portable TV. Siobhan was sitting on the floor between them, her back against the sofa, and every now and again she would roar with laughter at something one of the contestants had said, and bang her head on Juliette's knees and go, "Owww," and Juliette would ruffle her hair affectionately, as if she were a dog. Sissy was sitting bolt upright in one of the matching easy chairs, reading a book on Franco, seemingly oblivious to anything, yet every now and again giggling at one of the impersonations JoAnne would do of the presenter's accent. As the final ad break finished Natasha burst through the front door, hot and sweaty, Jane Fonda headband luridly pink, and plonked down next to Siobhan just in time for the bit where they talked about the date and Cilla would say things like, "Oh dear, no need for me to be buying me hat then, chuck," to try to add some levity into the air of mutual hatred.

Camilla bustled into the room, her face red and shiny with steam, her hair pushed back by a tortoise-shell Alice band, stripy shirtsleeves rolled up as if she meant business.

"Supper won't be long," she said.

"Thanks Mum," said Juliette, and they all laughed. "D'you need any help?"

"Well, if you could do the carrots that would be super," said Camilla.

"Sure," said Juliette. This was her favourite bit of the show, but she got to her feet anyway – she couldn't have Camilla doing everything, no matter that Camilla wouldn't have minded.

There was a knock on the internal door to the flat, and Juliette assumed it was a friend from one of the other floors, come to borrow something, or simply invite themselves in. Alison, one of the swotty physicists from downstairs, stood there staring mutely.

"Hi, Alison!" said Juliette. "Hey, what's up?" Alison heard the peals of laughter sounding from the living room. Still she didn't speak.

"Alison! Are you OK? What's happened?"

"Is Camilla all right?"

"Yes, come in, she's cooking as usual."

"Doesn't she know? Hasn't anyone phoned her?"

"Know what? We don't have a phone here."

"I take it you haven't seen the news then?" said Alison.

"No, what news?"

"Oh God, sorry, I can't say, just put the news on will you. I'm so sorry, bye." And with that she turned on her heel and walked away, as Juliette stood watching her in bewilderment.

6

East Coast of Australia

Sissy and Nigel's honeymoon in the earliest days of the 21st century was very nearly the best three and a half weeks of Sissy's life. She couldn't say she'd *enjoyed* the wedding as such – it had been lovely of course, but she'd become so stressed about all the arrangements, and then she'd hated being the centre of attention, and although everyone told her she looked beautiful she knew she didn't really, that's just what people said to the bride. Her dress was nice enough, but they'd done her hair like Princess Anne's and her face had looked garish, as if she'd been crayoned – she knew she should have trusted her instincts and done it herself – and she didn't need to wait to see the photos to know she looked terrible. The food had been OK and the speeches hadn't been *too* humiliating, but no-one had danced much – Sissy was worried that the space had been too big, the lighting too bright, to tempt anyone but the aunts and uncles out – and she'd found herself stressing, convinced people weren't enjoying themselves, wishing the evening would just hurry up and end. It had been a relief to collapse into bed, all thoughts of consummation abandoned;

they'd been together for years anyway so it didn't matter, not really.

It was only once they'd arrived in Australia that she'd begun to finally relax. They spent a week in a fancy hotel on Magnetic Island, where they had their own private terrace, complete with hot tub and smart wooden loungers, and sweeping sea views the colour of swimming pools, and where on the beach thirty yards away the sand was soft under their feet and coconuts fell like gifts from a more benevolent universe. And after that they took a trip in a Winnebago up the coast all the way to Cape Tribulation in the far north, not knowing where they would stay that night or what each day would bring. Sissy had adored it, even more than the luxury of the resort. Nigel made her feel safe, as though she didn't have to worry about everyone and everything for a change, and they found deserted postcard beaches where they set up camp and built fires and cooked fish they'd caught themselves, and she hadn't realised life could be so magical. She found herself falling ever more in love with her new husband, delighting that he was such a decent person, so optimistic about life, so practical and manly, so much fun, almost handsome with a tan, but mostly that he had chosen *her*. It was all too perfect.

So when on the third to last day Nigel told her over breakfast that he was worried about a mole on his left leg, just above the knee, it had seemed to really grow and darken while they'd been away, Sissy hadn't catastrophised like she normally did (especially after what had happened to poor Camilla while they were still at Bristol), and instead she'd felt sunny and positive and had reassured Nigel that it would all be fine. They agreed to get it checked out in Cairns though, just to be on the safe side, just so it wouldn't spoil their stopover in Hong Kong. So Nigel found a doctor, and when she'd taken one look at the mole and sent him straight to the hospital, that's when the river of dread had started flowing inside Sissy again, the one that had never quite stopped since, not since that sunny afternoon long ago, on the other side of the world.

7

Bristol

Camilla's father had the kind of fall from grace that had the Sunday tabloids whooping for joy, their reporters out sniffing round the corpse like a hyena waiting for the lion to clear off. His story had all the right ingredients for a front page splash – the oh-so-respectable peer, the dutiful wife, his droning sermons on public morals during the latest election campaign, the giant baby costume (with pictures), proof of his particular penchant for being spanked with a hairbrush for bad behaviour: too much crying, an inability to self-soothe etcetera. For anyone it would be horrific, but for Camilla, in her second year at university and a definite celebrity around campus due to her famously influential father, it was intolerable.

Camilla hid away in her room for days and days and refused to come out. She lay under her duvet and sobbed for most of the time, only getting up to shuffle across the hallway to the bathroom when she absolutely had to. And even then she would wrap the duvet around herself, as if it were a dressing gown, and it seemed it was her only protection from the world that before this had seemed rosy, benevolent, and now was rancid, impossible to navigate, the humiliation was just too great. She couldn't even go home, the press were camped outside, and anyway how could she face this man who until now she'd adored and revered, and her poor dutiful mother who must be dying from shame herself.

In the end it was Juliette who organised a weekend away in her friend Katie's uncle's cottage in Somerset, and they all went, and no-one remotely knew who Camilla was down there, and they took long walks and drank tea and ate chocolate, and being able to breathe the fresh, unsullied air and avoid the newspapers and the looks was a relief to Camilla, and when she got back to Bristol there was a letter from her father begging her forgiveness and it was so open and heartfelt she was tempted, which was just as well as the next day he was found dead, hanged in one of the trees he'd planted himself, in the thickening wood on their vast estate.

"Camilla? It's me, Tash."

"Oh. Hallo."

"I'm sorry to keep ringing, but I've left you so many messages."

"I know, I'm so sorry I haven't called back."

"Och, don't apologise. How are you just now?"

"Oh, you know..." Camilla trailed off.

"Look, I know this is terrible for you, but we want you to know we're all here for you. Did you get our card?"

"Yes, I... I've been meaning to reply."

"Don't be soft, we don't expect a reply... Anyway, we thought we may come and see you soon."

"Who?"

"All of us."

"Oh, Natasha, I don't think so."

"Aye, Camilla. We'll get a takeaway and watch a video or something. You just need a wee bit of normality. Please don't say no... Your mother thinks it's a good idea."

"You've been talking to Mummy?"

"Well, I've been trying to talk to *you* for the last three weeks, ever since the funeral, and in the end she picked up the phone, and she recognised my voice from the answerphone." Natasha sounded sheepish. She never had been one to take no for an answer.

Camilla didn't know what to say. She was touched that her friend had been so persistent. She hadn't known what to make of Natasha when they'd been put together as roommates – they were so totally different, from different worlds in fact. Natasha was from Glasgow and had an accent so thick that Camilla had struggled at first to understand it, and she'd had bright blonde, spiky hair that she'd never worn any different since, and she'd been madly into hockey and running and Prince's Purple Rain, playing it all the time, and she never seemed to have time to eat anything except Cup a Soups and Pot Noodles. Camilla on the other hand had brought her own slow cooker and prepared her evening meals before breakfast, and had an impressive array of stripy shirts and cashmere jumpers, even then. They were the odd couple of the kitchen group, but the strange thing was that in those days Natasha was so ballsy and ambitious that she didn't see Camilla's utter poshness as any kind of threat, just an opportunity to better herself. Camilla had found her guilelessness refreshing.

"So?" asked Natasha. "Can we come?"

"When?"

"Next weekend?" The question was assumptive.

"Can I call you back, Tash? I don't mean to be unfriendly, but..."

"I understand," said Natasha, and she found her voice was trembling suddenly. "But if you're coming back next year you need to see us all sooner or later."

"I – I haven't even thought that far ahead," said Camilla.

"No, but we have," said Natasha. "You can't let this ruin your life, Camilla."

"It already has." She said it softly, without self-pity.

"No, it hasn't," said Natasha. "You've got us, we're going to get you through this. We'll see you soon, bye," and she put down the phone.

8

Hyde Park

By 7.30 the picnic had been set up to Camilla's liking, who
had taken charge of the food as usual (fussing around like they
were at sodding Glyndebourne or something in JoAnne's
opinion), and even Siobhan seemed to be happier, having
actually shut up after little Katie's outburst. It turned out that
one of the folding chairs was a table so the food had been set
out on that, but no-one sat at it as there weren't enough seats
for everyone, which Camilla was privately cross about, she'd
specifically told them all to bring their own. Someone had
brought a miniature stereo and when Juliette put on Michael
Buble Siobhan said she adored his voice, so that kept her
happy, which was a relief to everyone.

The picnic was eclectic, despite Camilla's best efforts,
despite having created a pair of quite magnificent dishes
herself (fresh salmon and dill salad with rosti potatoes and
soured cream, a raspberry torte) and Sissy having made a
passable job of her pasta salad, but Natasha had come straight
from work and had cheated and spent a fortune at M&S,
which wasn't at all like her – she'd long since graduated from

Pot Noodles and would normally be up until midnight the evening before, she fancied herself as Superwoman these days. JoAnne stayed true to form and had brought nothing except three bottles of Prosecco and some crisps (she was the only one who could get away with it) and Siobhan had brought what was left of the profiteroles after her carrier bag had snapped under the weight of everything. They looked quite revolting now but no-one dared decline one, even though they were squashed and the chocolate had half-melted and the cream was thick and yellow – Siobhan didn't have a fridge at work and it had been a particularly hot day.

Katie had brought shop-bought sausage rolls and scotch eggs which Camilla just about managed not to comment on, despite Katie having ignored her explicit instructions to make a quiche. (Katie hadn't been part of the original group, hadn't been to university, so she hadn't realised quite how serious Camilla was being when she had called her re "the arrangements" – the kids had been fighting and Darren had been transfixed by the cricket so she'd had to dash off the phone to stop the children killing each other. By the time both kids were screaming and Darren had told her to fuck off out the way of the telly she had quite forgotten what Camilla had said, apart from that they were meeting at the Diana fountain at seven.)

The sun was sinking gently, and it left behind one of those rare English summer's evenings that were unmatched in the world. The atmosphere between the women was more jovial now, thank goodness, and when Camilla announced that the food was ready, even JoAnne sat up obediently. She poured herself another glass of Prosecco and grabbed a handful of crisps straight from the packet. Her eyes were shiny.

"How's Stephen, Juliette?" she asked airily, and Juliette still found herself bristling, even after all this time.

"He's fine, thanks," she replied. She paused. "How are you? Are you seeing anyone at the moment?"

JoAnne laughed. "Just the same old thing with Ed," she said. "He won't leave his wife, I don't want him to anyway, and we have increasingly mediocre sex the longer it goes on."

Juliette looked disapproving, although about exactly what no-one was sure, it could have been any number of things.

"Why don't you ditch him and go out with someone nice, Jo?" asked Camilla. "You might even like it."

"Well, it's not that easy," said JoAnne. "Ever since I hit 35, *I've* still thought I'm as gorgeous as ever of course, but the blokes I meet seem to think I'm desperate to go curtain shopping and get married and have babies, and a couple of them have even had the total cheek to dump me. So I'm quite happy with the occasional night with someone else's husband for the time being."

"Well, what about his wife, don't you think about her?" asked Natasha, and her tone was surprisingly stern, she didn't normally show it when she was riled. She had taken off her shoes to reveal nails that were painted glossy geranium pink, incongruous against her runner's bunions – like a plain girl in a prom dress, JoAnne thought bitchily. She looked coolly at Natasha.

"I think it's more for him to think about his own wife, don't you?" JoAnne said, as she topped up her glass again so it overflowed and the bubbles chaosed down the sides like slalom skiers, before lifting the bottle jauntily and saying, "More Prosecco anyone?"

9

Nashville, Tennessee

JoAnne dyed her fringe pink and flew to Nashville just six days after her graduation ceremony. She was apprehensive – she'd never been to America before, wasn't sure it would be her kind of place – but one of her best friends from home had managed to recruit her into his door to door bookselling team. Andy was taking a group of 15 students with him, mainly university friends from Cardiff, and he was hoping to make an absolute fortune – it seemed he was operating some kind of pyramid sales model that meant the more people he took, the more money he'd make. He'd done it the previous year too, and had come back bragging about how he'd made forty thousand dollars in less than three months, how it was so easy, how people had loved his accent, how complete strangers couldn't wait to let him into their homes, buy his books, serve him iced tea, even feed him lunch most days. JoAnne wasn't daft. She knew Andy was romanticising his experience, that selling encyclopaedias door to door must be way harder than that, but she didn't know what else to do now she'd graduated – she hadn't even thought about getting a job yet, she had no money for a holiday, and she couldn't face the prospect of going home to live with her father, in his big empty house near Clacton that was as good as falling down and looked as tired and unloved as he did. She had shuddered at the thought of the summer at home: silent meals on grimy trays in front of endless repeats of Morse and Frost, the atmosphere shot with dark resentments that were better left unsaid.

So when Andy had offered to lend her the money for the flight (he was that keen to have her on his team, sure that with her looks and wit she'd be brilliant at it) JoAnne had thought *why not,* it was something to keep her busy while she thought about what to do with the rest of her life, plus it would help pay off some of her debts.

What had surprised JoAnne was that it was Sissy of all people who first decided to come too. She never thought Sissy had it in her, or that she could bear to be parted from her lovesick boyfriend for ten minutes, let alone ten weeks. But Nigel was off to stay with his uncle in Sydney, had planned it months ago, before Sissy and he were even going out, and then he was going backpacking all the way up the East Coast of Australia with his cousin – and even though Nigel had asked her to come too, Sissy had said it wasn't fair on Brett, that it really wouldn't work with the three of them.

It was only when her best friend Juliette had finally caved in and said she'd come bookselling too (although secretly no-one had known how she'd cope) that JoAnne had felt better about going. What she hadn't been so happy about was Juliette's boyfriend Stephen deciding to tag along – although he always seemed nice enough there was something about him that JoAnne had never been sure of, and besides, he would only monopolise Juliette as usual. Andy didn't mind though – after all, it would mean more commission for him.

JoAnne had been irritated enough about Stephen, but it was made even worse when Juliette landed herself a fantastic job on the milk round and decided she wouldn't come after all. She was really sorry, she told JoAnne, but she didn't know that she'd be remotely any good at traipsing round knocking on strangers' doors trying to sell them encyclopaedias, and now she had a job and the promise of money to come, she could afford to go and chill out on a Spanish beach with her old school friend Katie. JoAnne forgave Juliette, knowing the real reason, although Juliette didn't explicitly tell her of course, she didn't want to be disloyal. But privately Juliette reasoned with Stephen that if they were going to end up together, like he wanted, the whole thing stood way more chance if they'd both had some time to date other people first. Stephen had been devastated, he wasn't used to being dumped, but for a change Juliette refused to be swayed – she said he could do what he liked, but she was going to consider herself a free agent. She had only just turned 22, she told him, she'd only ever had one proper boyfriend before him, and that just wasn't enough for a lifetime.

And so that's how it happened that the unlikely trio of JoAnne, Sissy and Stephen were squashed together on a United plane from London to New York one drizzly midsummer's morning. From there they would catch another flight to Nashville, where they would meet up with Andy and his friends from Cardiff. JoAnne had been in a foul mood from the moment she'd arrived at Heathrow, and when they boarded the plane she insisted on sitting by the window, even though that was actually Sissy's allocated seat, but she didn't want to have to sit next to Stephen – his rugby playing thighs were so broad he was bound to encroach into her space and she just couldn't bear that. Sissy sat in the middle, tense and irritating, fussing about ridiculously improbable potential catastrophes: insisting on picking up the peanuts she'd dropped down the side of the seat in case the cleaner didn't find them and the next person had a child who choked on one; wanting to know exactly where her lifejacket was, just in case; making sure her bag was lodged tight into the overhead locker so it couldn't possibly fall out and injure someone. Sissy was always so anxious about everything, so opposite in nature to JoAnne that JoAnne sometimes wondered how they were friends at all. But the thing about Sissy was how loyal she was, and reliable, and just an all-round good person, and JoAnne had recognised that quality in her from the day they had been put together in a shared room on campus. Sissy filled a need in JoAnne, a chronic need to be looked after that JoAnne did her best to hide but was there if you looked close enough, stamped forever on her little crumpled four year old face on the day her daddy had told her, as kindly as a man raging with resentment can, that her mummy had left and wouldn't be coming home.

Stephen sat in the aisle on the other side of Sissy, and to be fair to him, he just put on his headphones and JoAnne could forget for a while that he was there. She had never been quite sure what Juliette had seen in him – with those eyes and that hair she was so gorgeous-looking she could do infinitely better, but Stephen was one of those powerful types who always seemed to get his own way. He had set his sights on Juliette, had even admitted to her months later that he would watch for hours out of his window for her to leave her halls of residence, and as soon as he spotted her crossing the car park he would dash from his own room, and run all the way round the back of the buildings to the other side of campus, so that just as Juliette was making her way down the main precinct, he could be sauntering casually in the other direction – and he would be sure to stop her and say hi and get her chatting, until she really felt like she was getting to know him, like he was almost becoming a friend. When Juliette had confided this to JoAnne, not sure whether to be flattered or freaked out, JoAnne hadn't known whether to be admiring or scathing of Stephen's efforts either. One thing she had been sure of though, even then, was that Stephen was ruthless – he would go to limits beyond what other people would to get what he wanted. He was OK-looking maybe, and certainly he could be charming, but there was something about him that she didn't trust, and sometimes she worried about her friend Juliette, about how she may well even end up with him if she wasn't careful – and if so whether he would quash her eventually, she was infinitely more sensitive than people took her for. JoAnne sighed and put her headphones on and shut her heavily-kohled eyes, willing her mind to concentrate on the throaty thrum of the aeroplane's engine, as it headed relentlessly over the never-ending ocean below.

JoAnne found Nashville freaky. It felt alien, larger than life, especially through the prism of jet lag. She was shattered – they had endured two flights, been treated like criminals at immigration, taken a bus to the hotel to dump their bags, and then headed straight downtown to meet up with Andy and the others in a country music bar. For JoAnne it was like stepping back thirty years, back into the movies that she'd watched with her dad as a kid, into a world where people still wore cowboy hats and the men were butch and rugged-looking, and the women's boots were white and studded and their hair was golden and flowing under their Stetsons. The bar was warm and glowing, all tangerine lights and orange wood, with walls plastered with publicity shots of handsome men with fantastic names like Chesney or Kenny or Bud.

JoAnne felt weird, aloof from life, as they drank bottles of beer and the music twanged with life-lived sadness – almost as if she wasn't there at all. She wondered how Juliette was, whether she was in Marbella yet, what the others were up to, but mostly what on earth she was doing here. Had she made a huge mistake, she wondered. She was about to suggest to Sissy that they head back to the hotel when Stephen, who seemed to have had one drink too many, leaned in from nowhere and licked her face, big-tongued and slurpy, like a dog, and she realised with revulsion that now Juliette had released him he was going to be after her and Sissy, either of them or both of them.

That was the last the booksellers ever saw of Nashville. For the rest of that week they didn't even leave the hotel, the sales training was so relentlessly knackering, and on top of the jet lag the effort required to learn how to sell encyclopaedia sets to people who hadn't known they wanted them meant they felt far too exhausted to go out again. JoAnne still felt disengaged, worried that she'd done the wrong thing coming here. Everything was alien to her, even in the hotel, although it was just a modern block next to the highway that might as well have been anywhere. She had always dreamed of travelling eastwards before, to Nepal or Goa or some remote Thai island, and she imagined those places would feel more natural, less foreign than America somehow. It was the scale, the extremity of things here that made an impression on her: the two beds in their double room that could comfortably sleep three people each; the throaty clunking of the machine down the corridor that ejected fat glinting ice cubes, tumbling like coins from a jackpotting fruit machine; the toothache temperature of the Cokes from the mini bar (she had never known drinks to be so cold); the improbable proportions of the cars on the freeway; the sleek gleefulness of the morning TV presenters with drawls so sassy they sounded put on; the enormity of the breakfasts and the people who ate them. America seemed souped-up to JoAnne, as though it had to be bigger, better, colder, hotter, cheerier, louder, just all-round "er" than everywhere else. She found she was homesick, for her student flat in Bristol, for her life before graduation, for her group of best friends, for Juliette.

The sales course was attended by hundreds of students, mainly American, eager youths with springs in their steps and dollar signs in their eyes. JoAnne sat slouchily next to Sissy, unable to concentrate, surprisingly close to tears, as a short puppyish man (hair neatly side-parted, dapper in handmade loafers and an Italian suit) bounced around the stage, drunk on life, telling his impressionable audience how after five wonderful summers he was a paper millionaire at just 24, six whole years ahead of schedule. Greed wafted through the

42

room, all-pervading, like cooking smells. JoAnne wondered what on earth poor Sissy was making of it – if she felt this bad surely it was Sissy's worst nightmare – but Sissy just seemed dazed by everything, almost as if she were trying to transport herself back to England, like if she let her eyes glaze over enough then she could pretend she wasn't here at all. Most of the other students seemed to love it though, lapping it up, cheering in all the right places, happy to chant mantras like, "I feel happy, healthy, and terrific," which made JoAnne want to throw up. She barely ate any lunch, which was unlike her.

After the motivational talks of that first morning, designed explicitly to help the students equate volumes of books sold to future life happiness, it was time to get on with the business of learning how to sell them. They were split into groups and taken through exactly what to say and precisely what to do at every minute stage of the sales process. They were expected to learn the sales script verbatim, every last word, and not deviate from it, ever, and once they had learned it they were to practise how to say it with warmth and sincerity – you know, that learned, insincere kind of sincerity. For JoAnne it was like torture.

The students were taught plenty more slogans on that interminable afternoon, ones like, "Hey there beautiful, don't you ever die," and "I'm a fighter not a quitter," which they'd need to gee themselves up with when things "got a little tough," and as JoAnne looked around at the chanting masses she began to feel like maybe she had landed in some crazy religious sect rather than onto a bookselling course. Stephen was in her group and although he'd apologised for his lecherous behaviour of the first night, and behaved like a perfect gentleman ever since, she still found him grating – this afternoon especially he seemed to be lapping everything up, appearing to love the role plays and the motivational jingles, generally being loud and annoying. Surely he couldn't really be into this stuff, JoAnne thought in disgust, surely he was just thinking of the pay cheque at the end of the summer; that was way more likely, knowing him.

For the rest of that afternoon and over the next four days the students practised religiously what they would say and how they would say it, with no word changed, no careless deviation, no single opportunity to let the customer off the hook. And the more they went over the knock, the wave, the cheery introduction, the more Sissy felt sick with nerves, and the more JoAnne wished she could have gone to Kerala instead.

Exactly a week later JoAnne stood alone on the sidewalk in an ordinary middle class suburb of southern Cleveland, Ohio, bewilderedly looking round at the houses. She'd picked a cul-de-sac to start off in, they'd told her that people were more likely to know each other in those kinds of streets, but now she was here she felt exposed standing right in the middle, as if she were being watched. The gardens were large and well tended, the expanses of grass brilliantly green, lush with life despite the mid-90's temperatures, the sprinkler systems poking up like spies. The houses were well-kept too – in fact it was all rather perfect, movie-like, and it felt like she had seen it all before somewhere, maybe she was having her very own American dream, or nightmare, she wasn't sure which. As JoAnne hesitated she felt small and frightened, not at all her usual self, like it was her first day of school perhaps, and the heat from the sun poured into her like it was trying to cook her. She kept staring at the houses, trying to decide which one to pick first, which one would be the least unwelcoming. She wondered again at what she was about to do, it seemed insane now she was here – but then she remembered her training, how they'd been told that this was all part of the process, part of embedding themselves into the local community, of becoming a loved and trusted part of it for the summer. *As if*, JoAnne thought now, why had she listened to all that crap, why the hell was she here at all?

After perhaps two minutes of pacing, where her knees felt hot and unhinged, as though she really could fall over, she picked on the friendliest-looking house, the one with a couple of kids' bikes strewn on the driveway, and she marched on wobbly bare legs up the path, through the neat front yard, and knocked firmly on the door. She stood back six feet, exactly as she'd been taught, and looked sideways down the road: the least threatening position for the door-answerer apparently, the one most likely to grant you an entry.

The knocking set off a terrible racket. What sounded like a pack of dogs started jumping at the door, barking madly. JoAnne was about to run away when she heard a voice saying, "Now just you stop that Betsy, and you too Growler," and the door was opened four inches by a harassed looking woman in a very pink dressing gown, the colour of chewed up bubble gum, as unidentifiable dogs' teeth and paws scratched through the opening.

"Hi, are those your attack dogs?" said JoAnne and her

voice squeaked, as if she were being squeezed. This was one of the stock jokes she'd been fed for exactly this kind of situation, but her delivery was terrible. JoAnne swallowed hard and continued her patter.

"Errr, my name is JoAnne and I'm all the way from England! I'm on an educational programme here in Cleveland, from the University of..."

"Sorry, I'm busy," said the woman, and shut the door.

JoAnne stood still for a moment, feeling shocked, violated almost, unsure what to do – and then she walked self-consciously back through the front yard to the sidewalk, her ears glowing red with humiliation. She hated rejection, felt it like a punch. She thought of her mother in Paris for an instant and felt sick. She had to keep going. She walked straight to the next house and knocked, firmly, three times. A little kid answered, dragging his filthy muslin behind him.

"Mommy, there's someone at the door for you."

JoAnne waited and the roof of her mouth felt claggy, as if she were eating a peanut butter sandwich. After a couple of minutes a bright, friendly-looking woman with eyes so blue they must have been fake came to the door.

"Hi! My name is JoAnne and I'm on an educational programme here in Cleveland all the way from Bristol University in England! How are you today?"

"I'm good," said the woman politely, but she seemed a little impatient now, as though she knew what was coming.

"I've just arrived in Cleveland as part of an educational programme and I'm looking for somewhere to stay for the summer! And, er... do you have a spare room that I could possibly use?" As she said it she thought she might keel over with humiliation, but the woman smiled kindly and said, "No, you know what, our spare room is used as an office, so I guess I can't help you. Good luck though, have a great summer," and as she closed the door JoAnne could hear her yell, "Joey, get back up those stairs right now and clean your teeth. We're gonna be late for preschool."

JoAnne marched determinedly to the next house, refusing to give up now she'd started this. There was no reply at that door, but at the next three the people were friendly enough although for various reasons unable to help. Finally she approached the last house in the close, the least appealing one. It was tucked back further from the street than the others, and there was a big shady tree in the front yard and the paint on the windows was peeling a little. She waited for ages and was about to leave when she heard shuffling inside and several locks being opened, and eventually a man appeared at the door. He was in his forties, overtly unfriendly, with a big droopy moustache that seemed old-fashioned somehow, and certainly didn't match the smartness of his suit.

As JoAnne went through her patter the man said nothing, just stared at her hostilely, making her nervous. "So, um, do you have a spare room that I could, um, maybe stay in...?" she finished, her voice trailing off as she saw his face.

"You what?" he yelled. "What the hell d'you think you're doing? Coming round here asking if you can move in with me? Are you crazy?"

The man's aggression, rather than diminishing JoAnne, seemed to strengthen her.

"There's no need to shout at me!" she yelled back. "I'm

47

only doing what I've been told to do. You don't have to be so rude."

"Who told you to? What are you talking about?" asked the man, and after JoAnne started rambling on about bookselling and headquarters in Nashville and how this was all part of the programme he seemed to understand, and told her she'd better come in, and he led her (quite forcibly, he was obviously angry still) by the arm into a room where the curtains were closed, and it was full of tangly plants and the only light was what seemed to reflect off the white antimacassars. One of the armchairs had a plastic protective sheet on it, and there was a strong fetid smell of cats, although she couldn't see any in the room. JoAnne was freaked out now, but she started telling the man how she'd been specifically instructed by the bookselling company to go out and knock on people's doors and ask to live for free in their spare rooms, how her friends were doing it too, they were all only doing what they'd been told – and as she spoke she felt ridiculous, as if she really had been brainwashed, she was not normally nearly so suggestible.

"Have you any idea how dangerous that is?" said the man. "How do you know whose house you're going into? Anything could happen."

JoAnne privately agreed with him – after all she was here right now with this weird-looking raging man in his dingy stinking sitting room – but she didn't know what else she was going to do tonight. She'd spent the last of her dollars on her sample books and the bus fare from Nashville, she had no money left for a hotel. Her host got up and went over to the telephone table, next to an ancient-looking TV with a silver film of dust across its screen, and he found a pen and wrote down a number on a small sheet of paper that had, "Today I have to…" printed on it, and when he handed it to her it said "Father Duncan," and there was an address.

"Please call on him," said the man. "Tell him Larry Reynolds sent you, he'll help you." He moved towards the door and JoAnne got up and followed obediently. She thanked him in the hallway, and as she moved out into the sunshine she felt like she'd had a lucky escape, like the man had just rescued her from something close to madness.

10

Sissy loitered outside in the corridor (long, sky-blue, seem-ingly endless, as though it were the route to heaven itself), looking through the small square window, steeling herself to go in. It was as if every time she saw Nigel the shock returned, but worse than before. She couldn't believe how quickly things had changed for them – one minute they'd been on honeymoon, the next they were on the plane, not stopping over in Hong Kong after all, but heading straight back to London and directly into hospital. That had been nearly seven months ago, she realised now with a jolt. Nigel had been in and out of hospital ever since, enduring huge poisonous doses of chemotherapy that seemed to be sapping his soul, making him appear like a shadow-person, a shrunken ghoul from her worst nightmares. His hair, so thick and sandy before, had fallen out almost immediately the chemo started, along with his eyelashes and eyebrows, and although she loved him still she found it hard to look at him now, or at the bottle full of sickly brown fluid that lay hanging from his bed, or at his thin frail hand that could still just about hold hers, gently, as if he were reassuring her instead of how it should be, the other way round.

At the beginning she'd had no idea that one tiny mole could be responsible for such devastation. When she'd popped into Waterstone's in her lunch hour on the first day she'd gone back to work, gone back to trying to be a normal newly-wed woman – one who's excited at the life ahead of her, instead of terrified – she had picked out a reference book to read up on his cancer (she'd known so little about it back then), and after she'd read about the symptoms and treatment for a disease called malignant melanoma she had turned the page to the outcome statistics without even thinking of the implications, of what it might say. Sissy had stared hard at the "five year survival rates," which appeared to range from 11% to 90%, and had felt faint, as though she were leaking every last breath in her body, as if air was seeping out through her pores, not just her mouth and nose. She had sat down heavily on the floor, not caring what people thought (and besides she'd keel over if she stayed standing) and had rung him there and then on his brand new mobile to ask him what grade of cancer he had.

Nigel had been evasive. "You have to tell me," she'd shrieked. "I'm your wife!" She'd had to become almost hysterical before he finally confessed over the phone to having something called a Stage 2C, and when Sissy checked in the cancer manual it informed her that a 2C gave him a 45% chance of surviving five years. Or put another way, it gave him a 55% chance of dying. Sissy had stayed slumped on the carpet in the corner of the bookshop as the statistics loomed at her wherever she looked, as if they were stamped on her eyeballs, she couldn't shake them away. Eventually a member of staff had come over to ask her if she was OK, and he had looked at the book beside her and the misery in her eyes and realised that she wasn't OK at all, in fact was far from OK, and had gone to get his manager.

Standing there now looking at Nigel through the window, as if he were an exhibit in a freak show rather than her husband, Sissy reflected on how that had been before she'd even known she was pregnant, before she'd had to contemplate life as a young widow-mother-to-be. What was the name for that, she thought idly, is there a name for that? She looked through the tiny window again, saw he was still sleeping, and then she tightened something inside herself, as if she was forcing a dripping tap to stop, pulled her face into a small smile, and entered the death fug inside the room.

Nigel didn't stir. He was on so many drugs that Sissy sometimes wondered if he knew she was even there anymore, even when he appeared to be awake, had his eyes open. Nigel hadn't responded well to his treatment, and Sissy hadn't responded well to his illness. She wasn't able to tell anyone, it was so unlike her, but she felt desperate self-pity that her life had been plunged into misery and sickness so soon after their wedding, just when they were meant to be unwrapping their presents from John Lewis and looking forward to the rest of their lives together. She'd assumed she would be better at all this, and obviously so did everyone else, but she hid it well. People even kept telling her how stoic she was being.

Sissy had never dared hope for anything amazing in her life before – she'd always been the unremarkable middle child, the plain one with no special qualities, the average student, the nice but boring friend, the girl who made up the numbers; but not to Nigel. He had made something in her sparkle, given her life, courage to be herself, live a little – and when he'd finally asked her out it had all been so phenomenally fantastic she'd felt like the most special girl in the world.

And now he was going to die on her.

What was hardest to cope with was the depth of her anger – at her husband, at the hospital, at the world. She loved him too much to let him leave her, yet she hated him too, for his selfishness, for not getting checked out earlier. He had finally admitted after the diagnosis that he'd been quietly worried about the mole for weeks, but had never quite got round to going to the doctors, there had seemed so much else to do before the wedding; and besides, he hadn't wanted to risk spoiling everything. And so in Australia when the mole had started to weep and change shape, more quickly than ever, that's when he'd known he needed to do something – and still he hadn't told Sissy the truth, had claimed he'd only just noticed it. Sissy felt overwhelmed with loathing – of her own self-pity, of Nigel for lying to her, letting her down, of her friends and family who didn't seem to know remotely what to say or how to help; but mostly she was filled with loathing of the cancer itself, the creeping malevolent death-force, those multiplying cells so devilishly smart they couldn't be outwitted.

Sissy plonked herself heavily onto the bed (hopefully that might wake him) but she was uncomfortable there: her bump was massive these days, and she was up so high she had to dangle her feet, making her ankles swell. She put her hand on his forehead, and it felt odd, lifeless. She took his hand and it lay cold and limp, like it was already dead. She waited five minutes for something to happen, but nothing did. She felt like she would go mad. She lumbered herself off the bed again and sank into the blue vinyl armchair next to it, and found she preferred it there. The table that was meant to go over the bed was next to the chair, in her way, and it was cluttered with a box of tissues, a cardboard vomit tray (unused), a plastic jug of water and half-empty plastic cup, a Tupperware container full of grapes that looked soft and over-ripe, and an untouched box of After Eight mints (she wondered briefly who'd brought them, she thought people only had them at dinner parties). She scrabbled in her bag and pulled out the review section from Saturday's Times, reading the words without taking in any of the meaning, wondering yet again whether Nigel would live long enough to see their unborn child; and as she felt the baby kick, crossly, vibrantly, she was certain it felt the misery in the room and was trying to say, "Oi, you both, cheer up, don't forget about me."

Sissy was about to stand up, go and get another wretched excuse for a coffee from the machine down the corridor, when Nigel opened his eyes and smiled weakly at her. Her heart lifted. She'd always liked his eyes, they'd been easily his best feature, but without his hair and eyelashes they looked googly, and today they were faded and watery and he looked even less alive with them open than when he'd been asleep, if that could be possible. She got up to kiss him, to show him that she loved him still, no matter how he looked, and as she did so she tripped against the leg of the swivel table, and her bump brushed against the plastic cup, and it was so flimsy it tipped over, water spilling everywhere, careering across the table and down onto the sheets.

"Oh, sorry darling," she said, furious with herself as she took a handful of tissues and dabbed it up ineffectually. Nigel tried to shift upwards in the bed to help her, and as he did so he gagged suddenly, so she grabbed the cardboard tray and got there just in time to catch the green-coloured bile that poured out of him, shocking in its vividness, its intensity, his gut the most alive part of him now.

11

Hyde Park

Sissy filled her plate with food, not any of the fancy salads but just the sausage rolls and crisps, it was all she could face somehow, and she ate without noticing what she was even putting in her mouth (she sometimes wondered if her taste buds had died along with her husband). Juliette was trying to talk to Natasha about her summer holiday plans, but Natasha seemed angry, accusatory somehow, and instead of looking at Juliette she kept picking at her bunions, which was a revolting habit she'd never grown out of. Sissy felt sad that she wouldn't be going anywhere this year, but she just couldn't cope with the thought of taking the children away on her own. She felt it was a little insensitive of Juliette of all people to talk about holidays, but on the other hand she knew that people couldn't keep pussy-footing round her, just because her husband had died, and it wasn't Juliette's fault, so she tried not to feel resentful. Sissy still made an effort to come to these get-togethers, to keep in touch with everyone, even Juliette, who'd been as good to Sissy as she could be under the circum-stances – but she preferred not to see Stephen these days. Sissy just couldn't understand why Juliette would stay with a man like him. She'd actually quite liked Stephen once, especially when they'd gone to America together – he'd seemed quite decent when she'd got to know him better, beneath the bravado – but it had all become awkward when Stephen and JoAnne got it together. Although it was true he hadn't been technically going out with Juliette at the time – after all, she'd dumped him, said she wanted to enjoy a bit of freedom – Juliette hadn't been at all happy for one of her best friends to sleep with him instead. Not that it had lasted long – JoAnne had seemed to go off Stephen as quickly as she'd got into him, which was typical JoAnne of course, but Sissy always thought it had been more than that. Maybe JoAnne couldn't bear to risk losing Juliette's friendship, no matter how much she may have liked Stephen at the time.

Sissy sat quietly watching Juliette and JoAnne, who appeared to be talking to each other for a change (Natasha had stalked off to dunk her unlovely feet in the fountain, definitely upset about something). Juliette was being cool, distant, and JoAnne, although chatty enough, barely gave her friend a glance, and their conversation was stilted, over-polite, even though they'd been best friends once. It was ridiculous after all these years – it just made these occasions awkward, agonising even. Sissy couldn't understand why they both couldn't move on, it was all such a long time ago now, and although they pretended to get along, had never actually fallen out, it was obvious they didn't like each other anymore.

The worst part though, Sissy thought, was Stephen's role in all this. Over the years he seemed to have changed, lost any kind of morality – it was quite unbelievable the things he'd do in the name of journalism – and Sissy found that if she saw his smug jowly face appear on the TV she would have to switch it straight off; she couldn't bear to let him into her house, not even electronically, not after what had happened. God knows how Juliette stayed married to him; she'd been so sweet, so down to earth once, but now she seemed tainted by him almost. Stephen acted as though he was above everyone these days, above the law even. Sissy shuddered.

When Natasha came back from the fountain at last, obviously still smarting but with a small tight smile fixed determinedly across her face, Sissy shifted her bottom to make room for her to sit down, knocking over Siobhan's wine glass as she did so.

"Ohhhh, Sissy!" said Siobhan. "That's gone all over me! Why can't you be more careful?"

"Shut up Siobhan," said JoAnne mildly. "Don't be so obnoxious. You should've been holding it, it's too wobbly on this rug."

"But my jeans are soaking," wailed Siobhan.

"Just get over it," said JoAnne, more sternly now, and although Sissy felt bad for Siobhan she was grateful to her friend for sticking up for her. "At least it's not red wine – and look at the state of them anyway." JoAnne looked accusingly at the long dark chocolate smear down the front of Siobhan's trousers.

"But that was the last of the Pinot," moaned Siobhan, trying a different tack. "I don't like the fizzy stuff."

Sissy sometimes wondered whether Siobhan was actually all there, her responses were so childlike, disproportionate, and she seemed to be getting worse as she got older, not better. She just had no idea what was going on inside Siobhan's head these days. Did she know how she came across? Could she simply not help herself? One of these days, Sissy thought, JoAnne's going to tell her to just fuck off and that will be the end of it, which might be a relief to everyone in a way.

Camilla, ever the organised one, got a tea towel from somewhere and started mopping at Siobhan's jeans, but the chocolate mixed with the wine and dispersed into an even larger mess.

"Ohhhhhh, look, it's making it worse!" said Siobhan.

"Never mind, it'll be dark soon," piped up Katie, and Sissy wondered again what had got into Katie, she rarely spoke at all if there was any kind of conflict, she was normally so timid.

"It'll still show though," said Siobhan, seemingly not getting the irony. "I've got to get the tube home, I can't afford cabs everywhere, not like *some* people." And she looked accusingly at Camilla in her pearls, but Camilla ignored her, instead just gazed out towards The Serpentine as she took a sip of her drink. Natasha changed the subject, which was unusually diplomatic for her. She seemed to have made a monumental effort to cheer up. "Hey, has anyone seen that new Daniel Craig movie everyone's going on about?" she asked.

"Yes!" said Sissy and Juliette and JoAnne at the same time.

"Amazing," said Juliette.

"Shocking," said Sissy.

Siobhan looked upset. "Have you all seen it? Did you all go together?"

"Don't be ridiculous Siobhan," said JoAnne, not unkindly. "I went with a friend from work. Why do you always have to be so bloody paranoid?"

"Sorry," muttered Siobhan, feeling relieved and foolish at the same time. She knew she was acting appallingly tonight, and although the others probably wouldn't believe it, she actually wasn't like this with her other friends or with people from work. There was something about this group, perhaps that they expected so little of her, that she played up to, behaved like the useless undergraduate they thought she was still. Siobhan was well aware she wasn't like everyone else – her life definitely seemed more accident-prone and drama-filled than the norm. But it was as if her friends from college still thought of her as a child, seemed to put her down whatever she did, pick on her really. She felt her eyes starting to prick, and she hastily shoved her sunglasses down from her head, even though the sun had gone. She felt despairing suddenly – she'd got up especially early to make those profiteroles, and she wondered now why she'd bothered.

"D'you want another drink, Siobhan?" asked Sissy. "There's another bottle of white here, you don't have to have Prosecco."

"Thanks," muttered Siobhan. She sat quietly, staring at her nails which were ragged and had chocolate in them, feeling embarrassed. She took a great slug of the drink Sissy passed to her and then put it down, more carefully this time, holding her hands in her lap now, fingers hidden.

Michael Buble rather inappropriately started singing "Feeling Good," oblivious to the tension, but after a few moments of awkwardness his mood seemed to rub off on the group and everyone started to chat easily enough again (helped by the fact they'd got through the third bottle of Prosecco already), with even Juliette giggling despite herself at one of JoAnne's dating disaster anecdotes. Sissy had finally perked up and was talking quite amiably to Camilla and Katie about potential paint colours for her living room, but how the samples never looked like they were meant to, so she'd probably end up with just plain white. JoAnne was lying down again, flashing her knickers and eating crisps, and Siobhan seemed to have seen the funny side of her profiterole catastrophe, thank God. Only Natasha still seemed fed up: after her brief burst of sociability earlier she was back at the fountain now, sat facing away from them, kicking viciously at the water.

"Is she OK?" mouthed Camilla. The others shrugged, and Siobhan looked awkward.

"Maybe she's had a bad day at work," said Juliette.

"Yes, it's so unlike her not to brag about her marvellous fucking husband and genius children," said JoAnne cheerfully.

"Shhh," said Sissy. "That's mean."

"Oh Sissy, stop spoiling my fun," she replied. "What's life if you can't take the piss out of your oldest friends? She needs to be taken down a peg or two every now and again, she's so high and mighty these days – maybe I should remind her of her origins in the Glasgow slums, she seems to have forgotten."

"That's enough, JoAnne," said Camilla. "Don't be rude."

JoAnne went to say something, but thought better of it. Instead she got up and walked over to Natasha, and to everyone's surprise sat down next to her and put an arm around her shoulder.

"What's up?" she whispered, trailing her fingers in the water, but Natasha wasn't to be placated and shrugged her off.

12

Natasha found out about her husband's affair from a text message. It was that simple. One tiny four word message with two little kisses that popped up on his screen and that she would have avoided if she could have, she somehow knew these days never to check – but as she picked up the phone, thinking it was hers, to put it in her briefcase the message just appeared there, before she'd had time to drag her eyes away, and now it was in there, the knowledge, stuck in her mind, and whatever she did she couldn't make it go away, be unknown again. She couldn't think what to do, it was all so bloody inconvenient. The strange thing was that she was more upset about *the knowledge* than about the deed itself. What was she supposed to do now? Leave him? Confront him? Hit him? They had three perfect little children together, a whoppingly expensive house that relied on both their incomes, shared friends, lives so neatly intertwined that it seemed insurmountable to think about disentangling them. The fact that they hadn't had anything other than irregularly perfunctory, obligatory, lights out sex for years was something she preferred not to have to think about, and if that meant Alistair went elsewhere for affection, well what she didn't know couldn't hurt her. She was so busy, with her job, running, the kids, she barely had time to talk to Alistair anymore, let alone feel any kind of physical passion for him, and that was OK. She'd been quite happy with the arrangement, before.

And now that text had gone and ruined it all. It's not so much what it said but who it was from. It made her fucking furious, but bizarrely at the sender rather than at her husband: her betrayal felt greater than his somehow.

Natasha hadn't wanted to confront him, not now anyway, but how could she give him back his phone without him realising she'd seen the message? It was so stupid that she'd picked up the wrong one off the wooden counter top, but they both had the same model these days, the same bloody phone everyone seemed to have – plus she'd been busy doing up her emerald green work skirt and slipping on her court shoes whilst briefing the nanny on the children's various after-school activities before leaving for her breakfast meeting at the Landmark.

Why was her life so perfect on the outside and toxic on the inside? At what point had theirs become a phantom marriage, one where she and Alistair may as well be strangers co-existing in the same house, trying not to bump into each other in the kitchen? She'd loved him so much once, where had it all gone wrong? As Natasha put on her trench coat she thought that maybe this was the time to confront it after all, maybe it was a sign; and she thought about the conversation they would have and the depressing conclusion they would reach and she felt – what? She stood in the hallway, by the front door with the bright stained glass that the sun was pushing coloured rays through, and tried to analyse it. What was the feeling? Desolation? No. Sadness? Not really. The words that came to her instead were ones like *inconvenience, upheaval, embarrassment.* Surely she should feel more than that? This was her husband after all. What was she going to do?

And then the solution came to her, how could she not have thought of it earlier? She went back into the kitchen, picked up his phone and simply pressed delete, and the message was gone, disappeared into nothing. *He would never know she'd seen it.* Now all she had to do was delete it from her memory. That wasn't so simple, but maybe she could have a wee glass of wine while she was thinking about it. She knew she shouldn't, not in the morning, but it wouldn't hurt just this once – the nanny had taken the kids upstairs to clean their teeth and she had another couple of minutes before she absolutely had to leave for her meeting. The wine was so cold it was almost frozen: someone had turned up the fridge too high, and it hit a spot in her brain that didn't quite erase the memory of the interloping message, but it helped her cope better with *the knowledge* for now, just until she decided what to do next.

13

Bookselling didn't get better for any of them. Stephen got a dog so mad with his knocking it had flung itself straight through the screen door, ripping an Alsation-sized hole in it and causing the husband to call the police. The dog's legs ended up caught in the mesh, so it couldn't actually bite Stephen thank fuck, but the wife had chased him off with a broomstick and two little kids on their bikes had laughed at him, which he'd found hardest to take.

It was Sissy who proved to be the most out of her depth though. She must have been crazy when she'd said she wanted to go bookselling – she thought now it had been because Nigel was going to Australia, and she'd been distraught at the prospect of the summer at home without him. It had felt like two losses to her – of both her university life and her boyfriend – and so she'd stupidly just followed JoAnne. She tried to give it a go but it was a disaster – she was far too shy and unpushy to even hope to succeed.

It all went wrong for Sissy on her very first day in the field. Like every Tyler's student her initial task, before trying her hand at any selling, had been to do some investigative work. She'd been trained to pick a house where it was pretty certain there were no kids: old-fashioned curtains in the windows, primly neat borders, that sort of thing. If she was lucky she'd find a lonely old lady she'd be able to get talking, as long as she was charming enough – apparently the old dear would be glad of a nice English student to chat to (just start talking about the Royal Family, she was told, and you'll have her eating out of your hand). The conversation was meant to go something like this:

"Hi, my name's Sissy and I'm on a summer educational programme here in Cleveland and I've come all the way from Bristol University in England. Great to meet you, Mrs – ?"

"Smith."

"Oh, great to meet you Mrs Smith. You may be interested to know that I'm Lady Di's second cousin."

"Gosh, are you REALLY?"

"No, I'm just joking, but I did see her at a polo game once, and gosh she's pretty in real life." (Lots of laughing.)

"You know, I'm just really looking forward to spending the summer getting to know everyone around here, it's such an exciting programme for the local children. Now, those people next door (with basketball hoop over garage), they have kids, don't they? Great, and they're the – ?"

"Joneses."

"Ah, that's right, the Joneses. And what age did you say the kids were? And the ten year old, that's a boy right? Oh, a girl, and what's her name?"

And the patter was to continue for as long as Sissy could pump sweet obliging old Mrs Smith for information, and then she was meant to say goodbye and duck into a quiet corner somewhere to draw herself a map of the street and detail everything she'd learned – who lives in which house, how many kids they have, what ages the kids are, their names, hobbies etcetera, before she forgot.

Sissy wandered up and down the street, her anxiety threatening to escalate into full-scale panic, until eventually deciding on a house that seemed to fulfil the criteria: no basketball hoop, no bikes in the front yard, grass with weeds in and slightly too long, the paint on the front door faded and dusty. She clenched her stomach – *come on*, she had to do this, she couldn't come all this way and not knock on a single door, that would be pathetic. She hoisted her bag further onto her shoulder and teetered up the path. She put the bag down, exactly where she'd been trained to put it: to the side of the front door, butted up to the house, initially invisible to the person who answered.

She rang the doorbell, but it made no noise and she wasn't sure if it had worked. She stood back six feet, looking sideways down the street, just as she'd been taught, and waited. The house seemed quiet, lonely. She rang the bell again. As she was about to give up, the door creaked a tiny bit open, and a shrivelled face poked through the crack. Separated as the face was from its body its sex was unidentifiable.

"Yes?"

"Hi! My name is Sissy and I'm here all the way from Bristol University in England and I'm –"

"Whaddaya selling?" said the face.

"Uh, um nothing," said Sissy, flustered now. "I was just wondering if there are children living next door?"

"What are you, a paedo? Mind your own business. And if you ain't selling anything, what's that bag doing there? Get outta here, or I'm calling the police." And with that he, or was it she, slammed the door.

Sissy stood quite still, shocked, unsure what to do next. As her eyes started swimming with humiliation she made her decision. She put on her sunglasses, lifted her book bag onto her shoulder and started walking, fast, as fast as she could without actually running, cutting through residential street after street, oblivious to the heat, clueless to where she was going, never looking up from the ground, never slowing, for at least half an hour. Finally she happened across a grassy park, where she sat down under the single spreading tree that seemed welcoming, almost as though it had been waiting for her, and she took out Volume One of her handy educational book set and flicked through its pages until she found something she could concentrate on, and then she proceeded to try to memorise the names of all the American presidents, in chronological order, and when that inevitably all got too much she lay down and wept, desperate for Nigel, who was somewhere up the Gold Coast, unaware of her misery, uncontactable.

In the absence of any better options Sissy ended up staying in that little park, reading, weeping, sleeping, for hours and hours, until it was time to go home.

14

Many years later Sissy sat on the veranda of the apartment in Sardinia looking out across the low oleander hedge to the bold brash blue of the sea, and the rude red of the flowers sent electricity sparks through her eyes to her brain. It was all too obscenely beautiful, too alive, too vivid for her to believe that she could possibly be here, after the monumental absences, the living death she had endured with Nigel in London. She sat back against the warm cream canvas of the double deck-chair, but the sun was too hot on her face, so she got up and shifted the seat into the shade. She sighed, wriggled her toes, adjusted the seams of her costume, and, finally comfortable, closed her eyes and let her mind meander back, not accusingly this time, but gently, kindly, to the scene in the hospital, the one after Nigel had thrown up yet again from more horrific drug treatments and she'd finally flipped out, stormed out of the room to find a nurse and demand that they call the consultant, *now*. And when Sissy wouldn't take no for an answer, hysterical at last, they had sent for the on-call doctor, who was young and didn't know Nigel at all, and when he turned up he'd just looked at the notes and said impassively that it wasn't clear why her husband wasn't responding to the treatment, it was sometimes just one of those things. But the colour of Nigel's bile, the obscenity of its hue in the face of his impending death had made Sissy insistent that there was more life in him yet, she was convinced of it. And then she'd broken down and cried her heart out that she couldn't be a widow, not now, not with her baby due in just a few weeks, what was the matter with them, why couldn't they fix him, she *loved* him for God's sake. She'd caused such a fuss that the fresh-faced doctor became anxious and paged the consultant, so eventually Mr Tatchell had arrived too and they'd all been ferried into the patient's room, and although Nigel was no longer conscious Sissy had screamed that they must be able to bloody do something. Sissy had never been so demanding in her life, hadn't known she even had it in her. Up until now she'd never asked for anything much, not even from her parents, who lived on the Welsh Borders and had thought Sissy was coping admirably through all this, so although well-meaning hadn't been down that often – and besides, her mother was always so busy with the church Sissy hadn't even thought to ask them to come more. But now, finally, Sissy had had enough, and her anger was spilling out and she didn't care who saw it, and she knew the doctors were only indulging her because they were worried that all the stress might make her waters break, and they didn't want another death on their hands.

Sissy heard a seagull shriek above her and looking up she watched it fly across the peerless sky and land, like a precious object, on a terracotta chimney and the colours were screamingly vibrant, alive. Her eyes filled with tears, perhaps from the beauty of the view, or maybe from squinting into the sun – or was it something else, the memory of those next critical moments at the hospital, full of drama and passion she hadn't known was in her, and that had changed her life irrevocably.

15

Cleveland

JoAnne had found Father Duncan's house easily enough: the streets were mostly grid-like and she had a good map. She'd originally asked Sissy to come with her, but then when they'd got there she'd changed her mind, reasoning that one helpless potential rape victim might elicit a better response. Sissy loitered out of sight around the corner, looking like an overgrown boy scout in her baggy khaki shorts and Dr Marten shoes. She really should grow her hair, JoAnne thought idly as she trudged up the street towards the house, she'd look so much better with it a bit longer. The day was hotter than ever, and there was a heat haze that seemed to hover around the houses, glinting a keep out warning, or so it seemed to JoAnne. She walked more confidently than usual though – after all Larry Reynolds had sent her, it wasn't an unsolicited call for a change; and Father Duncan was a priest, he'd be nice, would definitely help them. She knocked and without even thinking assumed the position, perpendicular to the door, friendly turn and smile ready. She heard a noise within the house and after a few seconds someone came, but as the screen door remained shut and it was dim beyond, all JoAnne could see was a faceless shadow.

"Hello," she said to the shape. "Er, is Father Duncan there?"

"Yes, who is it?"

"I'm a, uh, I'm a friend of Larry Reynolds, he says he knows him? (Silence.) Oh, are *you* Father Duncan? (Silence.) Er, it's just I'm looking for somewhere to live and he said you might be able to help me..." JoAnne trailed off awkwardly. Father Duncan carried on standing there, featureless and impassive through the screen, saying nothing.

"Are you able to open the door please?" she asked. "It's just I'm finding it hard to see you."

"I'm afraid that won't be possible," he said.

"Oh," said JoAnne. She was confused. "Well, are you able to help me find somewhere to live? Mr Reynolds said you'd be able to suggest something."

"I'm afraid that's not possible," repeated the priest. "Good luck, my child. Please excuse me," and he turned away, and as she watched his dark frame leave the hallway to enter a light-filled room she caught the straight determined set of his back, and then he disappeared from view.

16

Sardinia

Sissy must have dozed off on the flower-tinged balcony, lulled into a hot semi-hysterical sleep, reliving the horror of the supposed last days of her husband's life. It was weird how she couldn't let it go, now it was over, now that she had room to live and laugh again. It was almost as if the further away she moved from the moment, the more intense it became – now that the fug of her emotions had lifted her mind was saying to her, "Feel it, damn you," but she couldn't see the point, not now. She was confused.

Sissy shifted in the deckchair and opened her eyes, and after adjusting to the brilliance she gazed out to sea. A boat was moving across the water and from here it looked modest, small even, but she knew that up close it would be titanic, owned by some Russian oligarch who had possibly once been in jail for fraud or corruption, but now judged his position in the world by the size of his bank balance or the length of his boat, and never worried about just how he'd made his fortune. *Terrible*, she thought, *how do people like that live with themselves?* It wasn't really her cup of tea, this kind of place, full of gorgeous exquisitely turned out people who made her feel dowdy in her canvas shorts and orange Birkenstocks – acutely, obviously English – but really, she was lucky she was here at all, Juliette and Stephen had been so kind to let them come, she shouldn't criticise it. She smiled wistfully, not quite back from the past, as she watched the boat disappear behind the oleander bush, and then she leaned back against the warmth of the chair and closed her eyes, just for a little while longer.

17

Cleveland

JoAnne had a thumping headache after her visit to the priest, and it reinforced her belief that the most overtly Christian people, like her own miserable father, were quite often the least charitable in their treatment of others. Sissy was tucked around the corner waiting for her, leaning into the shadow of the last house on the street, which had a big old-fashioned verandah running the entire width of its front, on which stood a huge wooden swing seat with faded blue and white striped cushions. JoAnne would have been tempted to go and sit down if she'd been the one waiting – no-one seemed to be in, plus the temperature must have hit 100 degrees in the sun – but Sissy hadn't, of course.

"Well?" said Sissy. "How did you get on?"

"He told me to get lost," said JoAnne cheerily. (She never had been one to show emotion, it was like she thought it was a weakness.)

"You're kidding," said Sissy. "What did he say?"

"Nothing. He wouldn't even open the door. I had to talk to him through the wire screen."

"What? That's dreadful! What on earth are we going to do now?"

"I don't know. I need to get something to drink," said JoAnne. "And some paracetamol, this heat is killing me. Let's get out of here, we can't think about it like this." She took Sissy's arm, as Sissy looked like she might cry.

"Come on, let's go and get a Coke," she said. "They do free refills at Pizza Hut." Sissy nodded, and despite her legs feeling hot and useless she forced them to work, and the two friends trudged together down the sun stricken street, their feet dragging listlessly, in the direction of the mall.

Although JoAnne assumed that most Americans in the service industry were only super friendly because it was the culture to say, "Have a nice day," the young woman in the drugstore was smiley and pretty in that rare way that was definitely completely genuine. Her badge informed them that not only was she happy to help but that her name was Nancy, and she even asked them where they were from – and it was a relief to JoAnne that someone was interested in her at last, that instead of having to force herself onto others she was able to have a nice chat about what she was doing here in Cleveland, without the conversation containing a currency. Sissy stood quietly as JoAnne described – nonchalantly deadpan – the book company's despotic training regime, the group exercises in the car park straight after breakfast ("Put down the bag, knock on the door, kick the dog," and so on, complete with matching actions), the hateful mantras, whilst Nancy looked increasingly horrified. But it was when JoAnne got to the part about trying to find somewhere to live – the expectation that they'd go round knocking on people's doors begging to be taken in, her run-in with Larry Reynolds, the visit to the priest – that Nancy became outraged.

"That is just so terrible," she said. "You poor girls! So what in hell are you gonna do now? Where are you staying tonight?"

Sissy and JoAnne looked at each other. They'd been trying not to think that far ahead.

"Probably in our car," said JoAnne at last, flashing an unconvincing grin. "It's really big, with luxury velvet bench seats front and back, so it'll be quite comfortable I reckon." She tried to laugh.

Nancy looked indecisive for a moment. "Are you in a hurry?" she said. "Can you wait awhile? I think I have an idea." She walked around the shelves of drugs immediately behind the serving counter, towards the back of the store, to the area where they made up the prescriptions, and they could hear her talking quietly on the phone to someone. Sissy looked at JoAnne, but JoAnne didn't dare look back, she didn't want to get her hopes up.

When Nancy returned her eyes were sparkling. "I've just spoken to my husband," she said. "We're moving into our new house in three weeks, but you're welcome to stay in the old one with us until then, and then when we move out you can have it to yourselves for the rest of the summer."

Sissy started prattling. "Oh no, really you don't have to do that. But are you sure? Oh my goodness, that is just too kind, how can we ever thank you?" She looked like she might burst into tears, but didn't.

JoAnne, always the more practical of the two, took over.

"That sounds great," she said. "Thank you so much... but, er, how much would you want us to pay each week?"

"Nothing," said Nancy. "Nothing at all. We would be glad to help."

"But why would you do that?" asked JoAnne. "Why are you being so kind?"

Nancy laughed. "That's how these things work," she said. "I know, 'cos my little brother did a similar programme a few years back. And you two are nice, I know I can trust you. You'll have to put up with me and Michael though, and we have a dog called Vinny – just for a few weeks until we move out."

As Sissy gabbled her thanks and started on about gas and water bills, cleaning the bathroom, mowing the lawn etcetera, JoAnne felt the tightness ease from behind her ears, just a little, and although she had no idea if it was the done thing in these parts, she probably would have hugged Nancy there and then, if only the counter hadn't been in the way.

18

Hyde Park

Siobhan is really pissing me off now, thought Katie as she packaged up the remains of her sausage rolls. She couldn't understand why the others put up with her, it was as if Siobhan was a child they'd adopted at university and were all too kind to shake off now, although in Katie's opinion they indulged Siobhan so much she seemed to get worse-behaved every time she saw her. Siobhan was moaning about the fact that they'd just been asked to leave the Diana memorial, going on and on and on about how they'd have to pack everything up and that it was so inconvenient, and anyway it wouldn't be dark for ages, why couldn't they just stay where they were, what harm were they doing?

For fuck's sake, thought Katie, does she really think she's so important that if she complains for long enough they'll bend the rules just for her?

"But we're all settled here," Siobhan was droning on to the park attendant as the others packed up around her. "What difference does it make? There are people who've come all the way from Surrey for this picnic." And Katie thought the way she said the word *Surrey* she might as well have said *Mars*.

"I'm very sorry, Madam," said the attendant, a sunny-faced young man with a Scandinavian accent and a patience greater than any of the others could bear. "Those are the rules I'm afraid."

"Well they're ridiculous rules – this is meant to be a free country."

"Just leave it, Siobhan," hissed Katie, and the youth looked embarrassed, as though he didn't want to have caused this friction amongst friends, he was only trying to do his job. Katie, furious now, pulled at her rug from under Siobhan's bottom, causing her friend to topple sideways, and as she fell she knocked over another glass of Prosecco.

"Owwwww," said Siobhan. "Katie!" She sounded puzzled, hurt even. "What on earth did you do that for?"

"Sorry," muttered Katie, the violence of her outburst dissipated now. She really needed to sort out this anger thing, she was beginning to think she may have a problem with her temper. Just yesterday she had yanked, way too hard, her youngest daughter Molly's arm, hauling her screaming out the bath after she'd shot Katie with a water pistol, squirting luke-warm sudsy water into her mouth and all down the mirror behind her. It had set off fireworks where her brain was, and she hadn't fully calmed down until the children were in bed and the guilt had had time to set in. Darren's rages must be rubbing off on her, she thought, and she was sufficiently self-aware to realise that she was beginning to turn into a bully herself: a sly, vicious bully who picked on emotionally retarded adults and little children, instead of standing up to the person she ought to be fierce with. She needed to get a grip, before she ruined her kids' lives too.

Natasha and Camilla helped clear up the spillage, and when Siobhan finally stood up the back of her jeans were wet too now, and the dark brown stain on the front had crusted where it was drying. She looked a mess. She sulkily followed the others out of the fountain enclosure, muttering on about pointless bureaucracy, to a spot near the cafe, where a patch of grass was just big enough for them all.

"This is fine," said Juliette, and she gave Siobhan a "Don't you dare" look, and to her credit Siobhan said nothing, although there was only a very limited view of The Serpentine here – she seemed to have got the hint at last. As everyone started spreading out their rugs again, Sissy held hers to her chest, like a shield.

"Look, I hope no-one minds," she said. "But I'm going to head off now. I'm tired, and my throat's beginning to feel a bit sore, I think I might be coming down with something."

"Oh, don't go, Sissy," said Siobhan, and the slur in her voice was noticeable suddenly. "We hardly ever see each other these days, let's all just have a good time."

"Yes, please stay, Sissy," said JoAnne. "At least finish off Katie's sausage rolls before Camilla chucks them at her."

Everyone held their breath, it was never clear whether JoAnne was joking or not – but then she cracked a smile, and fortunately Katie either didn't mind or didn't get it, and Camilla was as gracious as ever.

"Very funny, Jo," she said. "I know I can be a trifle bossy at times, but I'm only trying to make sure we all enjoy ourselves."

"I know, and we all love you for it," said Juliette, and she seemed more relaxed suddenly. "Please stay, Sissy, I want to hear how Nell and Conor are getting on at school. Flo and Jack are fine, but poor Noah's having a nightmare."

"Sorry, Juliette," Sissy said. "I just feel so tired, I don't know what's the matter with me really." Although of course she did.

It was JoAnne in the end who persuaded Sissy to stay. She took her by the arm and led her down to the water and whispered to her that this might all be difficult at times but they hardly ever saw each other anymore, and they had a history, a shared past, which Sissy was part of – she couldn't bail out now, before the evening had even got going. Everyone seemed to be settling down now, JoAnne said, maybe they could all have a good time after all. As Sissy listened the realisation hit her that JoAnne was right, they were *friends*, they'd all been through so much together – and so she walked with JoAnne back to the group, and she lay out her tartan rug once more and sat quietly in her flowery dress, sipping her sparkling wine, looking out towards the ever-darkening water.

19

Cleveland

Nancy's house was somewhere on a long straight main road peppered with little single storey wooden houses, which from the outside looked like hillbilly shacks from the olden days. JoAnne and Sissy drove slowly, trying to work out the unfathomable numbering system. After having to turn around a couple of times, they eventually found the correct mailbox, shiny in the sunshine, at the head of a long straight drive, and hidden beyond the hedge at the end of it was a little wooden house, smarter than the others, and in the yard in front of the garage stood a gleaming pink Corvette.

"Wow," said JoAnne, who liked to think she knew something about cars. "Wow."

The front door opened and Nancy appeared, her eyes shining and her hair loose. She was younger, prettier than they remembered, out of her white uniform.

"Hi, you found it!" she said. "Come on in, it's so great to see you. Would you like some iced tea?"

JoAnne and Sissy felt awkward entering Nancy's home, knowing they were going to be staying there for the summer, but that it wasn't a hotel or even a friend's house, it was just the product of one stranger's quite extraordinary kindness. And to think that this is what thousands of students up and down this vast country were meant to be doing, JoAnne thought, it was after all "part of the programme." Were American people simply more trusting, more giving, than the British, she wondered? Surely not, weren't people ultimately the same everywhere? But there again, would this kind of thing happen at home in Clacton?

Nancy's house was awesome. It had wood-cladded walls and the rooms were small and cosy, with thick sheepskin rugs on the floors and walls, like in a log cabin. The kitchen was an original from the fifties, repainted in diner-style candy pinks and baby blues, and there was a huge retro fridge with a clunky handle that you had to pull to open and that little children could get locked in. All the furniture was vintage and there were precious retro pieces everywhere – a jukebox that played 45's of Elvis and Jerry Lee Lewis and Hank Marvin; an old-fashioned vending machine that for just a quarter thudded out ice cold fizzy drinks in the original bottles; a two foot high Coca Cola neon sign above the sofa. There was even a waterbed in the main bedroom – it helped with the heat, Nancy said. And although it would be a squash for now they were going to have this perfect little house all to themselves in just three weeks' time! It was fantastic.

There was just one downside to the arrangement: when JoAnne told Andy they'd finally found somewhere, Andy had said that the only other girl in the group, Melissa, would have to join them. Melissa still didn't have anywhere to live, he'd said, and although the boys had found themselves a house that in theory had room for her too, the rules were that girls and boys weren't meant to live together, presumably to minimise any distractions from the business of selling books. Even Sissy wasn't happy. Melissa was a nightmare – she made their friend Siobhan from college look like the most considerate person in the world, but Melissa was stuck, and so JoAnne reluctantly asked Nancy, and Nancy was fine, at first.

JoAnne arrived back from her inaugural day as a bookseller and it had gone badly. She'd done everything she'd learned in training, and had discovered a natural talent for speaking to people, for worming her way into their houses, for selling them mediocre reference books their children would barely use. She'd stuck rigidly to the script and had made four sales, unheard of on a first day. She'd loathed it.

As JoAnne opened the front door, Vinny jumped up at her, standing on his hind legs, tail wagging furiously, licking her face – and it made her feel better, she adored the husky already. As she went to put down her bag, laughingly pushing Vinny away, Nancy appeared in the hallway, more in a manner of arrest than of welcome, and it was clear she'd been crying.

"Nancy, what's the matter!" asked JoAnne. Was she OK? Had she changed her mind about them staying there? Perhaps her husband had objected after all.

"I'm so sorry JoAnne, but I've had a few problems with Melissa," said Nancy. JoAnne knew what was coming then, not the details but the outcome.

"You shouldn't be sorry, Nancy," said JoAnne. "It's your house. *I'm* sorry. What's happened?"

"Well, first she told me to stop Vinny barking because she had a headache."

This was on their second day of staying in someone else's house, for free. What the fuck is the matter with that girl, thought JoAnne.

"Oh no! I'm so sorry."

"And you know, of course I would stop him, he just wanted to go out, but she demanded I do it, pretty rudely in fact, as if it was her house, not mine. And then half an hour after that she… she accused me of stealing her Walkman."

JoAnne put her hands over her face. "Oh God," she said.

"And the thing is," continued Nancy. "I think it must be there somewhere, but have a look at how she's left the living room." She opened the door so JoAnne could see the clothes strewn around as though there'd been a burglary, and there were greyed-out bras on the floor and twisted, taken off knickers, and a plate beside the sofa with a half eaten piece of toast from the morning, crumbs spilling on to the carpet beneath it.

"You must think we're horrendous," said JoAnne, her eyes shiny.

"Not you," said Nancy. "Just her."

JoAnne hesitated.

"Look," she said finally. "I think we've completely abused your trust and we should leave. Tonight."

"You don't have to," said Nancy, but JoAnne could see the relief in her eyes.

"Yeah we do," said JoAnne. "Don't worry, the boys have found a big empty house we can all share. We won't be homeless. And when you're all moved in, Sissy and I would

88

love to come and see your new place – and Vinny of course." She knelt down and buried her face into his fur so Nancy couldn't see her eyes glisten.

"I suppose we could give her another chance," Nancy started to say, but JoAnne stood up and told her no, she'd been kind enough already, and as she hugged the older girl she reminded herself that it wasn't the end of the world, it was only a house, only a husky.

JoAnne was becoming an expert at bookselling. She found her patter of, "Is that your attack dog?" when confronted by a chihuahua or anything small enough to obviously not be, followed by, "Hi, I'm JoAnne, I'm Lady Di's cousin," and then a laugh and a joke that OK, no she wasn't really, but she really was all the way from England, and she'd driven the whole way here (just kidding!), and she was so excited to be doing this great project helping all the local kids in the neighbourhood, and she'd had such fun with the Jordans' kids next door, and she was sure that little Johnny and Susie would love the programme too, and anyway did they have a place to sit down? And at that very point she would break the eye contact and move forward to pick up her book bag, the one she'd hidden down by the side of the door, next to the house, and the momentum of that movement would propel her towards the interior, and before anyone quite knew what was happening she would be through the front door and standing in the hallway, and then nice Mrs Smith or Jones or Adams would be leading her into the dining room or kitchen (after all they couldn't leave her just standing there making the place look untidy, could they), and she would sit down at the table and the kids would sit too, looking super excited at what this pretty fun girl with the pink-tipped hair and weird accent was going to take out of her interesting-looking bag. It worked almost every time, once she'd got the hang of it. It was when she pulled her master stroke of saying how she was going to ask the kids a general knowledge question and if they got it right they would WIN themselves a set of books, completely FREE, that the kids would be on the edge of their seats, frothing with excitement, and the mom would look a bit guarded, suspicious now, and her smile would fade a little (oh no, it must be a con after all) and JoAnne would sock them with the question: "OK, all you have to do is tell me the names of every single American president, in the correct order – and remember you have to get them all *exactly* right to get the prize." At this point the kids would giggle and say, "Shucks," and the mom would look relieved, and then JoAnne would flick straight to the exact page and there they'd be, every last American president from George Washington right through to Ronald Reagan, now isn't that a terrific book, and the kids would be nodding and Mrs Smith would be beaming, and then they'd talk a little more about the section for math (minus the *s* of course), and the great science chapter, and maybe the geography one too; and once they were all nodding and smiling *all* the time, JoAnne would very casually pick up her pen and say, "So this is Rockland Avenue, right?" and Mrs Smith would smile and say yes, that's right, and then JoAnne would nod, "And you're number 48, aren't you?" and Mrs Smith would agree, yes they were number 48, and JoAnne would confirm, "And it's Mrs Smith, isn't it?" and of course that was correct too, so JoAnne would continue, "OK, it's Tyler's Educational Handbooks Volumes One and Two," not as a question, more as a statement of fact, after all yes, they were Tyler's Educational Handbooks Volumes One and Two, and she'd go right ahead and fill that in on her pad too. Next she'd say, "And shall we add the dictionary as well, it's so comprehensive it's the only one you'll ever need," and again there would be no question mark in the statement, just an assumption that the dictionary would indeed be a welcome addition to the Smith family household, and at exactly that moment JoAnne would look up and smile reassuringly at Mrs Smith, before confirming, "So all three together will be just $117, and all I need you to do is sign right here," and Mrs Smith would finally acknowledge to herself, although of course she'd known all along, that she was being handed an order form, and she would take the pen that JoAnne would proffer and sign it, she didn't want to be rude, and besides they were all having such fun, and everyone would be happy, sort of. And still JoAnne would carry on relentlessly, absolutely word-perfect these days: "Now the way it works, Mrs Smith, is that I'm taking orders in the area over the next couple of weeks, and then I'll come back and see you, Susie and Johnny (big smile and often a wink), and I will deliver your books to you *personally* at the end of the summer – isn't that great, we'll get to hang out together again – so what I'll do for now is take a deposit, shall we say 50%? No cash? That's fine, a cheque is great," and Mrs Smith would say OK and go find her cheque book, and JoAnne would leave soon afterwards with enough money to more than cover the wholesale price the company would charge her for the books. And every Sunday the area manager would drop by to take all her deposits off her (minus just enough cash for her to live on for the week) so that she wouldn't be tempted to blow her takings, on self-indulgent nights out for example, and anyway she was far too tired for those, but instead would be sure to have enough dollars in her company account at the end of the summer to be able to afford to pay for the books she'd promised to deliver to her customers. She'd get to keep any remaining funds in her account of course, plus all the balances she collected off her customers at the end of the summer, and that would be her profit. It was genius how it all worked, how the company didn't need to risk one single teeny cent on a single one of their students, and yet still made millions.

JoAnne was so brilliantly sassy in her approach that on a good day she succeeded in sealing the deal at the point she first handed the pen over, often not needing to even get to the objection-handling part of the process, although she was pretty good at that too: those less suggestible people might refuse to take the pen at the first offering and instead be confident enough to spoil the party, maybe say something like they were sorry but they couldn't afford them. JoAnne wouldn't mind though, she was prepared, and she'd have her smiling reply straight-out-of-the-box-ready: "Ah yes, times are tight, aren't they Mrs Hughes? But what price can you put on a child's education? (Pause.) You know, Mrs Smith next door was worried about the cost too, at first, but when she found out that the Joneses at number 38 had got them for their kids she really felt she couldn't let her own children down by putting them at a disadvantage at school... Hmm, makes you think, doesn't it... (Pause.) So anyway Mrs Hughes, all I need you to do is sign right here." And most people would, after that onslaught. Sometimes the more strong-willed ones might resist still further and have another objection up their sleeve, perhaps along the lines of not needing the books because they already had a set of encyclopaedias. But JoAnne had an answer for that too. "Ah, yes, that's what Mrs Jones said as well, at first, until I explained to her that these aren't just ordinary encyclopaedias, these books are a brilliantly compact reference source specially designed to follow the school curriculum and take kids all the way from first grade right through to 12th grade. (Turns to child.) Wouldn't you like just two books that will help you do your homework for the whole of your school life, little Susie?" And little Susie would nod enthusiastically, before her mother had time to kick her under the table.

Some women were even more uncooperative and would try the needing to discuss it with their husband line, which usually worked in these kinds of situations, but they hadn't encountered a fully-trained Tyler's sales representative in full flow before. JoAnne of course would have an indisputable answer for that objection: "Yes, you do want to be sure you're making the right decision with something as important as this, don't you? But, you know, when your husband finds out that all the other kids in the neighbourhood will be getting these books in time for the new school year, I'm sure he'd have been happy for you to have gone ahead without him – in fact he might even be a little cross that you hadn't... (Pause.) After all, he'd want you to do the best for the children, wouldn't he?"

Most people could only stretch to two or three objections

before running short of ideas or energy, and besides the relationship would have become so utterly chummy by now there was no real opportunity for straight rudeness or eviction, and so JoAnne would just keep on going, giving perfectly pat guilt-inducing answers to each excuse, until the customer eventually ran out of steam, occasionally even getting a little cross and saying tetchily, "Look, I'm sorry, I just don't want them." And JoAnne would counter, "Yes, I completely understand what you mean, Mrs Brown. But there's a great deal of difference between want and need isn't there? I don't *want* to go to the dentist but I know that I *need* to go to keep my teeth healthy. And that's how it is with your children's education: you don't want your children being at a disadvantage to the other kids do you? (Pause.) So, anyway, Mrs Brown, all I need is for you to sign just here." And Mrs Brown would.

JoAnne grew to so despise the manipulation, the negative energy required for selling these books, that she developed a full-on phobia of the first front door of each day – apparently a quite common phenomenon in the direct selling business – and the strength of the phobia seemed to be directly proportional to how well the previous day's selling had gone, as though she loathed being successful and couldn't bear to inflict herself and her educational fucking books on any more undeserving people for another single minute. Every morning she and Sissy would drive to their allocated area in the beaten up old car they'd bought together, and JoAnne would come over all clammy and faint, and she'd stare with terror at the front yards she'd have to walk through and the houses she'd have to enter, and she'd think of the conversations she'd have to have and the dollars she'd have to take from the people who didn't want to give them to her and often couldn't afford anyway, and she would feel the tears prick obstinately behind her eyes; and it was as if she couldn't move, to even open the car door, and Sissy would try not to influence her, would just sit there patiently (after all, her tree in the park, the one she'd never quite told JoAnne about, would wait for her) until JoAnne either got it together and got out, and Sissy would drive off before JoAnne had time to change her mind, or else JoAnne's eyes would spill and the misery and self-loathing would pour down her face, and she would really really want her mum, although she hadn't seen her in years, and besides she never had been much of a mother to her anyway. At that point, when Sissy knew it wasn't going to be one of JoAnne's good days, she would put the car into gear and drive them up to the main road where they could sit in Pizza Hut and drink iced Coke all day, until the air conditioning became unbearable, but even that didn't matter as Sissy had learned to keep a couple of cardigans in the car for those kinds of days.

Wednesday had started off as one of JoAnne's better mornings, maybe not from a mental health point of view, but at least as far as the selling was concerned. She had sold two sets of students' handbooks and one cookery book by lunchtime, and had succeeded in largely not thinking, in simply fixing her brain to automatic for most of the morning. She'd had just one real failure, at the first front door as it happened, which had been opened by a waif-like woman with two scrawny girls hanging off her legs, wearing matching Barbie pyjamas and peanut butter round their mouths. (The woman had been very nice but alas unbending in her refusal, her kids wouldn't be in school for another two years, she'd said, it might have all changed by then, and JoAnne had replied with a cheeky smile that trigonometry hadn't changed for thousands of years, but the woman's responses had been equally smart and she wouldn't be swayed.)

JoAnne wasted no time wavering at the doors once she was fully into her stride – knocking, waving, entering, selling – and it was all working beautifully. She'd probably be able to work until six tonight, it seemed like she'd managed to switch off her mind for the day. That was how it tended to work for her – all or nothing.

So at exactly 1.15 she was sitting in the kitchen of a man who'd said his wife was out at the mall with the kids, and she didn't quite know why but she didn't believe him. He'd seemed so friendly when he'd first let her in, but as soon as she'd got inside she'd realised there was no evidence of him having any children at all: no scrawled pictures on the fridge, or scuffed sneakers by the front door, no toys lying around – and she began to wonder whether there was even a wife either. She just didn't like the feel of him, not at all, there was something definitely odd about him – plus it was harder to do her patter without there being kids to play off – and although at first she was smiley and flirty like she usually was with the dads, he was looking at her a little too keenly as she spoke about the comprehensiveness of the books' content and how it exactly matched the curriculum, and now he was smiling at her funny, almost like he was in pain, and he was leaning so far towards her she could smell his stale coffee breath, and his grin was twisted; in fact he was really beginning to freak her out big-time. When she stoically moved into the order form part of her routine (once she was in full swing she was a true professional) she went to hand him the biro, but he grabbed her wrist instead, and although he was laughing like he was only joking it hurt her, and as he pulled her to her feet she tried to escape, to shake his hand off her, but this seemed to annoy him – and before she knew what had even happened she was down on the cold hard floor and he was on top of her, straddling her, and his strong rough hands were fixed around her neck.

20

Hyde Park

Although Juliette and JoAnne used to be absolute best friends, the nucleus of the group really, things had never been the same since JoAnne had slept with Juliette's boyfriend in America – none of them had ever quite managed to move on from it, even though Stephen had sworn to Juliette that it had only happened the once, and besides they'd both been para- lytic, he'd said. Juliette had always known JoAnne was com- petitive about men, determined to prove how attractive she was, as though it made her a better person somehow, but she couldn't believe she'd targeted *Stephen* this time. Even now, over 20 years later, Juliette couldn't bear the thought of the two of them together, of where Stephen's lips and hands and, well, everything else had been, it was quite revolting really, and she'd very nearly not taken him back. She didn't care that she and Stephen had been on a break at the time, there are some lines you just don't cross, and besides privately she'd thought this could be her chance to make a fresh start. Stephen had had to get super-inventive to make her come round, and of course he had blamed it all on JoAnne, describing how she had flung herself at him, and frankly in Juliette's opinion and from the little Sissy had said about it, it was probably true.

Juliette didn't know what had happened to JoAnne. Since America she seemed to have changed into a total slapper – maybe, Juliette thought, it was some weird response to having been raped by that man she'd been trying to sell encyclopaedias to. She couldn't understand why JoAnne had never gone to the police, but JoAnne just seemed to be so ashamed of what had happened, as if it was all her fault, which was ridiculous. It had taken her weeks to even confess it to Sissy apparently, and by then, JoAnne had argued, there was no evidence, only the man's word against hers. She'd rather just get back to England and forget about it, she'd said, and Sissy hadn't known how to persuade her otherwise.

Juliette sighed as she looked down at her drink, and then across at the men tying up the last of the boats on The Serpentine. She still missed JoAnne, really missed her, even after all these years – they'd been so close once, like sisters even, and somehow them being here in each other's company, sat together on a patchwork of rugs, not quite touching, unsure how to reach each other again, just made Juliette more lonely than ever. Perhaps if she hadn't got back with Stephen she and JoAnne would never have drifted apart, and she wondered whether she might even be happier now, with a proper best friend rather than a husband she'd never really loved, not like she should do, she could see that now. Not that she and JoAnne had actually ever discussed any of it of course, it was all so fucking unspoken it was horrible.

JoAnne seemed to sense Juliette's thoughts, and she turned a little and looked, and Juliette appeared so terribly sad,

99

bereft even, it caused JoAnne a little jolt of anguish, and so she turned back to Sissy and complimented her on her pasta salad, on how it tasted so much better than it looked.

"You rude cow," said Sissy, and it was nice to see Sissy smiling again, she seemed to have lost all capacity for fun since Nigel had died, and suddenly Juliette was smiling too, and it felt almost like old times for a second, and JoAnne wondered whether they could ever be real friends again. She was sure in that moment that they all still needed each other in a way. Perhaps their friendships were worth fighting for after all. Maybe all they had to do was try harder.

21

Cleveland

JoAnne felt too scared, too ashamed to go the police. She must have been traumatised immediately afterwards, so although she'd been shaking and tearful she didn't think to call at another house, try to get someone to help her – and as people seemed to drive everywhere in Cleveland there had been no-one walking along the streets to even notice her state, just a couple of little kids who stared numbly at her, bewildered by her wailing. She hadn't known how to get home without the car, and she couldn't possibly hang around for hours until Sissy was due to pick her up. She couldn't bear to talk to anyone. She couldn't think what to do.

She wanted her mother.

JoAnne bent over double, her head reeling, and vomited into the gutter, and then she wiped her mouth on the front of her T-shirt and started to walk – her cries quieting as she moved, her steps in time with her snivels – not knowing where she was going, whether she was even going in the right direction, what the right direction was. She tramped relentlessly through suburb after suburb of detached family homes with neat front yards and shiny basketball hoops and massive untapped sales potential, jaywalked over six-lane highways, cut across pin-neat malls and the odd green space where no-one played. The day was stinking and her throat was rancid, but she couldn't cope with the thought of stopping, approaching anyone, of doing anything other than move her feet, one in front of the wretched other, not until she'd got home and showered, had rid herself of the taint of what had happened to her body, of the man's bulk on her, of the vile stench still in her nostrils. Eventually she reached one of the main highways through Cleveland, and at last she recognised where she was, knew she could get a bus home from here, and when it came she slunk on and hid at the back, in the corner, like a scolded dog.

The house looked empty as JoAnne approached it – all the windows were shut and there were no cars in the driveway. She thought perversely how it must have been a lovely house once – large, well proportioned, set in a generous plot, with great expanses of window that instead of letting light in from the outside seemed to absorb darkness now, so that the house felt unloved, dead. Inside it was passable – neutral colours, serviceable kitchen and bathrooms – except for the fact that it didn't have any furniture, not one piece. The booksellers ate standing up in the kitchen, and in the living room they lounged around on the floor, like in a refugee camp, until Greg, one of Andy's friends from Cardiff, bought a blow up sofa in fluorescent pink and some of them took to sitting in that, although it was horribly sweaty, until it inevitably popped.

As JoAnne opened the front door she was relieved that

she'd been right – no-one else was home yet. It was only half past three and even the students who never knocked at a single door, just found their own tree to sit under for the day, usually didn't risk coming back much before four, in case the area manager turned up on one of his spot visits. JoAnne went straight up to the shower and scrubbed viciously at herself, trying to get clean, and then she heaved herself to the very top of the house, to the room she shared with Sissy, and although it was stifling and furniture-free it was small and homely. Sissy had brought some pictures from England that she'd Blu Tacked up: that black and white one of the French couple kissing and some moody mono promo posters of Lloyd Cole and Paul Weller, plus a few Monet postcards she'd got in Paris. Their sleeping bags were laid out neatly side by side where the beds should have been, and Sissy had even rigged up a string across the corner of the room where their few pathetic clothes hung from wire hangers Sissy had got from the local dry cleaners. JoAnne wished Sissy were here now, she felt so helpless and alone in this boiling box of a room, and she lay down in her towel on her sleeping bag and sobbed until her chest hurt, and then she found she couldn't stop, it was as if some long-plugged gash had opened up inside her. She was just so scared, sickened, homesick somehow – but for where? Where was home anyway, now that she'd graduated, now that the safety of three years in Bristol were over? She hated going to her father's house in Clacton, and she hadn't seen her mother since that last trip to Paris, when it became clear to them both that JoAnne couldn't forgive her mother for choosing her lover over her daughter, and even though she'd only been 12 at the time there seemed little common ground between them anyway, they were both stuck in different places somewhere between childhood and adulthood, and it had all felt awkward, fractious. It had been a relief for JoAnne's mother to put the child back on the plane at Charles de Gaulle, and then the next year it had seemed easier for JoAnne to say no, she didn't want to go to Paris this year, she'd rather go to Cornwall with her cousins, and then after that she hadn't been asked again. It seemed perverse that it was *her mother* she pined for now, but maybe that's the way it works, she thought, it seems that when things are really bad only your mother will do, no matter how useless they may have been before then.

JoAnne tried to work out what she should do. As she lay on the floor, her revulsion and hatred grew, and she found it was aimed as much at herself as at him. It was as if the stranger had unlocked all the holed up neuroses within her body, and they were haemorrhaging out of her from where the pain was. She knew she should have listened to Larry Reynolds, who'd warned her about walking into strangers' houses, had tried so hard to save her from danger. She should have trusted her instincts, she'd known from the start that last guy was a creep. *It was all her fault.* She started sobbing again.

There was a knock at the door. JoAnne sat up quickly, wiping her eyes on the edge of her sleeping bag. She checked her watch – it was just past four, still a bit early for anyone to be back yet. She adjusted her towel as the door edged open.

"Oh. Sorry. Are you OK?" asked Stephen, retreating a little. "I could hear you from outside the house."

"Oh God, sorry," said JoAnne. "I... I just had a really shit day, that's all."

"What happened?" asked Stephen, obviously concerned. He hung outside the door as if he didn't want to intrude, she was half-naked after all, but didn't want to leave her either. He looked like an anxious little boy somehow, and it was endearing.

"Oh... just some arsehole customer," said JoAnne, and she decided in that moment not to tell anyone what had happened, not even Sissy. She knew it was mad, she'd done nothing wrong, not really, but she felt ashamed somehow.

"Look, I was going to have a quick shower and then go for a swim at the lake," said Stephen. "D'you want to come?"

JoAnne didn't want to spend time with Stephen, he still irritated her for some reason, but she needed to get out, she'd go mad if she stayed in this room on her own for much longer, and she had no idea when Sissy would be back – Sissy would soon be driving around the suburb JoAnne was meant to be working in, looking for her, not realising she was home already, and knowing Sissy she wouldn't give up for ages, she'd be beside herself. It could be hours before she got home.

"OK," JoAnne said. She still felt so tainted; maybe a swim would cleanse her, help hose off the revulsion the shower hadn't reached.

"The bus goes right there, it's quite quick I think. Looks like you could do with getting out. I won't be long." He disappeared, pulling the door gently closed, and JoAnne sat there for a while, wondering what she'd just agreed to.

Stephen had a surprisingly good body. He always looked so beefy in clothes, solid rather than fat, as though he'd been over-inflated, but in his Speedos his skin was smooth and hairless, his legs well-defined, his form nicely triangular, like he was on the way to becoming a body-builder but before the steroids had kicked in. JoAnne was almost beginning to see what Juliette saw in him, especially as he'd been so kind since he'd found her crying. Maybe at last she, Juliette's feisty, kick-ass best friend, wasn't a threat to him, had shown her sensitive side, and on the bus he was concerned but not prying, and he genuinely seemed interested in how she was, what she had to say for a change.

JoAnne felt overly aware of Stephen as she took off the sundress she'd thrown over her bikini. She still felt distraught, traumatised, and it seemed to be making her super-conscious of her body and his body, almost as if her hideous ordeal earlier had heightened rather than diminished her sexuality. It was peculiar. She tossed the dress onto her towel and careered down the beach, feeling self-conscious of her pale exposed flesh, towards the waves that she found hard to fathom were not part of a sea or an ocean but were just a lake, a huge landlocked mass of unsalted water where you couldn't even begin to see the land on the other side. As she ran across the sand, the splashes felt icy against her overheating body, but she didn't slow down, instead she half-jumped, half-waded in, as fast as she could, until the water was deep enough for her to dive into the waves and then she put her head down and swam, out away from the shore, breathing hard, doing her schoolgirl front crawl, trying to swim away from the cold, away from herself, from Stephen, away from America.

Finally she stopped, panting, and turned to look back towards the shore. She was surprised at how far out she was, and although Stephen had got into the water he was still close to the beach, watching her.

"Are you OK," he yelled, and she just about heard and shouted back yes, she was fine although she wasn't really, not in her head anyway, and as she started to turn back the cramp hit her, hard, as if her left leg were made of wood, she couldn't move it at all, and then as the pain shot down through her spine she panicked and tried to scream, and as she did so she took a mouthful of water and it tasted disgusting, dieselly, and now she was waving her arms frantically as her head bobbed under the waves, and eventually Stephen seemed to understand and started swimming towards her, but he was taking too long, she couldn't be that far out, surely, and she took another gulp of filthy water and then another and she really thought she was drowning now, she couldn't stay up with just her arms, she was tired, the waves were too big, she was sinking, definitely, was this really how it was all going to end, here in this lake after all she'd survived – and then at long long last there was Stephen, and he grabbed her round the neck and turned her over, and started swimming back to shore, towing her behind him, and she could feel his body hard beneath her even though she was about to pass out, and it seemed to be taking so long, surely she hadn't swum that far out, and then everything went black for a second until another wave slapped at her and they still weren't there, and then finally, *finally* she could feel the sand grazingly under her legs and her heart was double its size, pounding outside her chest, and her mind was blank and her eyes were glazed.

22

Dagenham, East London

Terry Kingston emptied the kibble into Hugo's bowl and told him to sit. Hugo looked at him, eager, adoring, as their eyes locked.

"Down," said Terry, and the dog went to the lino, head between his feet, eyes still looking up into Terry's. The tension built.

"Go on, then," said Terry at last, and Hugo lurched to his arthritic feet and padded over to his dinner. His name tag tinkled against the metal of the bowl as he ate, and Terry found the noise strangely soothing.

"Dinner's nearly ready," said Maria, from behind him.

"OK," he replied. He wondered briefly how his wife still had such a strong accent, still said dee-ner: she'd been in East London longer than she'd ever lived in Italy. He sat down at the oval dining table, which she'd covered with a transparent plastic cloth, so the wood could only peer through pitifully, as if desperate for air. Two faded stripy placemats sat on top of the plastic, the knives and forks laid out haphazardly either side of them.

"This looks nice," he said disingenuously, as she put the bowl of gnocchi drowning in an unidentifiable sauce in front of him. He paused. "By the way, I won't need dinner tomorrow night thanks, I'll be out."

"Oh, where?"

"Private job," he said. Maria didn't ask more, simply nodded her dark head and started to eat.

Terry couldn't think of anything else to say to his wife. He was annoyed with his client, dragging him into such a sordid business, and he didn't want to tell Maria, implicate her in any way.

"I think I'll clean out Sid and Vicious after dinner," he said eventually, as a way of starting conversation.

"Really, Terry, do you have to talk about such things when we are eating?"

"Oh – sorry," he said.

Terry Kingston adored his pets, almost certainly more than his wife these days, which was a shame for both of them. His love for his animals was allocated in a strict pecking order, starting with Hugo the spaniel, through Achtung the cat (unremarkable in all but name) onto the pet rats Maria had been horrified by when he'd brought them home a couple of months earlier. He dished out affection for these creatures like it was school dinners – love piled high in metaphoric mounds of mash and custard, hill-shaped, squidgy, comforting. He found it helped somehow.

Maria didn't like animals, thought they were dirty and pointless, but she hated the rats especially, which Terry found faintly pleasing, although he hadn't deliberately wanted to upset her of course. The sight of their pink eyes and whip tails made her stomach turn like a cranked engine, and she banished them to the spare room, the one where the babies had been meant to go, the ones that had never come, even when they'd been trying. He debated now if he should get rid of them, for her sake.

Terry finished his dinner and sat watching his wife. She looked like a little bird, small and delicate, although not pretty exactly, and he wondered again what she'd ever seen in him. He knew he still had a pleasant enough face, but it seemed to drift downwards these days, gravity-compliant, and although his eyes were a beautiful brown they looked like they were going to cry, like they might soon be brimming with tears, but they were often like that, he suffered terribly from hay fever. Otherwise he was nondescript: average build, average height, mousy wavyish hair, and he prided himself on being the type of person that could meld into the background and just observe, and he found he enjoyed this, it was less stressful than trying to think of things to say.

Terry sometimes wondered how Maria put up with him – he'd always found women so alien that even his own wife was a mystery to him – but she seemed happy enough, and she definitely enjoyed mothering him, had spotted his vulnerability right from the start. What he knew she couldn't understand though was his increasing obsession with fantasy war worlds, the hours and hours he spent painting the figures, and he dreaded breaking it to her that he wanted to go to another convention in Nottingham next weekend. But, he reasoned, she seemed to be pretty busy herself with the choir these days, so hopefully she'd be all right about it. He just needed to pick his moment to ask her.

23

Hyde Park

The skies had darkened over Hyde Park and most of the pic-nickers were well on the way to drunkenness now, a dangerous destination for this particular combination of women. Sissy was the only one trying not to drink (she found she couldn't face it these days, plus she had to get the kids up and out early in the morning, Nell had a school trip, and it was all too grue-some after even a couple of glasses of wine) but JoAnne kept insisting on filling up her glass. Sissy was relieved nothing serious had kicked off between anyone, although as the eve-ning continued it was an increasing possibility, and Siobhan in particular kept threatening to cross into danger zones now she'd had a few drinks – she kept moaning on about her boy-friend Matt, how he would never commit, and how the others were so lucky to have husbands, and then she'd said, "Oh, sorry Sissy," and Sissy could have throttled her. Natasha seemed pretty uptight too, which was unlike her, normally everything was fucking marvellous in her world, and she seemed to have the arse with both Juliette and JoAnne for some reason. And of course Juliette and JoAnne didn't get on and hadn't for years, so there was that to deal with too. Only Camilla was being normal, now she'd got over the presence of shop-bought scotch eggs and the absence of sufficient picnic chairs. Honestly, thought Sissy, I think this is the last time we should do this, it's just too stressful – we've got to stop living in the past, we've all got our own lives now. She looked out towards The Serpentine and wondered idly whether it was a river or a lake, she didn't actually know, and she wondered what it was like to swim in, she knew people did but it looked dirty to her, unappealing.

"Sissy," said Natasha, obviously not for the first time, her tone was the one Sissy took with her own children the fourth time of asking. "Would you like some cheesecake?"

"Oh, sorry Natasha, no thanks, I'm fine," said Sissy. "I'm going to have to think about going soon, I've got an early start tomorrow."

"Oh, come on Sissy," said Siobhan. "Why can't you just let your hair down for a change? You've got to start enjoying yourself again. It would do you good."

"Siobhan, shush," said JoAnne. "Don't be so bloody insensitive."

"Yeah well, we can't all pussy-foot round her forever, it's not good for her. And at least she's had a husband," said Siobhan, and she'd obviously had far too much wine now, and not just down her trousers. "No one's ever wanted to marry me."

Everyone was silent for a moment, stunned.

"Well, I'm not surprised with that attitude," said Juliette in the end. "You are quite possibly the most selfish person I know."

"Well, I hardly think so," said Siobhan, and her tone was more sober suddenly. "I think we all know you're married to the person who wins that prize."

"Siobhan, shut up," said Natasha. Her tone brightened, like the school nurse with a sad sickly child. "Now, who's going to have this last piece of cheesecake, it's a shame to waste it."

"Yeah well, Sissy would still have a husband if it wasn't for Stephen, wouldn't she?" said Siobhan, as though Natasha hadn't spoken, and as she said it she tried to stop herself but her mouth wouldn't cooperate, and everyone knew she really had gone too far this time.

There were at least three involuntary intakes of breath, and then there seemed to be no breathing at all, and nobody said anything for long empty seconds that even the irrepressible Michael Buble failed to fill. Sissy looked back out to the water and it lay still, seemingly breathless too, and she wondered whether everything was slowly dying in her world, and she tried to work out what would be the quickest way to get home, so she could pay off the babysitter and go straight upstairs and hide under her duvet, and never come out again.

24

Cleveland

JoAnne lay on the beach and belched a great flood of lake water into the sand. Stephen was just getting off her, he must have been pumping her chest, and she was dimly aware that he had saved her life. She lay still, her breathing shallow and irregular, as she heard other voices now – American, loud, concerned – saying they were going to call an ambulance.

"No, no, I'm OK," she mumbled. "I'm fine, I don't need one." And she tried to sit up and found that she could, in fact she felt surprisingly normal, just a little giddy perhaps.

"Well, let's get you inside and fetch you a drink, and see how you are then," said one of the voices, and she looked up to see it belonged to a man with a fierce-looking face, like a wrestler's, and he had long straggly hair untamed by a baseball cap, and he was wearing huge hitched-up jeans and an open shirt. A gold medallion shone through the hair on his chest, like treasure.

Stephen and the stranger helped JoAnne up and wrapped her in a towel. Even though it was still so hot she felt shivery, it must have been the shock. A woman gathered up the rest of their belongings from the beach, and she was little and sinewy in a tiny skirt and cut-off top, with deeply brown tattooed skin, as if she were wearing her hurt on the outside. Stephen held JoAnne under one arm whilst the burly man took the other, and as she was propelled between them she felt like was floating, not drowning anymore. They walked her one block back, helped her up some concrete steps and into a big empty bar which had a terrace that looked out over the tops of buildings and the main lakeshore road, towards the drabness of the water. They sat her on a vinyl bench seat inside, and the air conditioning was so fierce someone turned it off, to try to stop her shaking. Stephen gave her his T-shirt, which she put on over her bikini, keeping the towel wrapped around her like a skirt. A drink got shoved into her hand, and when she took a swig the liquid was warmly brown and strong-tasting, and instantly the blood in her veins felt a little livelier, as if it were being chased around her body now rather than creeping reluctantly.

"Stephen, I'm so sorry," she said, as he came back from the restrooms, involuntarily half-naked still, towel draped over his brawny shoulders. "I don't know what happened, I just got such excruciating cramp I must have panicked."

"That's all right, you don't need to apologise. I'm just relieved I wasn't towing a corpse, I honestly thought you were about to die on me." He smiled, looking young and nervous, his mid-brown hair beginning to curl at the ends where it was drying – and she thought again that she must have misjudged him, it seemed he was quite nice after all. She was still aware of him in a way that she recognised with a shock as maybe the reason why she hadn't liked him much before, and she pushed that thought aside – after all he was her best friend's boyfriend; they might be on a break but she was sure Juliette would have him back, once they were both home; and she was also sure he would go back, he adored Juliette, who didn't? And why the hell was she even thinking like this after what had happened just a few hours earlier with the stranger in his kitchen? JoAnne shivered again and took another slug of her drink, a larger one this time, as she tried to process the events of this unimaginable day, tried to work out precisely what impact they had had on her, what she should do. When finally it came to her she couldn't believe she'd only just thought of it.

She needed to go to the police – that's what she should have done in the first place, as soon as it had happened. *Why hadn't she gone to the police?*

She stood up, ignoring Stephen's protestations to take it easy, and walked unsteadily to the bathroom where she gazed at herself in the mirror, shaking with cold, or was it fear? Her mind was racing. There would be no evidence now, only the faintest of marks on the left side of her neck – it would be his word against hers, and she'd already sussed what the local police thought of booksellers, she'd been moved on enough times despite having her licence. They probably wouldn't believe her, and even if they did it could just prolong the ordeal – they might want to keep her there, for the court case or something, she might even have to miss her flight home. No, there was no way she was going to risk that.

JoAnne continued to stare in the mirror, barely recognising herself, hardly believing she was there. *She had escaped death twice in one day.* She was lucky to be alive. Surely that was enough? She washed her hands again, holding them for forever under the dryer, and then she made her way back to the bar, just as Stephen was coming to check she was all right.

25

Soho

The restaurant was small, charming and candle-lit, the perfect backdrop to the start of an affair. Natasha's husband looked across the table at his companion's lips, as red and vital as newly spilt blood, even in the half-light, and decided she'd looked better before she'd excused herself and gone to the bathroom to apply it – it aged her. It didn't matter though – he found he didn't really care what she looked like, or what they ate, or what they spoke about, he just wanted to get her back to his hotel and fuck her senseless. It was quite extraordinary really – that he should be at this table with one of his wife's oldest friends, that she should have been the one to take the first step with him, and he wondered how much the chronic lack of sex in his marriage showed through, in the starvation in his eyes. She must have guessed about that, he was sure Natasha wouldn't have spoken about it to anyone, Natasha was too proud, she wore her life like a trophy – *look at me*, look how far I've come, with my three adorable children, my fucking brilliant career, my handsome novelist husband, my detached house in Barnes, my sub-45 minute 10K

118

runs. Life was just wonderful as far as Natasha was concerned, she would never admit otherwise. Alistair often wondered when he'd first regretted marrying her, and he thought it may have been even before the wedding, once the sex had started to dwindle – around the time the preparations had been fully cranked up: Invite List A minus four months from the Big Day, Invite List B (finalised and mailed minus two months according to acceptees off Invite List A), separate spreadsheets for hotels, menus, flowers, thank you gifts, transport. She'd made them have weekly meetings, with an agenda and every-thing, to discuss it. And then immediately afterwards there'd been the baby-making to get on with: no more wild abandon, no letting nature take its course, just those offensive ovulation sticks from the get go, dictating their appointments with pas-sion, purely so she could have autumn or at worst December babies – they had so much better an outcome in life she'd read somewhere. The biggest bang he'd had on his Mauritian honeymoon was on Day Eight, exactly when Natasha would be ovulating, and she'd made him endure abstention for three whole days beforehand to ensure his sperm was top-notch for the conception. He'd nearly bloody exploded. He'd always known she was competitive, and it had served him well in many ways, but he'd preferred her when they first met, when she'd channelled it into who could have the most orgasms (her) and finding him an agent – she'd been unstoppable at both in the early days.

"I think I'll have the sea bass," his wife's friend was saying. "What about you?"

"Um, yeah, sounds good," Alistair said, and his nostrils filled with fishy smells and his mind crawled with visions of her with her legs apart and him going down there for the first time, like an explorer, and he forced himself back to the little restaurant behind Carnaby Street and told himself, "Just a couple more hours," and as he looked at her he thought he might even blow right there with the agony of it all – so he tried to think of something else, recalled his wife bossing the nanny around this morning, going on about the importance of a nutritionally-balanced packed lunch, and that settled him down again.

Natasha's friend shifted in her seat and looked shyly down into her wine glass, as if the answer to something lay there. "So were you surprised when I texted you?" she said. "I hope you didn't mind, I just really needed someone to talk to about... about..." She trailed off.

Alistair thought then that maybe he'd got it wrong, maybe she simply wanted to go out with him as a friend, wanted some advice, about writing perhaps. Maybe he'd imagined she wanted the same thing as him, had imagined that she too was after dirty messy uninhibited sex with a nice smear of guilt to top it off. He started to feel insanely edgy, like he really needed to get this over with, one way or the other.

"Um, well, of course not. Though I was a little surprised," he managed. He wondered then, for the first time, as if a revelation, why he had never thought to be unfaithful to his wife before. It would have solved so many problems (and inevitably caused a few others, but he wasn't concerned about those at this precise moment). He must have just got caught up in the frustration of it all, and of course there was the internet these days and his almost obsessive level of wanking which meant he did it at least three times in the en-suite on a bad day. But surely that was better than cheating on her, he'd always thought, not even consciously really – and then he'd got THAT text and it had given him ideas, but maybe he'd misinterpreted it; and now here he was feeling unsure, and he didn't want to sit and eat dinner or chat about anything, large or small, he just wanted to go and fucking finish himself off if she wasn't going to go through with it. Maybe he had some kind of a problem, a little voice whispered, and he looked up desolately and as he did so she took a sip from her glass, seductively, and her red lipstick smeared bawdily, and she reached her foot under the table and rubbed it against his ankle, and as she smiled at him with her smudgy crimson mouth he felt relief gush over him like he'd already ejaculated. "Shall we go?" he asked urgently, and although she looked surprised she acquiesced and there was no more messing about thank God, and since then he'd got laid at least once a week, and he thought it was doing them both good.

Less than half an hour after leaving the restaurant Natasha's friend lay on her back next to Alistair and wondered just what she'd done. She felt wracked with guilt, but funnily enough more because of Natasha than anyone else. What the hell was she doing sleeping with someone else's husband, no matter how miserable her own circumstances? What had happened to female solidarity? It didn't help that Alistair had proven something of a disappointment in that department – it had been over so quickly for a start. She'd initially hoped he would talk to her about her writing, give her some advice, but he hadn't seemed interested, not at all; in fact he hadn't even wanted to stay in the restaurant for long enough to eat, and she felt cheapened now.

Just as she was about to get up, get dressed, try to get the hell out of there, Alistair turned over in the bed and opened his eyes, and as she stared at him, as if he were a stranger rather than someone she'd known for years, he grabbed at her again (his recovery time was miraculous, she had to hand it to him), and this time it was slower, quite nice even, and he *was* so handsome, a famous writer, and it did seem to help heal the aching loneliness in her heart – so somehow she agreed to see him on a second occasion, and before she knew it they were meeting every Wednesday, and she dreaded the next time she'd have to see Natasha.

26

Cleveland

Stephen and JoAnne found themselves getting on better, even becoming friends, after the drama at Lake Erie. They had a bond now, he'd saved her life after all, and JoAnne thought she must have misjudged him all along, that maybe he wasn't as ruthless and selfish as she'd always thought. They often found themselves sat next to each other at breakfast, it just seemed to happen that way, and the others began to notice, and Sissy even said something once, but JoAnne told her not to be so ridiculous, he was Juliette's boyfriend, not hers. But Sissy seemed anxious about it, as though she could sense the trouble to come, and JoAnne privately thought that Sissy was worrying about her own boyfriend Nigel, about what if he met some nice bronzed girl in Australia – and anyway JoAnne didn't even fancy Stephen, he wasn't her type at all. She just got on well with him these days, and what was wrong with that?

The waitress stood patiently in her short brown tunic, beige frilly apron tied neatly, white bobby socks and sneakers over American Tan tights, grey permed hair tucked tidily into her matching cap, waiting for Melissa to order. The booksellers breakfasted here every morning now: out of all the local diners this one did the best hash browns by far, and Melissa's performance had become something of a ritual they all bizarrely enjoyed, in their own ways.

"Have you got cereals?" asked Melissa, studying the menu, which was large and laminated.

"Yes, ma'am, we have Corn Flakes or Rice Krispies."

"Have you got muesli?" asked Melissa.

"No, ma'am, we only have Corn Flakes or Rice Krispies."

"Ohhhhh, I wanted muesli," said Melissa. "I wish you had muesli," and she said it sulkily, as if the restaurant not having muesli was a personal slight on her.

"I'm sorry ma'am, that's all we have. What would you like?"

Melissa couldn't help herself. "I'd like muesli," she said, like a five year old. "Why haven't you got muesli?"

"Just shut up, Melissa," said JoAnne mildly. My God, she's even worse than Siobhan, she thought. "Do we have to go through this every single day? Just pick something else." She turned to the waitress. "I'm sorry about her. I'll have two eggs over-easy please, and some coffee."

"Same for me," said Stephen, and everyone else ordered whilst Melissa slumped moodily in her seat. Finally the waitress turned back to Melissa.

"Have you decided yet, ma'am?" she said.

"I suppose I'll have to have Corn Flakes," said Melissa, with a harumph. "If you haven't got *muesli*. And tea please, but not with the teabag left on the side of the cup, in a pot so that the water's boiling, like it should be."

"I'll see what I can do, ma'am," said the waitress and whisked the menus away. JoAnne rolled her eyes at Stephen, and she wasn't sure if she imagined it but he seemed to press his knee against hers, under the table.

The following Saturday everyone was getting ready for a rare night out. It had been JoAnne's idea originally, and as she'd seemed so jumpy and not herself since the day she'd nearly drowned, Sissy thought it might do her good to get out. She wondered whether JoAnne would ever be able to recover her selling stride; although she usually seemed all right at breakfast (when Stephen was there, Sissy couldn't help noticing) she'd had first door syndrome for the rest of that week and the whole of the next, and had spent hours and hours sitting tearfully with Sissy in Pizza Hut sipping icy drinks with unlimited free refills. The waitresses were good though and never said anything, not even when JoAnne and Sissy paid the bill with a five dollar note and always took the change.

Stephen took over the evening's arrangements, of course, and insisted on choosing the venue, but JoAnne didn't appear to mind, it seemed to Sissy that Stephen could do no wrong in her eyes now. They went to a bar in the next suburb, another of those places where everything was old-fashioned and wood-cladded and they played old country tunes on the jukebox, and old men sat silently with just their bourbon for company, and Sissy thought the barmaid had that tired look in her eyes like she'd seen enough of sadness and ruination, but she had two kids to feed so that's just the way it was since her bastard no-good husband had upped and left her. (The truth was actually quite different – the barmaid was very much married, and this job helped pay for their annual trip with the kids to visit her sister in Florida, but Sissy didn't know that of course.)

JoAnne sat at the bar with Sissy and stared morosely into the bottom of her glass. Sissy tried to distract her with stories of Nigel in Queensland, she'd had a letter that day, but JoAnne seemed vacant, uninterested, and so Sissy fell silent. The others were standing in a group, laughing at some story their manager Andy was telling about how he'd managed to sell the complete set of Tyler's books, from the toddler nursery rhymes all the way up to Grade 12, to a couple who hadn't even given birth yet. Sissy found the story upsetting somehow – that Andy seemed to be mocking these people he'd befriended; that who knows what may happen to them or their child in the next sixteen years or so; that bookselling appeared to be sapping Andy's soul, he seemed more driven by money than ever these days. JoAnne's melancholy must be rubbing off on me, Sissy thought, and again she felt a stab of panic, that she was in the wrong place, that she needed to go home. But Nigel wasn't in England anyway, and her flights were firm-booked, she wasn't sure she could change them even if she wanted to, and she had settled into her days under trees, dreaming, drifting, reading, even writing again, to pass the time. It was only sometimes that it hit her, the head-filling, heart-emptying loneliness, usually when she was in a crowd rather than on her own, funnily enough.

She turned to JoAnne, who looked like she might cry herself.

"Are you all right, Jo? What's wrong? You're not at all yourself these days, I'm worried about you."

"I'm OK," said JoAnne. "Apart from hating bloody bookselling." Sissy didn't look convinced, so she added, "I'm sorry Siss, I don't know what's up with me really." She felt tempted, for just a moment, to tell Sissy about the man on his kitchen floor, the horror of the attack, how close she'd been to perhaps being killed, but she stopped herself. She still couldn't face talking about it, not even with Sissy.

"Well, nearly drowning can't have helped," said Sissy. "You're just so lucky Stephen saved you."

"I know," said JoAnne. She hesitated. "You know, I'm not sure he's as bad as I thought."

Sissy looked across at Stephen, beefy arms stretching the sleeves of his too-tight T-shirt, head thrown back with laughter, and she tried to think that perhaps JoAnne was right, maybe he was all right really, now his initial desperation to get his own back on Juliette for daring to dump him had faded, and he'd stopped trying to get off with them both. But she didn't like the way he was showing off now, it was almost like he thought he was David Hasselhoff or something since he'd saved JoAnne's life. It was funny how Stephen instilled such mixed emotions in people, he seemed so nice sometimes and then an utter tosser at others, she really couldn't work him out.

"Well," said Sissy. "You'll always be grateful to him, that's for sure."

"I know," said JoAnne, and she took a swig of her drink as Stephen turned and caught her eye, and when she smiled at him he seemed to puff up even further, like a snake who's just eaten a mouse. But Sissy was wrong, JoAnne would not be grateful to Stephen for always, not at all.

27

Hyde Park

The atmosphere was poisonous now, and not even the languidly liquid disappearance of the sun into a cooler, more peaceful place could rescue the evening. JoAnne and Juliette sat stiffly next to each other and didn't appear to be speaking at all anymore, there may as well have been a fence between them, and poor Sissy looked as though she was going to faint with the stress of it all. Natasha was sullen (as she had been most of the evening) and Siobhan was trying to paper over her appalling insult of Juliette's husband, daring to imply that Stephen had somehow had something to do with Nigel's death. Katie started tidying up, grimly, as if she were picking up dog-shit – tipping the remaining quarter of Sissy's pasta salad into an M&S bag she'd designated for rubbish without even asking Sissy whether she wanted to keep it; scraping plates like they were potatoes to be scrubbed (or perhaps children to be bathed); scrunching used napkins with unnecessary force into tight mucky balls that were tossed into the carrier bag too, not bothering with recycling, just chucking the empty wine bottles in with the mess;

flicking stray flakes of sausage roll towards Siobhan, perhaps deliberately.

It was JoAnne in the end who said it. She tried for a chummy tone but it came out strangled, and although it was clear she was suffering too, she was drunk enough to not care about the consequences.

"Look girls, I'm so sorry but I'm just sick of this atmosphere. If it's going to be like this every time we see each other we might as well not bother trying to get together anymore."

"All right, JoAnne," said Natasha. "I don't think we need to discuss it here."

"Oh, but I disagree," said JoAnne, more airily now. "Here's as good a place as any. Why do we all pretend we still get on for a start? Who's to blame for this whole *horrid* situation? Is it just the passing of time, the natural growing apart we can't seem to accept, or is it something more, more... *sinister*? Siobhan, you seem to think Stephen's responsible for all this, why don't you start?"

"Shhhhush, JoAnne," said Siobhan. "I said something out of line, I take it back."

"Ah, but maybe you shouldn't take it back," said JoAnne, and her eyes were flashing warnings and no one had ever seen her like that. "After all, it's true, isn't it, Juliette? Stephen killed Nigel, didn't he?"

Juliette stared at her former friend. "Don't be so bloody ridiculous, how on earth can you say such a thing?"

"Because it's true!" said JoAnne. "If it wasn't for Stephen, Nigel would be alive now, Sissy wouldn't be struggling on her own, she'd still have a husband who loved her, way more than yours ever has. But Stephen fucked it all up through his greed and selfishness. He's such a fucking cheat and liar, as well as a –" She stopped.

Juliette looked horrified. "What the hell are you trying to imply, JoAnne? Don't *you* start now, not after Siobhan's outburst."

"What has become of you, Juliette?" said JoAnne, and she said it quietly now, almost as a caress. "Where has your sweet beautiful heart gone?" Juliette looked broken for a second, and then she looked away, towards The Serpentine.

It was Natasha's turn to speak, to break the loneliness of the silence. "Leave her alone, JoAnne. I don't think you of all people have the right to lecture anyone on morals."

"Well, I think I have more right than most of you," yelled JoAnne, inflamed again. "Just take a look at your husband for a start." Everyone gasped as JoAnne blushed. She carried on hurriedly. "Sometimes I think Siobhan's the only one round here who's honest, who says it like it is."

The incriminations continued on in the downy dusk, where the air was soft and summery and there were no strangers to inhibit them, where the alcohol had finally dislodged stuck feelings, like years-old plaque set free by mouthwash. Sissy sat rigid on her auntie's rug, bought as a wedding present in a far ago, happier time, staring at her ankles below her unflattering flowery dress (why hadn't she just worn shorts like she preferred) and they appeared to be swelling, trying to drown the bones out. She wanted the screaming to stop, she didn't much care what they were saying anymore, she didn't care who was to blame, after all maybe *she* was, and anyway Nigel was dead, none of this would bring him back, no matter how loud any of them shouted.

28

Barnes

Alistair had just come back from the en-suite feeling a little better, but he still couldn't bear to even sit down at his desk, let alone make contact with the keyboard. The room was large and bright and looked out onto their garden which backed onto the common, so the view was sunny and cheerful and they'd both thought it would be a wonderful place for him to write. In London yet out of it, Natasha had said when they'd been to look at the house with the weaselly prick of an estate agent that Alistair had always felt like punching. Alistair hated the house now. He especially loathed his writing room. It made him feel trapped, locked in an airless hostile space with just the deeply irritating Shouty Mouse and Rude Rabbit for company. He thought if he had to do this for much longer it would drive him insane – but his agent was breathing down his neck, threatening that if he didn't come up with Volume Six soon the publisher would be taking back part of his latest advance for breach of contract. As if. Alistair Smart, king of children's fiction, author of the best-selling series about behaviour-challenged furry creatures, a poor Tourettes-ridden mouse and an autistic rabbit. Child psychologists had queued up to fete him, he had made "different" children feel normal, had created tales of such moral fortitude he'd helped parents and children alike gain empathy and understanding for these all too common conditions. His writing was acerbically, charmingly witty. He was a modern day Roald Dahl, a fucking hero!

Alistair finally stopped pacing, sat down and clicked onto one of his favourite porn sites, and as he watched two big-breasted girls cavorting in baby oil he felt his desire build all over again. What the hell was wrong with him these days? Just how much sperm could one man produce? He heard a noise on the stairs and quickly flicked over to his email, and he swore he was going to get rid of their housekeeper, what did they need one for anyway? He loathed her being around – even when Natasha was at work and the kids were at school he felt like he had to be on his guard, behave himself, almost as if he were just visiting, in his own fucking home. There was always someone in the house to intrude on his loneliness – the cleaner, the housekeeper (what was the difference between the two, he wondered idly), the gardener, the nanny. And how much did they all bloody cost?

The idea came to him in an instant then, and he kicked himself that he hadn't thought of it before – he would get a lock for his office door! Then he could browse lesbian porn and wank to his heart's content without even leaving his desk, whenever he was bored rigid (quite literally, he sniggered, always the master with words) or stuck on Shouty Mouse's latest tedious adventure he couldn't give a shit about.

Alistair was so excited by his idea that he thought he might go to Homebase right now, so he could buy a lock and a drill and fit it himself, it couldn't be that hard, surely. That would give him something to do. He was about to get up from his desk in a rare burst of energy when his email refreshed and two new ones appeared: the first from his agent which he ignored of course, and then one from someone called Smartfan, entitled: HELP ME ALISTAIR. Alistair was used to getting fan mail, mainly from 7 year olds, saying things like: "Dear Alister Smart, thank you so much for riting Showty Mous, he has mad me so hapy that I am not the only won lik him, love Oliver," or, worse, from gushing mothers saying, "You have made my darling Lucy one happy bunny (pardon the pun!), she no longer feels so isolated by her condition, and you have made one very happy mummy!! Thank you so much, and please keep on writing your wonderful books." They made Alistair puke.

This email however seemed a bit too shouty (he couldn't bring himself to snigger again), too desperate, to be just another fan letter, and although he usually left this kind of correspondence to his agent's assistant Xavier, he found himself opening it – he didn't dare go back on the internet while Mrs Cole was outside hoovering, and he couldn't face even looking at his hopelessly overdue manuscript today.

"Dear Mr Smart," it said. "I am a budding new writer and I have written a new children's book about a boarding school for dogs. All the dogs have different characters and the book is the first of a series that deals with all sorts of issues for the "Tweenie" market, from for example bullying, to how to cope with not having the latest must-have possessions, to realising you might be gay. I haven't sent it out to any agents yet because I would so love to have your view of my book first, and perhaps even a quote to put on the cover. You are the absolute champion of children's issue-based fiction and I have admired you for many years, from when I was a behaviour-challenged child myself. I am 19 years old and this is my first novel.

Yours excitedly

Lucinda Horne"

Normally Alistair ignored these kinds of emails, but there was something about this one: was it her name, or maybe her age (totally legal) – he still hadn't quite settled down in the trouser department – or was there something interesting about her story? He opened the attachment and started reading about Bottersley Dog School, with its three houses Barkers, Howlers and Sniffers, and its key characters Fluffy, T-Bone and Wowser, and as he whipped through the chapters he found the story surprisingly compelling, and so he settled down on the sofa under the window, his back flat, bare hairy feet up and over the end of it, and he felt himself relax for a minute, and then tighten – and then he felt his heart rate whoosh as the idea came to him, devilish and fully formed.

29

Cleveland

The music in the bar was loud and twangy, and although it wasn't the type that people usually dance to, there was so much pent up energy in the room that before anyone knew it Stephen was pulling the girls up and twirling them around as if they were in a salsa bar in Rio – Juliette had dragged him to classes in their final year at Bristol and he was surprisingly adept at it. Sissy had mildly protested and gone bright red, but hadn't actually stopped him when he'd grabbed her, she must have been drunk for once; and although the dreadful Melissa complained loudly when they accidentally barged her during a particularly complex over the head manoeuvre, once it was her turn she joined in with gusto, giggling up at him, even smooching a little, until he pushed her off with an expert flick of his wrist that sent her spinning away from him towards the bar, where the barmaid with the dead eyes looked on inscrutably.

JoAnne sat in the corner, propped on a high padded bar stool next to Andy, drinking steadily, and she found she couldn't stop herself from watching as Stephen twirled

Melissa (who was griping and moaning that he was hurting her back, and then as she came up from an admirably athletic backwards lunge was mooning at him with her silly simpleton face). Since the day at the lake when JoAnne had felt Stephen's flesh solid beneath hers as he towed her out of the waves – what, almost two weeks ago now – she'd been aware of him in a way that surprised, no, not surprised, shocked her. She tried not to think of Stephen in that way, Juliette was her very best friend after all, and whatever people might think she was not the type to steal other people's boyfriends – but more than that she'd never much liked him before, let alone found him remotely attractive. It was bizarre.

JoAnne tried to force her mind away from strange thoughts about Stephen, but combined with the drink the effort of doing so seemed to make everything worse somehow, mixed everything up. Suddenly, as if he were there, she experienced the stranger on top of her, saw the twisted look in his eyes, smelled the sour stench of his breath, felt the hairy sweat between his legs, the hardness, of him, of the floor... and now she was back in the lake, stinking dieselly water filling her mouth, lungs burning, Stephen's thighs beneath hers, waves slapping at her face remonstratively... and to drown out these sensations, stop the spinning in her head, she took another deep draw of her beer. She shuddered. She wished she could feel normal again.

JoAnne knew within herself, in somewhere locked and fragile, that this peculiar mind set wouldn't simply go away, couldn't be cleansed by the water of Lake Erie, by pretending nothing had happened – or by becoming attracted to *Stephen* of all people. She tried to process it. Just how had the man's attack left her? Naked and lacking in self-respect, that's what. She knew she should have gone to the police, but it was too late now. *What if he does it to someone else though?* It would be her fault if he did, she'd be as culpable as him in a way. She stared at her hands and willed herself not to go and wash them again, they were getting so dried out, but it was as if they were tainted by what they'd done, where they'd been. It was as if the attack had been on her hands as well as her body. She shivered, although it was hot in the bar.

"Are you OK, Jo?" asked Stephen, as he walked over and stood casually next to her in the dingy light, having managed to shrug off Melissa at last, who was now propped further along the bar droning on to Andy about the inadequacies of American food establishments.

"Sure," said JoAnne, and she looked sideways at him and smiled, and then she felt nervous so she looked down again, back into her beer. "Enjoying swinging the girls around are you?"

Stephen laughed. "It started off as a joke, but Melissa seems to think she's on bloody Come Dancing."

"That girl is so unbelievably stupid," said JoAnne. "It's like there's a part of her brain missing or something."

"That's a bit harsh," said Stephen. "You're not jealous are you?"

JoAnne coloured, and they both stared at their drinks now. Stephen shifted as Andy roared derisorily at something Melissa had said, although she hadn't meant it to be funny, throwing his head back, narrowly avoiding knocking into Stephen's drink. Stephen budged up and JoAnne could feel the comforting warmth of his arm against hers. She thought about moving away, about creating some space between them, but she stayed there, not quite knowing why.

"Remember, he's Juliette's boyfriend," she told herself, but the thought drifted away and her brain replaced it with another: "She finished with him, they're not together anymore." She looked into his eyes and they were large and deeply brown, like muddy puddles, kind even. She smiled shyly at him, and Stephen moved in a little more then, so his leg was pressing against hers under the bar and they remained like that for ages, half-enjoying, half-dreading the physical contact, the possibility, as the music blared around them.

30

Hyde Park

In a park in central London on a perfect summer's evening it was a close call who could become the most hysterical. Amongst the group of picnickers there was a woman who was tired of living with her bully of a husband, a man who had just been called a *murderer*, in effect; another whose husband was dead; one who had recently found out hers was having an affair with one of her supposed best friends, who happened to be right here too, apparently unaware that her secret was out; one sobbing drunkenly about having been raped years ago; and a fifth who usually managed to be the most melodramatic without having to try too hard, so was feeling a bit put out, she really wasn't used to this level of competition. Siobhan was confused. Her skinny jeans were ruined, she was mortified by her outburst about Stephen, there was a sick feeling in her stomach that Matt still hadn't called her – and she was far too drunk to deal with any of it. She leaned over and picked up a glass near Natasha, she had no idea whose, and drank the contents straight down, although she knew that wouldn't help. Camilla was getting up, being all mumsy and sensible, draping her jumper over her shoulders, going on about how they should all go home; and Siobhan had a sudden dread of the evening ending, despite how horrifically it was turning out, of going home to her empty flat and her absent boyfriend and her over-fed cat Norris – and all she wanted was for the others to look after her, like they used to. She started bawling, mainly because she was pissed and couldn't think what else to do. It was dark and the park was nearly empty now, and the sounds seemed to travel further than they should, ringing out rancorously across the water, as if they would reach over the grass and through the trees all the way to the Bayswater Road, they were that ragingly loud.

"Oh just shut up, Siobhan," said Juliette. "For God's sake. If it wasn't for you and your big mouth none of this would have happened." Siobhan looked shocked at Juliette's outburst, she never used to snap like that. Juliette stared across at Sissy, who appeared to have deflated, was just sat with her head on her knees on her fancy woollen rug, shoulders shaking gently.

"Look what you've done to poor Sissy," she added, as if for emphasis.

Siobhan lost it then.

"Look what *I've* done to her," she yelled. "I've done nothing! She wouldn't even be a widow if it wasn't for your lying bastard of a husband, and you know it." Even Siobhan looked shocked at what she'd said, for a second – and then her tongue ran away with itself, as if it were operating unilaterally and had decided there was no going back now. "In fact most of your husbands are pathetic," she continued. "They're either scheming bullies," and she looked pointedly at Katie and Juliette. "Or they're adulterous perverts." She flashed a look at Natasha at this point. "And you're all too wrapped up in your posh houses and fancy cars and private schools to do anything about it. You know, sometimes I think me and Sissy are the only ones left with any morals at all."

"Morals," snorted Natasha. "You've got to be joking."

"And I don't live in a posh house," said Katie, somewhat pointlessly, but she always did seem to have an inferiority complex about her social standing, about never having gone to university perhaps. "Stop tarring us all with the same brush, will you – and what's where people live got to do with anything anyway? You are just so ludicrously hung-up that you've never managed to hold down a relationship. It's always the same when I see you. If you didn't bitch and moan and go on about yourself so much maybe you wouldn't be so bloody lonely." Katie was on a roll too this evening – she just hoped she'd be able to maintain it when she got home to her husband.

Juliette was standing now, looking like she might even punch Siobhan, and she was so shocked and humiliated that she was debating whether to just dump her massive picnic hamper and go home, flag down a cab on the bridge and leave the lot of them, this was unbearable. In the end it was Sissy who spoke.

"Please can we stop this," she said quietly. "None of it's going to bring Nigel back, and I'm sure no-one did anything deliberately. Please let's not make everything worse by all screaming and shouting at each other. All I want to do is go home, *please*, let's just get packed up and go."

Sissy stood up and shook out her rug and even in the fading light it was clear that tears were running down her cheeks and she looked small and hunched, like a little girl who's been smacked by her mummy, undeservedly. No-one spoke as they packed up, and the atmosphere was sullen, brittle, utterly irreparable; and each woman was aware that their life would never be quite the same again, not after this, although at that point they didn't realise in what way.

31

Cleveland

Sissy looked over into the corner of the bar, where the lights were dim and the music was loudest, and she didn't know whether to feel annoyed or anxious. What the heck was JoAnne thinking, she was really going too far now. Stephen had found himself a bar stool and was sitting next to JoAnne, his dirty mid-brown head bent close to her sleek dark one, and even from here Sissy could see that their feet were intertwined underneath the counter. What on earth would Juliette say? The funny thing was that Sissy had asked her, back in Bristol, if she was worried about Stephen meeting someone else over the summer, and Juliette had replied that she'd even be quite glad if he did – what would be would be, she'd said – and Sissy had wondered at the time if Juliette would ever get back with Stephen, she'd seemed almost desperate to be free of him.

"What *would* upset me, though," Juliette had continued. "Is if he got off with one of my friends – but you're far too in love with Nigel, thank goodness, and JoAnne doesn't even like him."

"Juliette!" Sissy had said, shocked. "That's not true; of course she does."

"Darling Sissy," Juliette had replied. "You're so sweet and that's what I love about you. But Jo's not keen on Stephen and never has been, and if I'm honest that's always made me a teeny bit wary about him too. I do tend to trust her opinion, deep down."

"Don't you think it might be that..." Sissy had stopped.

"What?"

"Oh, nothing."

"Come on, Sissy, what were you going to say?"

"...Don't you think... she might be... a little bit jealous of him?" Sissy had said finally.

"What on earth do you mean?"

"Well," she'd floundered. "You do see him quite a lot."

"Oh," Juliette had said. "Do you think so? (Pause.) I suppose I do... Oh God, I feel awful now.

"Anyway," she'd continued, changing the subject. "Let's see what happens over the summer – and with any luck I might meet a hunky Spanish waiter in Marbella, ha ha."

Just as Sissy remembered the end of this conversation, she saw in the orange glow Stephen lean in and caress JoAnne's face, and JoAnne stop and look at him, as if trying to make up her mind what to do; and now she was laughing at something he'd just said and they were almost rubbing faces, it was quite revolting really, and although Sissy tried not to look she was almost transfixed; and now, no, oh my God they were, they were fully, full-on, mouth-open tonsil-munching snogging, and she could see his revolting darting tongue, and he was wrapping his arms around her clumsily, like a bear – and, oh no, now he was standing up and virtually dry humping her. It was disgusting.

Melissa noticed next, and started going, "Ooorgh, have you seen Stephen and JoAnne?" When they realised everyone was watching they stopped snogging for a while, and Stephen sat back down on his stool with his hand in his lap, as if he were concealing something, but after a little while they started laughing and smooching again, until eventually Stephen stood up and hoisted JoAnne off her seat too, and Sissy noticed that she staggered a little – and then they left, and didn't come back.

32

Hyde Park

Terry Kingston was fed up with prowling around in Hyde Park, like some kind of cottager, chasing after a group of middle-aged women having a *picnic,* for God's sake. It seemed obvious to him that his client's wife was on a girls' night out, and a pretty tame one at that, rather than taking part in any clandestine extra-marital relations, for tonight at least. Terry was tired now and wanted to go home, get back to painting his fusiliers, he needed to finish them before the convention in Nottingham the following weekend. It had been more difficult to observe the women since they'd moved from Diana's fountain, there was no obvious place for him to sit here, plus it was getting very late for him to still be in the park alone, he'd look like a ruddy pervert if he wasn't careful. He'd ended up having to hide behind a tree near the cafe, meaning he couldn't actually watch them anymore, but he could see along the path to the bridge, would know if anyone came or went – and although he couldn't hear the detail of what they were saying now, it was pretty obvious no-one was having much fun. What are women like, he thought to himself. Why oh why did he ever marry one, he'd have been so much happier with just his pets and his pastimes for company. And then he felt a flash of guilt about Maria – his view of women wasn't her fault, he knew who to blame for that one.

Terry shifted on the patch of grass he'd made his seat for the past hour and looked at his watch for perhaps the twenty-fifth time. He'd been specifically told to wait all evening to see where she went afterwards. His client was convinced that she wouldn't be coming straight home as she'd said – she always got in so late from her supposed girls' nights out these days – and so Terry was stuck here. It was very tedious, normally he wouldn't take on a domestic job, creeping around in the bloomin' bushes like this, but he was doing it as a favour, it was for his half-brother after all.

The dark was descending quickly now, and what little of The Serpentine he could see streaming away towards the bridge appeared blackly thick, like liquid mud. There was hardly anyone around – just a wiry middle-aged woman with over-sized head-phones and well-defined muscles who jogged elegantly past, her breath effortless, like a Kenyan marathon-runner's; and twenty minutes later a couple walking along the bank arm in arm, chatting comfortably, almost like they were still in love.

Terry was sleepy. He rested his head against the tree and felt himself dozing off in the summer haze. He was tired of listening to all the bitching and moaning, glad he couldn't make out the exact words – apart from the occasional louder one every now and then (*murder* he was sure was one, which had made his detective-ears prick up, and surely *rape* another). And then it went quieter suddenly, as though someone

147

had told them to shush. He yawned. His eyelids started to stretch involuntarily downwards, his long lashes fluttering indecisively, as though debating whether or not to succumb to sleep – and then he flicked them up again, briskly. He'd been startled by a scream; well, not a scream exactly, more of an anguished roar, as if an animal had grabbed a woman's baby perhaps, and was running off with it. He shrank into the shadows as a woman came careering past, sobbing. He watched as she threw herself down by the side of The Serpentine, her identity unclear in the darkness, and despite himself he felt a pang of sympathy as she knelt at the water's edge and keened, head between her knees. What the bloody hell was going on? He thought he'd been hired simply to find out if his client's wife was having an affair, and now it seemed he'd stumbled into a potentially more explosive situation.

Terry tried to make sense of it. He stood up and hopped from side to side, like a little boy who needs to go to the toilet, indecisive as to what to do. He sat down again, and waited. After a few minutes, he heard voices coming closer to him, and he shrank back into the bushes as he heard a well-spoken one slurring, "My God, I can't deal with any more of this tonight, let's just leave her to it. All she's doing is trying to shift the attention back to herself as usual."

"But do you think she's OK?" said another voice, and it was timid, anxious-sounding. "She's hysterical... how's she going to get home?"

A third voice cut in then. "D'you think she hasn't been in this sort of state enough times before? She always manages to find her own way home eventually. And after the things she's said tonight, I don't think we owe her anything."

"But she's right by the water," the timid voice said. "And she's so drunk..."

"She'll be fine, she always is," said the voice. It paused. "And anyway, if she does fall in she can bloody drown for all I care."

The timid voice went to object, but the drunk posh voice said, "NO. Let's go, I need to get home now, I've just about had enough for one day. I'm sorry but I'm NEVER EVER doing this again, it's all just too awful."

Terry pressed back into the undergrowth as the women started leaving, and he counted six of them – although one was quite a long way in front, walking fast, as though she couldn't wait to get away – but it was too dark to be sure from here whether his target was amongst them. Perhaps it was her who'd run off into the night – he wouldn't put it past her, he always knew she had some kind of screw loose, like most women. One of the group seemed to be limping, and another two were carting the enormous picnic basket and carrying folding chairs across their backs, like bows and arrows. They were nearly at the bridge now and he could see the outlines of five of them, a good hundred yards from him. It was probably safe for him to start following now. He hesitated again. Maybe he should double-check it wasn't his target down by the water after all, just in case – his brother would give him hell if he lost her, and it would only take a minute. After a few more seconds of dithering he finally made up his mind, and moved carefully along the shadows towards The Serpentine.

33

Cleveland

Stephen and JoAnne staggered home from the bar along the deserted sidewalk next to the busy main road – arms draped around each other, stopping continuously to snog, then carrying on walking, still kissing and stumbling, almost falling over. JoAnne felt euphoric. Even through her drunkenness she could feel the acute sadness of the past two weeks twist and lift, as though it were spiralling away from her, leaving her free again. She realised now what part of her distress had been: unbridled loneliness. She'd felt isolated and disorientated anyway since graduation, but it had got acutely worse since the attack. She realised she'd been missing college life, her best friend Juliette, the home they'd made in Bristol which was forever gone now, even her mother who she never saw anyway – and it felt so good to be held tight and safe. It wasn't just a sexual feeling, it was more one of feeling alive, of being important, relevant again in the world, at least to someone. She didn't think much beyond that, she was too hammered.

As they reached the house and started dragging themselves up the driveway Stephen went in for an overly-ambitious embrace, and she stumbled in her heels, and finally, inevitably, they lost their footing. They collapsed together onto the packed red dirt, and the dust flew up accusingly.

"Owww," laughed JoAnne, but she didn't get up, just lay there winded, knickers on show, her knee burning and sticky. "Are you OK?"

"I'm fine," said Stephen, and as he nuzzled into her she could feel the grit sticking to them both, like breadcrumbs on schnitzels. They rolled around for a bit, but JoAnne was uncomfortable, the stones were digging into her − so she pushed him off and straddled him instead, leaning teasingly down and saying that she was filthy, she needed a shower first. She hauled herself up and managed to pull him to his feet too, which was no mean effort, and although he went to grab her again she told him he'd have to wait, and she ran giggling upstairs to the bathroom, and locked the door.

34

Hyde Park

Even as Terry crept closer, he still couldn't be sure whether the woman by the water was his sister-in-law – clouds had drifted in, obscuring the moon, and with her head between her knees like that it was difficult to be certain. His eyes were watering now, one of those bushes must have set off his hay-fever again, and he rubbed at them which just made it worse. He was feeling increasingly agitated – the longer he hung around here the more likely he'd lose her if she *had* left, was with the group after all. His client would give him hell. He had to be quick. He moved a little closer. As if on cue, the moon came out and she lifted her head and looked up.

Shit! It wasn't her – she must be with the others after all, he was going to lose her. He ducked away and legged it past the reed beds towards the bridge, his heart hammering in his ears.

Terry was in luck – the women were moving so slowly, weighed down as they were by their picnic paraphernalia, that they were still on the path. As he got nearer he slackened his pace and edged along carefully, discreetly following them.

The arguing had stopped but he could hear soft crying now, although he wasn't sure from whom. No-one was speaking, and the fury in the air, even from a distance, felt tangible, like dust. They were almost at the bridge and he could see five of the women clearly, a good hundred yards from him still. Just as the first one made it onto the stone steps there was a noise: a thud and then a loud undignified splash, resonating into the night. They stopped.

"What was that?" one of them asked, the timid one Terry thought.

"It must have been a bird," said the posh voice.

"Don't be ridiculous, that wasn't a bird," said a third voice. "It must have been her."

They all stood still, weaving a little. There was silence, no splashing, just the dull thrum of the traffic along Kensington Gore. Precious seconds passed.

"We need to go and look," the timid voice said, and she spread fear into the air.

They listened again, but it was quiet still.

"It's nothing, come on."

"Maybe we should check," said another voice and although it was posh too it had a slight edge to it, like maybe once it hadn't been.

"I've told you," said the first voice. "I'm not going back, I'm going home. She'll be fine. I didn't even hear anything if anyone asks me; ten more yards and we'd be up on the road with –" Terry didn't catch the name.

"I can't believe you!" said a new voice.

"Well, what are you going to do? Call the police?"

"Yes, maybe I will."

There was more silence then, as if they were all hesitating, not sure what to do next. Finally, one of the earlier voices spoke and said, "Well, I don't think we can do anything now. It must have been nothing, we would have heard her screaming otherwise. Let's go."

And it was like an unspoken pact, a group brainwash. They appeared to make a decision en masse and, as if connected by a long invisible rope, they slunk up the steps together – heaving picnic baskets and rugs and chairs – and shuffled away into the night. The whole thing had taken less than a minute. Terry hesitated himself now, his instinct telling him to go towards the water – and then he thought of his brother, of his brother's temper, of his, Terry's, fee, and he came out from his hiding place, and he looked up and down the bank seeing nothing, just moonlit nothingness. He went to hurry away from The Serpentine, after the women, and then he remembered himself, someone could be *drowning* down there, and he turned and ran back towards the water's edge, and as he stared down into the stillness, willing himself to see something, a ripple, anything, he reached into his jacket pocket, for his mobile phone.

Part Two

35

Bristol

JoAnne knocked gently and, hearing no answer, slowly opened the door into Juliette's room. Her eyes took a while to adjust to the half-light, but soon she could make out the clothes still strewn on the floor, like the wind had got to them, and the lump in the single bed, one cold-looking foot protruding from the pink gingham duvet.

"Oh, you are there," she said. "I thought you might have stayed at Stephen's last night."

"No, he tried to get me to," said Juliette, turning over and yawning. "But I need to do an essay today, so I wanted to get back."

"Why didn't he come too?" said JoAnne. "After all, you two are officially joined at the hip these days."

Juliette looked uncertain for a second. "Oh, you know," she said, stretching her arms above her head. "I hate sleeping in a single bed with him, he's too big, so I sent him home."

"Well, well done," said JoAnne, and she smiled to show she was being kind rather than sarcastic, Juliette could sometimes take things the wrong way.

"And anyway," continued Juliette. "I thought it would be nice to spend some time with my flat-mates. I feel like we never get to see each other anymore."

"Well, whose fault is that?" said JoAnne, and it came out more harshly than she intended, and Juliette definitely looked offended now. JoAnne changed the subject.

"Are you going to the economics seminar this morning?" she said. "Can I borrow your notes? I'm not going, I need to finish my sodding psychology assignment."

"Sure," said Juliette. "Although I don't know why I bother, I never understand a bloody word of it. I don't think maths is in my genes." She stopped and looked lost suddenly, as if she'd forgotten something important. JoAnne spotted an opening.

"Listen, I saw this thing in the Guardian yesterday, there was this article about how to track down your birth mother. I think it's quite easy."

"Jo, I told you before, *I don't want to*," said Juliette. She shifted in the bed and sat up against the pillows, resting her head awkwardly on the bare wall behind her. JoAnne went to speak but Juliette stopped her. She'd only recently confided in JoAnne that she was even adopted – even though they'd hit it off immediately and it was mid-way through the first term already. She'd seemed ashamed of it somehow. JoAnne had told her not to be ashamed – after all, it was less of an insult to be given up at birth, before her mother had got to know her, than to be left at four years old for a lover in Paris. Now *that* was a rejection if ever there was one, not that JoAnne voiced the comparison of course.

"Please stop going on about it Jo, she's my mother, not yours."

"Sorry," said JoAnne, aware she'd gone too far. "I just thought it might help you, that's all."

"I'll decide if and when I'm ready, thank you very much," said Juliette, but she sounded softer now, as if she knew JoAnne meant well. "I know *you* think there's one, but *I* don't feel like there's a gap in my life, in fact my life feels quite full enough right now without anyone else getting involved in it." She swung her legs out of bed and they were blue-mottled, like an over-cold baby's. Her pink-eared rabbit lay forlornly on the pillow, abandoned. She stood up and tugged at her T-shirt, pulling it over her bottom, then she bent over and shook her auburn curls so dust and dandruff flew up and danced in the sunshine drenching through the curtains.

"Ugh, I need a cup of tea," she said.

"I'll make one," said JoAnne, and fled to the kitchen, where no-one had done the washing up as usual, so she'd had to rinse out two mugs that still had faint brown rings inside them even after she'd washed them. As JoAnne left the bedroom Juliette moved through one hundred and eighty degrees to stand up straight, and behind the tumult of hair there were fat sparkling glycerin tears forming at the very edges of her eyes – although of course they were gone by the time her friend returned.

36

Fulham

The home phone rang in South West London but Juliette ignored it, just sat at the solid oak kitchen table nursing her mug of tea, staring into its contents, trying to look beyond the surface at what lay beneath. She'd barely slept the night before, and she'd obviously drunk way more Prosecco than she'd realised: her head was throbbing and she felt empty, as though her stomach had been hoovered perhaps. She wondered just what they'd done the previous evening. Had they been totally nuts, abandoning their friend like that when she'd been so drunk, especially near water? What on earth had happened? What if that splash had been her after all, what if she really had fallen in, had drowned, was *dead*? It was too horrendous to contemplate. OK, they may have had an almighty row, but no-one wanted anything bad to happen to her, they hadn't wanted her to *drown* for God's sake.

Juliette's mind raced. *What had caused the splash?* It was too loud to be a bird, she knew it now. *It was her friend, she was dead.* Of course she wasn't. *She might be.* She wasn't, those things don't happen, not in real life. *What if she's dead?* They'd left her – would it be their fault? *What would happen to them?* Would they have committed some kind of crime, especially knowing the state she was in? It was unthinkable.

The only thing Juliette was sure of, through the throb in her brain, was that she would never ever go out with those women again – getting together had become increasingly fraught over the years anyway for all sorts of reasons, but last night they had mined a new seam of hatred and envy, of poisonous secrets uncovered, of tragedy beckoning and maybe having occurred. She'd discovered things that were surely too hideous to be true, things that made her sick.

Radio 4 blared obliviously in the background, going on about something called a double-dip recession, and it made her think idly of a fairground ride, a roller-coaster that left your stomach in the downward bit, before it swept upwards again away from it, leaving you screaming with terror.

Noah slunk back into the kitchen, although she'd sent all the children upstairs to get ready, unable to cope with the noise levels this morning. He stood there silently, just staring at her, dangling his revolting-looking bear by one arm beside him. His pyjamas didn't match and there was a wet patch in the front of his trousers, Ireland-shaped. Juliette looked up from her tea. She tried to stay calm.

"Noah, sweetheart," she sighed. "Have you wet your trousers again? I thought I told you to go upstairs and put on your school uniform."

"I haven't, Mummy," said Noah, trying denial as a tactic this morning.

The panic was rising in Juliette's throat.

"Yes, you have! Don't lie to me, Noah."

"Sorry, Mummy," he said, taking a conciliatory approach now, but rather than help it seemed to enrage her. Juliette let rip, she couldn't help herself.

"Well sorry's not good enough is it? *Not* wetting your trousers is good enough. *Getting ready* for school is good enough. Anyone would think you were still three years old."

Noah looked as if he might cry at that onslaught, but he didn't answer, just stood there silently, teddy trailing, eyes wide, the patch in his trousers getting bigger.

"Oh, for God's sake," said Juliette. "Just get into the toilet will you," and she stood up and dragged him by the arm towards the downstairs cloakroom, and he started screaming at this treatment, and she couldn't stand the noise, so she shoved him in and pulled the door shut, leaning heavily against it, so he couldn't get out. She closed her eyes and tried counting to ten, but by the time she got to six she heard a noise, and when she opened them Flo was standing there.

"What?" she said crossly.

"Mummy, are you hurting Noah again?" asked Flo.

"No, I am *not*," said Juliette. "He just can't stop wetting his trousers. It's disgusting.

"And what do you mean, again?" she added, realising what her daughter had said. She felt inflamed with shame. "How *dare* you?"

Flo stood looking at Juliette, and somewhere in her nine-year old brain she was aware that her mother's temper and Noah's incontinence were quite firmly related, but she knew better than to say anything more, she was lucky her mother's reaction hadn't been worse. Noah sat on the toilet seat behind the door with his Spiderman trouser bottoms around his ankles – he found he needed to do a poo as well now for some reason – and as he kicked his legs the word kept repeating in his head, over and over, although he tried his hardest to stop it. The phone started up again and even the sound of that changed into the word, and it went on and on, through the hallway, echoey with its high ceiling and fancy light fittings and solid parquet floor, as his mother still didn't go to answer it – bring bring, bring bring, disgusting, disgusting, disgusting.

37

Bristol

"D'you ever wonder what she's like?" asked JoAnne. It was nearing the end of their first term and she was lying curled up at the bottom of Juliette's bed, the end of the duvet folded over her feet against the winter cold. Juliette was still in the bed, even though it was nearly midday and she should have been at a psychology lecture, and as usual she was propped up against the wall with a mug of milky tea under her chin. A deluge of clothes lay flung across the floor, and it was impossible to tell whether they were clean – just tried on and carelessly rejected – or actually in need of washing.

"Yes, sometimes, I suppose," said Juliette. "It's just very weird, knowing that there's someone out there who gave birth to me and then..." She stopped.

"Have you thought any more about tracking her down?"

"God no, what would my mum and dad say, I'm sure they'd think of it as some kind of betrayal."

"I'm sure they wouldn't," said JoAnne. She thought of her own mother then, who'd done the same thing in effect, had relinquished her too, only she'd taken a few more years to do it. Maybe that's why she and Juliette were so close – they both had "abandonment issues," and it was weird how that had never occurred to her before. They were similar in so many ways, it was uncanny.

"What do you think she looks like?"

"How would I know?" said Juliette, but she didn't seem cross to be asked these kinds of questions for a change, so JoAnne carried on.

"She must have been beautiful," said JoAnne. "Look at that hair she's given you."

"Shush," said Juliette. "I hate my hair." And she did, although she had tumbling corkscrew curls the colour of ginger biscuits that people always stared at, because what with her dark lashes and deep green eyes she was just so unimaginably stunning.

"Maybe she was a film star," JoAnne continued. "Maybe she was Chantelle Dauphin, she's about the right age. YES, you look just like her. Maybe she was over here filming when you were conceived, and then she thought she'd have you adopted by an English couple."

"Don't be so bloody silly," said Juliette, trying to smile, but JoAnne knew she'd perhaps gone too far, her friend was obviously still quite fragile about it. She shifted a little on the narrow bed, away from Juliette's foot, which had been poking her in the ribs anyway, and as her head hit the wall the pain was concrete, unpleasant.

"Why don't you think about it, Juliette," she said gently. "It might do you some good... and I'd be happy to help you."

"I don't know, I'll have to consider it," said Juliette. "And even if I did do it – which I'm 99% certain I won't by the way –

even then I'd only do it if you agreed to us going to Paris next summer." She paused, and her tone became softer. "Surely it would be good for you to see her Jo, she is your mother after all." JoAnne almost recoiled from the word. "And... and we could go shopping," Juliette continued, flustered. "Drink cafes au lait, hang out in the Louvre chatting up French boys – just so we could practise our French of course. It would be amazing."

JoAnne's face hardened under her bleach-tinged fringe, which Juliette secretly thought looked a bit odd against the black of the rest of her hair, she'd preferred it when it was purple.

"We'll see," JoAnne said. "But I've told you what she's like – even if she did agree to put us up she'd probably charge us for breakfast."

"Well, we should think about it," said Juliette. "Even if we don't track my mother down – which I repeat I officially do NOT want to do, before you start packing me off to Somerset House. We wanted to go inter-railing anyway, it would be mad not to start in Paris, and I'm sure we'd have a great time."

"I don't know about that – you haven't met my mother," said JoAnne, and her tone wasn't quite as jokey as she intended.

"I haven't even met my own," her friend replied, and JoAnne wasn't sure how to respond to that, Juliette had seemed so vulnerable before – but then Juliette started to giggle, and as she did so she slopped her tea onto the duvet and kicked her feet in mock-rage, sending JoAnne sprawling off the single bed, onto the blue-striped nylon carpet.

38

Fulham

Katie lay in bed in Juliette's house with a pillow over her head. All she could hear downstairs was screaming and shouting and the phone going on and on and on. She'd been looking forward to this break from Darren and the kids, but it had gone so horribly wrong that now all she wanted was to go home, to her family. She was appalled, disgusted by what they'd done last night, that they'd just left and gone home without going to check on their friend. She was certain now it wasn't a bird that they'd heard, it was a bloody big woman-sized splash. But if that was the case why had there been silence afterwards? What could have happened? Surely if it *had* been her she would have splashed around theatrically, screeching for attention?

As Katie shifted in the bed her bones felt heavy, like they were trying to burrow into the mattress, which was soft and pocket-sprung and ludicrously comfortable, but the comfort somehow made her feel like an imposter, like she shouldn't be there, like she should be lying still and drowned herself.

Drowned. Surely not, *no.*

Katie took her head out from the pillow and opened her eyes, attempting to work out from the light what time it was, debating whether she should get up yet, go downstairs, try to call her, get her to answer. She lay still, too afraid to move, trying to quell the dread, think of something, anything, else. She tried reflecting on her life, on what she'd achieved – but couldn't think of anything besides having become a downtrodden wife and mother with no career, no prospects, nothing. That didn't help, just made her feel worse in fact. She tried concentrating on her surroundings instead, taking in every detail. The curtains at the bay were thick and silky and hung all the way to the floor, pooling luxuriously. The chaise longue in front of the window was upholstered in dove-grey velvet that seemed to absorb the shadows thrown from the monstrous crystal chandelier hung high above the bed. The floor was painted linen-white with gorgeously thick sheepskin rugs slung casually across it, perfectly positioned to keep visitors' toes warm as they stepped out of bed. The fireplace was large, white marble, with arty black and white photos of the family arranged across the mantelpiece, below the muddy-hued artwork of a naked man and woman abstractedly embracing. It's an original, Katie thought, it must be worth a fortune. The room was twice the size of hers and Darren's, even though this was just the guest room. She sighed to herself, finally distracted from her hellish visions of The Serpentine: Juliette did have good taste, at least in home furnishings if not in husbands, she'd give her that.

It seemed calmer downstairs now, the kids seemed to have stopped crying at last, maybe she'd get up in a minute. But the feeling of doom, of fear and recrimination, just wouldn't go away, so when the home phone started up again, for the third time now, and then her mobile rang straight afterwards, Katie didn't even look to see who it was, she just dived under the covers and lay there, luxurious between the Egyptian cotton sheets, cold and shaking.

Darren O'Connell swore under his breath as his wife's phone went to voicemail yet again. Where the hell was she? He *knew* she'd been lying about going to Juliette's, and he wanted to kill her, the bitch. He hung up, and again tried Juliette's home number (which he'd copied off his wife's phone two nights before), in the hope that someone would answer, give him definitive proof she wasn't there – but having rung out just before, the line was engaged now. He howled with frustration and slammed his mobile onto the counter top, so hard he was lucky the screen didn't break, before he picked it up again and went to dial a third number.

"When's Mummy coming home?" said Molly, toying with her toast. She hated her father's tantrums, found her mother's moods easier to deal with – and she wished her mummy didn't go out so much, especially on a Wednesday when she should have been picking her up from Brownies.

"Your guess is as good as mine, Molly," said her father, and as both kids started to cry he continued, "I'm joking love, she'll pick you up from school," although privately he thought that that was if he hadn't throttled her first.

39

Bristol

Juliette abandoned her essay and scrabbled in the bin for the leaflet JoAnne had left in her room, feeling like she was cheating on her parents, even unscrewing it. She found she couldn't help herself though – JoAnne had seemed to unleash in her the desire for knowledge at least, if not reconciliation. *Who was she? Where had she been born? What name had she been given? Who was her real mother? What did she look like? Who was her father? Had her parents loved each other once?* It was very strange, almost like now the questions had been asked, they wouldn't go away, couldn't be un-asked, although she didn't dare tell JoAnne that of course – before she knew it JoAnne would be rushing her off to find out, given half a chance.

Juliette looked again at the leaflet. She needed her place of birth, her adoptive parents' names, some proof of ID and £5 in cash. That was it, to make a start at least. That's all it took. There was only one problem: Juliette didn't actually know where she'd been born, had never even asked her parents, which was odd now she came to think of it. Why hadn't she asked? Had the subject just been completely off limits, or had she simply not been interested? Or maybe she'd asked when she was younger and been brushed off, so had given up. It was weird. It seemed even odder now, to ring up her mother and ask about the weather and her jam-making and the Women's Institute, and, "Oh and by the way Mum, where did you get me from?" Aaaaagh, why did JoAnne ever stir this up? Juliette hadn't thought about it for years, and frankly she didn't have the head space for it at the moment, they had their end of term assignments due in soon, plus Stephen was taking up so much of her time these days, monopolising her really. Mostly though, she didn't want to risk hurting her parents.

She got up from her desk and walked over to the window and gazed out across the roof-tops, and she couldn't believe that she lived here in this fantastic city, with such brilliant friends, a doting boyfriend, doing a course that she loved, and she really should be fantastically happy. But instead she felt a growing sense of detachment, and she was vaguely aware that the space she had now, away from her family, was giving her the freedom to question who she really was. She moved across to the mirror next to the bed. Where *had* she got these extraordinary curls from? What if it turned out her birth mother really was a film star? She looked at her nose sideways in the mirror. It did have a conk to it, exactly like Ms Dauphin's. Don't be so bloody ridiculous, she told herself, it's just JoAnne putting ideas into your head. She thought again of Somerset House, of how London was only an hour and a half away by train, of how she and JoAnne were planning a trip there anyway to stay with JoAnne's aunt for the weekend. Maybe it wouldn't hurt to ask Mum, she thought. It's such a simple little question, surely she wouldn't mind. She could pretend it was to do with her course, having to research her birth-place or something, so as not to upset her. Yes, that's what she'd do, next time she rang.

"Hello, darling, how lovely to hear from you! I thought you weren't going to call until Saturday."

"Yes, I know," said Juliette. "But I was walking past the phones and they were empty for a change, so I thought I'd just give you a quick ring to see how you and Dad got on during your gardening trip." (This was a rare lie, she'd been queuing for over 40 minutes at exactly the same spot where a couple of months earlier she'd been befriended by a solid-looking sporty type, Stephen he'd said his name was, who she now seemed to be going out with, although she wasn't quite sure how that had happened.)

"Oh, you're such a sweetheart," continued her mother, pleased. "Yes, Wisley was super, thanks. It was terribly cold but I'd made a thermos of homemade soup, leek and potato, the cafes are so expensive in those places, and that kept the chill out."

"Great," said Juliette. "And how's McGee?"

"Oh, he's fine, darling. He's eating at last, thank goodness, and he's taken to chewing your father's slippers again, so he must be on the mend. Anyway, how are you, Juliette? How's your course going?"

"Oh, it's good Mum," said Juliette. She paused, she couldn't think what to say.

"Juliette, are you OK?" said her mother. "Is something the matter?"

"No, nothing Mum, honestly." Her phone card started beeping. She had to be quick. "Mum, we're doing a project as part of Psychology." She stopped again.

"Ye-es," replied her mother, aware now that something was definitely up. Surely Juliette wasn't homesick, she'd seemed so happy when they'd spoken the other day.

"Well, we're meant to research the town where we're from, where we were born I mean, and... and, well I... Mummy, I don't know where I'm from."

"Oh," said her mother, and her voice changed, still warm but wary now, although no-one but Juliette would have noticed. "What are you asking, Juliette dear?"

The phone started beeping again. Juliette spoke urgently.

"Mum, where was I born? Can you tell me?"

Her mother replied and then the phone cut out and between the beeps Juliette wasn't sure whether her mother had said Acton or Clacton.

40

Barnes

It was Friday morning, the day after the picnic, and Natasha had been back from her run for well over ten minutes. She was standing in her kitchen fuming, absolutely bloody furious with Juliette, but she was dimly aware that that was easier than being angry with herself. Every time she rang it, Juliette's mobile went straight to voicemail and she just wouldn't pick up her home phone either, although Natasha knew she'd be there, it was still too early for her to have left to take the kids to school. Surely one of her many domestic staff should be there at this time, why weren't they picking up either?

Natasha let Juliette's home phone ring – it didn't seem to go to answer phone, but just kept ringing and ringing until finally a loud continuous parp parp would signal that even BT had had enough of waiting, and then Natasha would call it again, as dogged as ever. She debated whether to simply get in the car and go round to Juliette's, after all they really needed to get their story straight before they spoke to anyone, just in case something had happened – but the traffic would be terrible and she needed to be at work early, she had a board meeting to prepare for, and Juliette would almost certainly have left for the school run by the time she'd be able to get there. As she stood staring at her mobile, ready to hurl it across the room in frustration, an idea came to her. She'd leave Juliette for now, she obviously didn't want to talk to her, or to anyone else for that matter. Natasha wouldn't talk to the others for the time being either, it might make it worse, and anyway Juliette was the one who would have known what to do; she was the one with connections.

Eventually Natasha decided on her strategy – hopefully she was just catastrophising anyway, but if needs be she would go to the police by herself, after the weekend. *She* hadn't done anything wrong after all, and then if anything bad had happened to her friend – whose phone incidentally also went straight to voicemail (*that's because it's waterlogged, at the bottom of The Serpentine,* said a little voice she tried to ignore) – she, Natasha, would be in the clear. She heard a noise from the hallway, and flinched. The kids had already left for school with the nanny, and the cleaner hadn't arrived yet. *Alistair.* Christ, she could do without seeing him this morning – she'd snuck out of bed while he was still pretending to be asleep, his back to her, hostile as ever. The sounds went away, thank God, he must have heard her too. The kettle finished boiling and she made a strong instant coffee, no milk, three sugars, and when she drank it it burned her tongue and the sensation, that her tongue was rough and sanded, stayed with her for the rest of that terrible day, like an imprint of wrongdoing.

41

The Bristol to London train

The 17.35 train was crowded with a mixture of people – commuters, day trippers, students – and the carriages had been incorrectly labelled, so everyone was sitting in the wrong seats and passengers were having to stand up again although they'd already got settled in for the journey, resulting in much clutching of disrobed coats and scarves and hats to chests, and people were struggling with Walkmans and glasses and books and already unfolded newspapers, trying not to but bound to drop things. Although it was freezing outside the train itself was hot and airless, almost feverish in its atmosphere – it was Friday night and people were in that very specifically jolly mood of work being over for a while, and what with the carriage mix-up strangers were being forced to interact more than they usually would, and they were rolling their eyes at each other good-naturedly, saying things like, "Bloody British Rail," and even offering to swap seats in an abnormally magnanimous fashion.

JoAnne and Juliette were sitting crammed in by the door next to the buffet car, and it kept opening and closing and there was the occasional whiff of toilets, and Juliette found her mind was racing, absolutely bloody motoring, faster than the train even. She sat there pondering all sorts of important issues: wondering what mark she'd get for her economics assignment, it had been so rushed in the end; trying to picture what kind of train designer would put the toilets right next to the food, surely that's unhygienic; questioning who had chosen the vile green pattern for the seat covers, was it the same person, or would that be someone else's job; noticing that JoAnne seemed to have put on weight lately, was looking fuller around the face, or maybe it was just the effect of her new orange fringe; observing that the guard in the buffet car had that faraway look in his eyes, as though he were on a journey somewhere, which of course he was, and what must it be like to trundle from one side of the country to the other serving coffee and sausage rolls as your job; and what was his accent, it was so distinctive but she couldn't place it, where did he actually live, east or west, or maybe in-between, Swindon perhaps. Juliette thought of absolutely anything she could, anything that might stop her looking at every passenger who passed by her seat and thinking, "That could be my mother," or "Maybe that's my brother," and she wondered again what was going on inside her head these days. Why were all these questions and fanciful theories surfacing now? Was it just that nineteen years of self-denial had dammed up, like water reaching a frozen waterfall, unable to go anywhere, and now the sun had come out and the waters had started to melt, just a little, until the onwards force had become inexorable and the water had started fully flowing again, down into the icy river, waking her up from herself. Don't be so bloody pretentious, she thought. All she planned on for now was trying to have a look – and even if she found it, which was unlikely anyway, just a little peep at a birth certificate wouldn't make much difference, surely? She'd just have a peek, and then she'd leave it all alone again, most definitely. And even if she did find she wanted to carry on further in her search she'd wait, for months or years even, until she'd worked out how to talk to her parents about it, made sure they were all right about everything. No, there was no harm in just having a look.

"You all right, Jules?" said JoAnne, glancing across from her Marie Claire article about ten ways to say no to your man without him losing interest.

"Yes, I'm fine, thanks," said Juliette, forcing a smile.

"You'll like my Auntie Linda. She is one feisty woman."

"Where did you say she lived?"

"In Camden, not far from the market."

"Oh," said Juliette, and she couldn't recall having been told that before, surely she would have remembered. She wondered what kind of place Linda had – she'd been to Camden once before and it had just seemed full of dirty-looking people with parrot-red mohicans and rings through their noses, or else drunks with uniformly grey beards and filthy overcoats, like they'd been dipped in ash, or dreadlocked hippies straight off the plane from Goa in tie-dyed trousers with the crotch around their knees. She thought it seemed an odd place for an auntie to live, and one who was a doctor at that. She thought of her own Auntie Deirdre and Uncle Peter in their neat semi-detached house in Amersham, and decided Linda sounded nothing like them.

"Did she ever get married, or has she always been single?" asked Juliette.

"Hmm, I don't think marriage is her thing," said JoAnne.

"What do you mean?"

"Well, you'll see," laughed JoAnne, and Juliette felt even more uneasy then. It all felt a bit much – going to somewhere as edgy as Camden, staying with an odd-sounding stranger, *taking the first step to maybe finding her mother.* She leaned back against the seat and shut her eyes and willed herself to feel the vibration of the train, the steady clackety clack that grounded her again, made her feel more normal, and as she did so the buffet man said, "Two coffees, there you go Sir," and she realised with a jolt that he was from bloody Birmingham, how could she have missed that.

42

Hyde Park

Terry Kingston seemed like a dodgy sort of bloke to PC Ryan. What was he doing hanging about by the Serpentine cafe at this time of night anyway? How could there possibly have been a splash but then no other noise, as he was claiming – surely if some drunk woman had gone and fallen in the water Terry Kingston would have heard a commotion, or seen some splashing, would have known where it had happened at least?

PC Ryan was fed up. It was his wife's birthday the next day and they were meant to be going away, down to Ramsgate for the weekend, and he wanted to get home on time tonight of all nights, so he could get up early and not be tired and grouchy for a change. He walked up and down the river bank (was it actually a river, he wondered, does London have other rivers apart from the Thames?), but he knew that there was no real point to it – if she really had fallen in at around 22.35 as Terry Kingston had said, then that was over 20 minutes ago, there was no way she'd still be alive by now. He sighed. He'd probably have to call in the frogmen, which meant he wouldn't be getting home for at least a couple more hours. He thought he would try one last time.

"Mr Kingston," he called.

"Yes," said Terry and as he came over he looked timid and frightened, his sallow face twitching, suspicion pouring out of his eyes like magician's smoke.

There's something not right here, thought PC Ryan. But if he pushed her himself, why on earth would he call the police? Surely he'd have made a run for it.

"Are you absolutely certain that a woman fell into the water?" he asked.

Terry hesitated. His mind crawled across the facts as he knew them, like a beetle over dung. Seven women. An annual picnic. One of them suspected by her husband of having an affair. Terry assigned to discover whether it was true. A row, a humungous one at that. Accusations flying, too numerous, too hysterical, too incoherent, too muffled mostly to understand. Someone being raped? Someone's husband being murdered? Just a load of hysterical nonsense, surely?

Terry knew it was better to say nothing about any of it. It could get messy. He regretted now that he'd even dialled 999, it had obviously been too late to save her if she had fallen in, or jumped deliberately, or even been pushed, whatever might have happened to the unfortunate woman. She'd be dead by now, and the thought filled him with dread. Implicating the others wasn't going to help either – as they'd said themselves, they could simply deny they'd heard anything. 30 seconds later, 50 yards closer to the road, and they never would have heard it. Even if there was CCTV here, and Terry wasn't sure about that – it was bloody everywhere else – no one knew that they'd heard the splash.

Someone does. *You.*

Terry felt increasingly panicky. This was a bloody mess. He'd definitely be a suspect if it turned out she was dead. His half-brother would get dragged into it, and that would go down unbelievably badly, would cause him, Terry, all sorts of problems. And conversely, what if she hadn't fallen in at all, what if it had been a bird or an animal like one of the women had suggested? This could all be a blinking wild goose chase. He might even get done for wasting police time.

Terry became more furious with himself, the more he thought things through. He *knew* he should have turned down this job, held out against his brother's bullying, he could sniff trouble a mile off on this one. What the hell was he going to say to the police? What explanation was he going to give as to why he'd been in the park? He'd be the prime bloody suspect, he was sure of it, if there really was a dead body in there. Well, if it does come to that, Terry thought, I'll have to sing, regardless of who I implicate, after all *I've* done nothing wrong. That will get me off the hook at least.

But will it? Terry knew that his brother was clever, too clever to mess with, too powerful, in with the right people these days, a stitch-up could be just what he needed to keep his own nose clean – they might be brothers but that wouldn't stop him, after all they'd never liked each other.

"I said, what were you doing in the park, Mr Kingston?" asked PC Ryan, and his tone was definitely accusatory now.

"Um, well… it was a nice evening," said Terry, his palms sweating and his heart pounding, much like at key moments during war-games conventions. "I, I thought I'd go for a walk."

"And you live *where*?" said PC Ryan. He was sounding even cockier now that his colleague, a little round Asian man (was there no minimum height for police these days, Terry thought), had joined him, and PC Ryan obviously fancied himself as the senior of the two.

"In Dagenham," said Terry.

"And so on a summer's evening you come all the way from Dagenham to Hyde Park, on your own, just for a *nice little stroll*?" The sarcasm was unbridled.

Terry didn't know what to say. It was too late to admit he'd been lying, so he decided he'd just have to go with it for the moment. He felt sick. He knew he should have left it, just followed his target as he'd started to do, made sure he got his money, kept his client off his back, and be done with silly drunk women who ran around shouting and screaming and drowning themselves.

"Yes," said Terry in the end, and that one little word was the official beginning of his nightmare.

43

Camden, North London

Outside the tube station it was noisy and dirty and full of people who were just hanging around, looking either like they had dodgy business to do or nowhere better to go. Juliette wished she hadn't put her purse in her rucksack now, she felt vulnerable with it tucked inside the outer pocket, readily accessible for anyone to steal. She kept swaying from side to side as she walked – the bag following an awkward semi-circled arc – in an attempt to make pickpocketing her too tricky, but people were getting hustled and jostled, and someone even told her to mind the fuck where she was going. She struggled to keep up as JoAnne marched confidently through the throng, seeming to know the way – left out the station, straight up a grotty litter-lined street, past an unappealing pub with a horrible little courtyard teeming with black-drainpiped people with gravity-defying hairdos and painful-looking piercings, over the dankly pungent canal – until after four or five minutes they turned right into what seemed to Juliette like another world entirely, one of smart Georgian terraces and lit-up Christmassy trees, and the house they were looking for was just a few doors up, on the left, and the door they knocked on was painted pale pink, the colour of a fairy's costume. They waited for maybe 20 seconds, and then there was a deep loud, "Coming," and the door was thrown back so the warm air could come gushing at them, as if to say hello, and on the breeze drifted the smell of percolated coffee and freshly baked cakes.

"Hallo Jo!" said Auntie Linda. "And you must be Juliette! Come in, welcome. Don't worry about your shoes, just get inside out the cold." She was smallish but stocky, neatly oblong, her white T-shirt tucked into hitched up Levis, bottoms turned up neatly to show off her polished Dr Martens. She beamed a smile across her oval face, and it sent her forehead creasing up towards her cropped dark hair and the skin around her eyes darting out as if to meet her ears. Her nose was straight and her lips were thin. Juliette thought she must be quite old, over 40 even.

"Hello," Juliette said shyly – she had never met a lesbian before, not properly anyway. She shrugged off her rucksack in the hallway and unzipped her boots, and followed the other two into the kitchen at the back. It was small and cosy with painted floorboards and an old pine dresser full of floral crockery, and the tablecloth was wipe-clean and polka dotted, and the chairs had chintzy seat pads, and Juliette couldn't believe that Linda was so boyish-looking yet lived in such a pretty house, in so delightful a street, a mere stone's throw from the revoltingness of Camden, and which according to JoAnne she'd bought, owned, all by herself.

"Now what would you girls like – tea or coffee?" asked Linda.

"Oh tea please, Auntie Linda," said JoAnne.

"Um, yes, the same for me, please," said Juliette.

"You sure you don't want coffee? I've just made some."

"Uh, yes, coffee then please, thank you. Um, no sugar... oh actually no sorry, one sugar, please... I have it with coffee but not with tea." Juliette was embarrassed by her gaucheness, she wasn't usually like this. She was still nervous about the real reason they'd come to London, and now she was here she was wondering whether she really was making a huge mistake – taking on way more than she could handle, and betraying her parents to boot. She could hardly change her mind now though, JoAnne would go mad.

JoAnne was asking how Linda's job was going, and Juliette thought it was amazing that she worked in A&E, Juliette couldn't even cut her own finger without fainting. People like Linda tended to make her feel inadequate somehow – she seemed to have such a strong sense of purpose, a belief in who she was, in where she was going, Juliette thought she'd never feel like that. *You won't know where you're going until you know where you come from*, said a voice, and Juliette didn't even know where that had come from. She felt sad and vulnerable here, in Linda's charming little kitchen with its warmth from the oven and optimistic glow, and even though there was chatting and laughter and Tracey Thorn singing softly in the background, at that moment Juliette had never felt so alone, although she wasn't quite sure why.

44

Hyde Park

PC Ryan had called his sergeant, and his skipper had initially told him to just have a bloody good look round first – if this odd-sounding bloke was now saying he wasn't even sure someone had fallen in the water, they didn't want to waste time calling in the frogmen. It all sounded very strange to Sergeant Hunter from what PC Ryan had said. Flasher type calling 999, saying he'd been enjoying a stroll in the park when he heard a woman fall in the water, now saying that perhaps he'd imagined it, that maybe it was a sodding bird instead. What the heck were they dealing with here? In Sergeant Hunter's experience it sounded most likely that this Kingston bloke was an attention-seeking weirdo, but in theory he could also be a murderer – or he could actually be telling the truth and there really had been a tragic accident that he'd happened to witness. It was all a bit annoying, as he wanted to go off shift and get down his snooker club for a few frames and a couple of well-earned pints. Typical, he thought, it's only when he'd got something planned that anything interesting happened – usually it was just routine stuff like domestics or burglaries. He decided he couldn't take any shortcuts on this one though, not when there was potentially a body involved, just in case.

"Call up more units," said Sergeant Hunter. "Get a load of officers down there with torches. Call India 99, and the Marine Support Unit I suppose. We can't take any chances."

Terry Kingston stood in his cheap grey suit watching PC Ryan's bumbling response to this barrage of requests across the radio waves, and although he didn't know what India 99 was he could pretty much deduce everything else, and he knew that he'd well and truly had it now. The skin between his top lip and nose was moist and the twitch in his hands had grown into a full-scale tremble. He desperately wanted to be at home, in front of his miniature armies in the bedroom cum office that Maria never came into, ever, with Hugo curled at his feet and Achtung purring on the easy chair behind him, the rats whirring madly on their wheel to nowhere. He badly needed to relax, badly needed not to be here, and he wished he could just leave now, make his way home so he could get back to his Prussian general, which needed its final coat of varnish before the weekend.

"Er, do you still need me?" he said to PC Ryan.

PC Ryan looked perplexed, not knowing what to say to this – he couldn't let his potential murderer just wander off, could he?

"Um, well, can you wait for a while, just until we've completed our search," he said finally. "We may need to take a statement from you – if we do find anything," and he said it in such a way that it was clear he thought this was all a complete waste of everyone's time.

Terry acquiesced meekly, and went and perched on a stone step outside the cafe, and as he watched the park fill swiftly with officers searching in the bushes, torches bobbing, and a van turn up with a load of scuba equipment in the back, and heard the ominous thrum of the helicopter overhead, he put his head in his hands and wished with all his heart that he had never called 999, even if she had bloody drowned.

45

Berkshire

Juliette's mother looked across the table at her husband, well, at his hands anyway, which peered elegantly around the edges of The Times. She had debated whether to tell him, in fact had put it off for over a week, but she knew she couldn't risk him finding out through anyone else, it wouldn't be fair. She coughed delicately, but Giles didn't appear to hear her, just carried on reading the paper, occasionally tutting, the newsprint rustling gently. She normally liked to leave him alone at this time, just after breakfast in that brief moment of peace before he had to leave for work, but for some reason she found she couldn't put it off any longer.

"Giles," she said. "Giles, darling... *Giles!*"

"Oh, sorry dear," he said finally, angling the paper downwards, so he could look over the top of both it and his reading glasses, at his wife.

"I need to talk to you," she said.

"Yes, dear," he replied, and waited, and when she didn't say anything, he hoisted the paper up a little, as if he were going to start reading again.

"Juliette wants to trace her birth mother," Cynthia said, as if it were one word, one fast uninterrupted stream of letters, and this time Giles sighed and put the newspaper flat on the table, its edge settling into the remains of the milk from his corn flakes in the shallow beige bowl.

"Oh," he said. "Oh."

"Exactly," replied Cynthia. "What on earth are we going to do?"

"I don't know," said Giles. "What can we do? We knew this would probably happen one day."

"Yes, but not now," said Cynthia. "She's not long been at university, she's not ready for it."

"Well, what happened?" said Giles. "How do you know she wants to? Did she actually tell you? Maybe you've got it wrong."

"She rang me last week and I knew there was something up, she sounded funny, and it wasn't even the right day to ring. But she kept chatting on and I was even quite pleased that she sounded interested in my boring old WI stuff, and I assumed she was just homesick – and then she came out with this story about needing to research her origins for an assignment, but it was obviously rubbish..." Cynthia's voice started to crack a little.

Giles took his wife's hand across the table, and the sleeve of his crisp striped shirt got a smudge of newsprint on it, just above the cuff link.

"It's all right, dear," said Giles. "What did you tell her?"

"The truth. I told her where she was born. I didn't know what else to say. What can she do now?"

"I'm not sure. I think she can go to Somerset House and

look up all the births on the day she was born, until she finds her own certificate."

"And then what?"

"I don't know, Cyn. I suppose once she knows the name though she can go about trying to trace her."

Cynthia looked down into the dregs of her coffee and it was strange, they seemed to have settled into a human shape: two eyes, a sad downward mouth, the exact opposite of one of those yellow smiley faces that were everywhere these days. She couldn't look up at her husband again, she knew that if she saw the kindness in his eyes she'd be unable to stop the tears coming. Cynthia was a reserved woman – she hardly ever cried, and if she did, it was always in private. She certainly wasn't ready to let her emotions out about this, not even to her husband. Maybe Juliette wouldn't even go through with it in the end, and they could all forget about everything again for a while. As Cynthia sat there gazing at her diamond-ringed fingers, she knew she was being over-optimistic, like she always used to be, every single relentless month, yes, every single one, until every single bloody hateful month it had come (and she was sure it had all been her fault, not poor Giles'), until eventually it had stopped forever, and she'd thanked God she'd been blessed with Juliette instead.

46

Hyde Park

Elijah was excited. His daddy had just said they could go on the boats after all – he had definitely clocked that if he nagged his parents for long enough they usually caved in in the end. His mummy had already promised him an ice cream so there was that to look forward to too – he wasn't going to let them forget that, no way Jose.

Elijah's excitement didn't last long however, once his brief sense of triumph had dimmed. As they stood waiting for the next boat he thought the water looked brown and dirty on closer inspection, and actually rather scary; and then when the little boat turned up it was all old and decrepit and there was water in the bottom of it, like it was leaking; and when his dad got in it rocked wildly, and he was a large man so how would they all fit in anyway – and so Elijah decided maybe he didn't like the look of rowing after all.

"Right, in you get sweetheart," said his mother.

"No," said Elijah. Now he'd spotted that his father's big fat bottom was already wet he definitely didn't fancy it *at all*.

"Come on Elijah darling," she said. "D'you want to hold Mummy's hand?"

"No!" he said.

"What d'you mean no?" said his father. "I've just bloomin' well paid for this. Get in."

"I don't want to," said Elijah, snivelling.

"Oh come on angel, it'll be fun," cajoled his mother, as she stood next to him on the bank in her high heels. She tried to push him gently towards the boat.

"Noooo!" screamed Elijah, and as she went to take his arm he made such a commotion everyone looked over. Perhaps they should leave it after all, she thought, this was becoming embarrassing.

"Elijah," said his dad, in a low voice, as patiently as he could manage (although it still sounded unmistakably tight, not far off temper-losing pitch). "If you get in the boat we'll take you to get a milkshake after."

"As well as an ice cream?" said Elijah, smelling an opportunity.

"No, not as well, either or," said his father.

"Then *no*!" said Elijah, folding his podgy arms defiantly. Other people were still looking over, with a definite whiff of parental superiority now. Elijah's mother really couldn't cope with yet another scene, they were meant to be having a nice day out as a family, and she was sure he'd enjoy it once they'd got going.

"Oh, OK Elijah, just this once," she said quietly. Her husband threw her a look and shifted crossly in the boat, and as Elijah stepped in jauntily (his fear miraculously dissipated despite the new rocking his father had just created) she caught the tell-tale shape of his tongue poking through his right cheek, and she saw the victory in his eyes.

47

Battersea, South West London

JoAnne heard the thrum thrum of the landline and willed it to be answered. Why isn't she answering? Why isn't she home? Maybe she'd gone off to a bar last night, JoAnne wouldn't have put it past her, especially when she was in that kind of mood. Or perhaps she'd passed out on a bench somewhere and been picked up by the police – she must have been pretty drunk to have run off into the night like that, even she wasn't usually that rash, so yes, maybe that's what had happened. Normally JoAnne would be appalled at the thought of one of her friends being arrested, but it was a hell of a lot better than the outcome she kept trying not to think about, the one where the reason she wasn't answering her home phone was because she wasn't home at all, was because she was lying cold and dead at the bottom of The Serpentine. It was like a nightmare, like something you saw on the news that happened to other people.

Finally JoAnne decided yes, she would call one of the others, but still she hesitated, as if voicing her concerns verified them, or, even worse, implicated her. She'd been just so utterly hacked off last night that she hadn't been thinking straight, and of course the bottle and a half of Prosecco hadn't helped. She knew in her heart that the splash had been too loud to be a bird – it must have been her, what else could it have been? In the end she dialled Juliette's number, but at first it was engaged and then the second time it connected but just rang and rang, and JoAnne cursed her, not knowing that Juliette wasn't deliberately ignoring it this time; she was simply too busy ripping off Noah's Spiderman pyjamas as he lay screaming and writhing: while doing his poo, his willy had shot upwards and, to his mother's outrage, he had weed all over the cloakroom floor.

In the end none of them talked to each other that Friday morning, which may or may not have made any difference in the long run. Juliette never had answered her phone. Once she'd finished cleaning up after Noah, she'd collapsed behind the cloakroom door and sobbed for a good five minutes, and then she'd gone up to his room and found him hiding under his duvet and she'd tried to hug him, tell him sorry, that it was her fault not his, but he'd turned his stiff little body from her which had made her cry again. When she'd eventually got him dressed, she needed to rush all the kids to school, they were horrendously late, and as she still hadn't charged her mobile that just went straight to voicemail, and so finally the others had given up.

48

Hyde Park

Seven-year-old Elijah Button was a clever little boy. Not only did he have his mummy and daddy firmly wrapped around his little finger, he'd soon got the hang of rowing a boat too, quickly realising that he could send his parents into even more of a spin than usual with just the little boat's right oar. It was all tremendous fun – skimming the surface of the water with the paddle so a mini wave could form, and then if he changed the angle just a *teeny* bit, the water could travel the length of the oar and soak his mummy (eliciting a plaintively ineffectual, "Oh, Elijah!"); banging the top of the water so that the noise was hollow and eerie, water spraying everywhere like an aquatic firework while his dad yelled, "Stop that, you little bu–," before just about restraining himself or, perhaps best of all, simply digging the oar vertically into the water, so that the boat began to rotate and his dad would start ranting that they weren't bloomin' well going anywhere.

"Elijah, just stop that," said his dad, for the hundredth time. "Otherwise I'll take that oar off you and I'll row the ruddy thing on my own. Look, we're heading right for the bank now – *be careful* or we'll flippin' well hit it."

"Sorry, Daddy," said Elijah, as he lifted up the oar and dove it towards the bottom, exactly as his father had just told him not to. His dad roared at him and he grinned happily, desired outcome achieved, and then he shoved it in again, just for fun. As the oar stabbed down into the tea-coloured water for perhaps the fifth unapproved time, Elijah felt it hit something, and in his young brain he assumed quite sensibly that it was the bank or even the bottom. But when he looked over the side he saw, through the opacity, trailing light brown hair tangled like weeds, and one hollow eye gaping at him hopelessly, and a flash of colour, and although when they finally got back to shore he did eventually get his ice cream, his parents never bought him the milkshake, and as he grew older his behaviour worsened if anything, and he never ever stopped seeing that image.

49

Sardinia

Sissy had fallen into a deeper sleep this time, and when she awoke her face felt hot and tight, like maybe she'd had a face-lift. Delighted squeals that carried in on the hot breeze from the car port below were almost certainly what had roused her, and as she shifted in the double deckchair she heard the key in the lock and two little children come stomping through, flip-flops thudding, sand going everywhere, she was sure of it, how many times had she told them?

"Hello Mummy!" cried Nell, her eldest, as she ran onto the terrace. "We went snorkelling and I saw a huge fish and it came swimming right by us. It was brown," she added proudly.

"I had a ice cream," announced Conor, and she could tell, there was chocolate all round his face.

"Did you have a lovely time, my darlings?" said Sissy, her head throbbing as she scooped them towards her. Nell snuggled in whilst Conor wriggled away giggling.

"I think they did," said her husband, coming out onto the balcony after them. He must have gone into the kitchen first – a tall glass of water was shimmering in his hand, like a mirage in the sunlight.

Sissy turned and smiled up at Nigel. He looked blondish and fit, larger than life through her sunglasses, and it seemed almost impossible that they were here in Sardinia, on holiday as a family, celebrating ten unbelievable years of life after cancer. She was so grateful to Juliette and Stephen for lending them their holiday apartment, she'd never known Stephen to be so generous before, at least not without expecting something in return – maybe she'd misjudged him after all. He'd been delighted for them according to Juliette, calling it an absolute bloody miracle, and it was him who'd suggested they borrow the apartment, saying it was only sat there unused at the moment. They'd been reluctant to accept, but Stephen had insisted, saying he needed someone to give it a trial run now it had finally been done up.

Sissy knew she would never understand what had caused Nigel's journey back from the very edge of death. She often found herself going over that pivotal day at the hospital, the one when she thought he was actually about to die on her, fail to hold out long enough to even see their baby. She never stopped wondering what had saved him. Was it her outburst itself, the heart-wrenching, long-overdue outpouring, irrefutable proof at last of her love for her husband, of rage and bewilderment that he would just fade away, unchallenged, that he would leave her without a damn good fight at least, and with the doctors just stood around watching, doing nothing. Or was it the new drugs the doctor had put him on, their barely legal experiment on the half-human she still called her husband; or perhaps it was simply a miracle, a benevolent gift of life sent to them by almighty God himself. She guessed she'd never really know, and anyway it didn't matter now – she had him back and she'd always be grateful for that. He'd even rallied enough to see their daughter on the day she was born, just a week later – Nell had been delivered in the very same hospital, and they'd taken her straight over to the cancer ward when she was less than an hour old, and Nigel's joy at meeting his daughter had even the stoniest of ward sisters dabbing at her eyes. And when five years later they'd finally had a son too, it was all so fantastically miraculous that Sissy swore she would never take anything for granted ever again.

Sissy squirmed to the edge of the deckchair and, her bottom firm against the wooden strut that held the canvas, hauled herself out of it. As she stood up her head throbbed even more and it felt perversely weightless, spinny. She'd definitely had way too much sun. What time was it, how long had she been asleep?

"Could I have some of your water?" she asked Nigel. He passed it to her and as she leaned against the railing she lay the cool of the glass against her forehead and then against the top of her chest. When she drank it the water was over-chilled and her teeth twinged, and it hurt the back of her throat as she swallowed.

"Are you OK?" said Nigel. "How long were you in the sun? You're very red in the face."

"I fell asleep," said Sissy. "The sun must have come around – I was in the shade before. So much for me trying to give my skin a rest." She seemed anxious now, and they both knew that it was Sissy who suffered most these days, worrying about every last mole on her freckly body, or the slightest fever one of the children got – and she still found it hard to go to the beach, but the kids loved it, so usually she managed, as long as they were in full sun suits (which looked odd on these beaches, no-one else wore them). But today, because the weather had been due to be so hot, she'd said she fancied just a quiet couple of hours writing her diary on the balcony, she hardly got any time to herself these days.

Nigel took Sissy's arm and led her inside, helped her onto the bed – and by now she'd started to feel sick and her insides felt watery, as if they were being liquidised, and she thought she might even pass out. It was gone five, Nigel had told her, so she must have been asleep for over two hours, and now she was lying down she felt like she couldn't get up again. Her limbs felt heavy and independent, as if they belonged to someone else. The children had the TV on and the Italian voices were fast and high-pitched, young-sounding, and there was laughter from a live audience of excitable minors, and although Nell and Conor would have had no idea what was being said they were being swept away on the outré vitality of it all, and laughing in all the right places.

Nigel came back in to check on his wife and was alarmed to find she could hardly lift her head now. He either needed to keep her cool and get her to drink lots of water, or else he would have to call a doctor – he'd already spotted the signs of heatstroke, his cousin had got it all those years ago in Australia. Nigel turned the air conditioning to full, and the unit swept up and down rhythmically, blindly squirting out cold air, but the room was so hot the air was warm again by the time it reached her. He got a couple of towels and soaked them in the sink, then he wrung them out like he was strangling someone and took them still dripping into Sissy, and placed them on her forehead and over her body, but she didn't react to him at all now. Her face was red like soup and burning up, and she seemed barely conscious. As he raised the glass of water to her lips, her head was bowling-ball heavy under his arm. It was alarming how quickly it had happened; she'd seemed OK when they'd first got home, just flushed and a bit groggy perhaps. He'd already been debating whether he needed to call a doctor, but when he saw her eyes start to roll towards the back of her head he knew he couldn't wait any longer, and he yelled to his daughter to bring him his phone.

50

Balham, South London

On a sunny Sunday afternoon, in an unloved-looking Victorian terraced house just in from the Emmanuel Road side of Tooting Bec Common, Sissy felt like she was going mad. Since Thursday night she hadn't been sleeping at all well – she still hadn't heard from her friend and was desperately worried about her now. She had that familiar feeling of dread that she'd harboured for so long about Nigel, and everything else for that matter, but if anything it was worse than ever today. The kids were playing up and she couldn't quite deal with them at the moment, so she went into the lounge to put on the Disney channel while they ate their tea; it wouldn't hurt just this once. After messing about with two remotes for what seemed like ages the TV finally sprang into life, causing Sissy to shriek so loudly that both her kids turned their wide sad eyes on her, and Conor said over his boiled egg, "What is it, Mummy?"

Sissy didn't even need to listen to what they were saying. As soon as she read the caption, "Live, Hyde Park," and saw the white police tent and the grungy brown of the water, she knew they'd found her friend. It had actually happened, she really had drowned – and as Sissy flicked the channel frantically to a re-run of Top Gear she felt as faint as she had on holiday in Sardinia, the time she'd nearly died of heatstroke.

Her poor, poor friend. *Siobhan was dead!*

Sissy felt the grief as if she'd been punched in the stomach, hard. When Nigel had died it had been too quick, too unbelievable to take in, so her feelings had been stuck for days, weeks even, her brain unable to comprehend what had happened. On this occasion she'd been prepared for death, had dreaded it, whilst also hoping desperately that Siobhan would turn up at her desk on Monday morning with a comical tale of a wild weekend. It had happened before – but not this time.

Sissy tried to think logically through her grief and panic. Siobhan had drowned, was dead. But not only that – she, Sissy, *had left her to drown*, had heard the splash and done nothing. What on earth had been wrong with her? How had she convinced herself that it wasn't Siobhan, a great big splash like that? She *knew* she should have gone after her. Why hadn't she gone after her? *Why?* She'd let her friend drown, had just walked off and gone home to bed, and left Siobhan helpless at the bottom of The Serpentine. They'd all left her, Sissy tried to remind herself, it wasn't just her; and maybe it wasn't really anyone's fault, the splash must have sounded like a bird after all, they can't all have been wrong – but inside she knew she was as complicit as the rest of them.

Sissy sat down on the faded stained sofa and dropped her head between her knees to try to stop the roar in her head. The children watched Top Gear mutely, even though Nell especially didn't like it, all the cars looked the same to her. Another thought came to Sissy then, and it made her feel physically sick. She knew she was at fault morally, was sure of that, but what exactly was she culpable of in the eyes of the law? Obviously it wasn't murder – but did her inaction constitute a crime, even manslaughter perhaps, through negligence or something? Was she *legally* at fault for Siobhan's death, for not going to her aid? Could she even be arrested? As she tried to control her panic, aware the kids were watching her, she remembered a couple of the others saying if anything had happened they were going to pretend they hadn't heard the splash – but they wouldn't do that now Siobhan was actually dead, surely? No, they would all have to go to the police, file a report, admit that they'd left her and gone home.

Sissy's thoughts turned to her children next, which made her feel worse. What if she ended up in prison over this, left them without a mother or a father? She started panting, hyperventilating almost, and although she'd thought she'd never cry as hard again as she had over Nigel's death, she'd been wrong. Her children looked desolate, already aware, as children usually are, that there was yet more sadness and heartbreak to come in their poor young lives. And as Sissy sobbed she remembered all over again that Siobhan was *dead,* and she cried even harder – mainly for her lost friend but also for herself, for her children, already so damaged, for what the fallout from her madness that night might ultimately prove to be. Sissy could bear no more. She stumbled from the room and ran upstairs to run Conor's bath, leaving her children in the lounge, shocked, but safe for now, in the capable hands of Jeremy Clarkson.

51

Barnes

Alistair Smart was getting extraordinarily fed up with his wife now. Over the weekend she'd been even more of a bitch than usual – moody, monosyllabic, forever shouting at the boys. Even when Rebecca from next door had popped round to invite them to a barbecue the following weekend, Natasha had seemed unable to put on her normal "everything's-fucking-marvellous" front, and Rebecca had left assuming Natasha and Alistair must have had a row, she'd never seen them like that before.

Unknown to Natasha, there was another reason Alistair was so uptight – he hadn't heard from his lover all weekend, she just wouldn't answer her phone, and nearly a week had gone by since he'd had sex (well, proper sex, with a woman anyway), and he realised how addicted to the real thing he seemed to have become of late. Even relentless wanking just didn't seem to do it anymore.

Alistair thought he may as well pretend to do some writing, mainly to get out of his wife's way – plus he had a nice sturdy lock on the door now, so his web browsing was that much more relaxing, although it did lack a certain frisson which he missed a little. As he made his way up to his sunshine-filled office overlooking the common, with its cheery fucking pictures that Natasha had chosen and that made him want to vomit, his hairy little toe caught on something, and when he looked down he saw that the stair carpet was threadbare, unravelling in fact. They desperately needed a new one, this one was bloody ancient. He smiled to himself. Once his little arrangement with Ms Lucinda Horne (Horne by name, horny by nature as it turned out, landing as she had in his inbox like manna from heaven) was sorted out he wouldn't need to worry about paying his half of the ludicrous mortgage, or about replacing the car or the carpet, or even about paying for winter trips to Courchevel or the Cayman Islands – just to complete the alliterative landscape of their financial future. (*Yes! He was a writer, an artist at heart, he hadn't lost it.*) Although no money had actually come through yet it was definitely on the cards, the deal was about to be done, worth absolutely loads his agent had assured him; and it was such a relief to have got his publisher off his back at last.

"You little bugger," Sebastian had said, when Alistair had presented him with three full volumes of Bottersley Dog School's Woofy Adventures. "I thought you were going to give me one almighty heart attack, winding me up like that, giving me the impression that you'd done absolutely sod all for 18 months. This new stuff is going to *fly* off the shelves, kids aren't going to be able to get enough of these characters, it's like Harry Potter with dogs, but without the magic." Alistair had looked at his agent witheringly at this point, he couldn't help himself, but he knew better than to say anything – and to be fair to Sebastian, he was on the cusp of landing Alistair a sensational deal, one that would enable him to replace the carpet in the whole sodding street if he wanted to. It was bloody miraculous.

The whole thing had been managed so neatly, so seamlessly, had turned out to be a complete doddle in fact. It seemed that little Miss Horne was so in awe of the great Alistair Smart she would have agreed to pretty much anything. He'd been generous, he felt – a full 30% to her, 70% to him, and besides, sales would be absolutely huge with his name on the cover, far more than she'd ever hope to achieve on her own. So he was doing her a favour really. They had met to discuss things in the Holiday Inn at Brent Cross – she was coming down from Stevenage and was scared of driving in central London, and to make sure there was no chance of them being overheard he had booked a room, and when she'd walked in she'd been so cutesily pretty, so child-like, but with the most voluptuous assets, that he felt himself explode inside; and having spent years and years being faithful to his wife (and *for what?*), managing his extreme sex starvation as best he could, he found that having already taken one lover it was just too easy to take another. Lucinda had been so impressed by him, so naive and giggly, and although in truth it did creep him out that she'd grown up with his stories, was one of his original fans (she even had a signed photograph from 1996, she'd told him), once they'd agreed terms in principle, which only took one cup of room-made tea and a shortbread finger, he found that her age and immaturity didn't put him off after all, in fact it was a bloody great turn on, and it most definitely didn't stop him pulling her down with him onto the just-too-convenient bed, and as she squealed delightedly he'd groaned and then come, all over her amazing tits.

"*Alistair,*" said his wife, for maybe the fifth time, and as he turned and looked at her she just stared at him open-mouthed, slack, like a rubber band that has been pulled too tight, and then she nodded mutely towards the flat screen TV on the wall behind the dining table, and he looked vaguely at the news, but he was so mesmerised by thoughts of the marvellous Miss Horne that he had no idea why his wife wanted him to watch a body being pulled out of The Serpentine.

52

Somerset House, Central London

Juliette felt like a child again as she stood in the middle of the vast building, clutching the knowledge (adoptive parents' names, recently learned place of birth) inside her head, the fee (one folded-up £5 note) tight in her fist, and her passport (humiliating) deep inside the handbag slung over her shoulder.

Now Juliette was actually here at Somerset House she felt an uncomfortable obligation to go through with the search – JoAnne would never let her leave at this point, not without at least trying. JoAnne was doing her best, but she couldn't hide her ridiculously over the top excitement, and it upset Juliette that it almost seemed like entertainment to her friend, as if Juliette's past of rejection and abandonment was some kind of treasure hunt, with the fantastic prize of a mummy at the end of it. She privately thought that JoAnne ought to sort out the issues with her own mother rather than keep chasing after hers, but she didn't want to hurt JoAnne, she knew she meant well.

At the enquiry desk Juliette spoke quietly, there were

other people around, and she felt a bit like she was asking for something embarrassing, pile cream perhaps, in a crowded chemists' shop. The clerk was sensitive though, and once she'd intimated why she was there he came straight round from behind the counter and led her towards a private room that smelled of furniture polish and stillness. JoAnne gestured to ask whether she should come too, but Juliette shook her head apologetically, suddenly aware she needed to do this herself − and that seemed to annoy JoAnne, as if she were being left out of the best bit.

"So, let's see," said the clerk, peering over the top of his glasses as he settled into his chair behind the massive desk. He wore a burgundy cardigan with a grey bow tie, and was like a friendly old uncle, and Juliette started to feel a little better, despite a twinge of guilt about making JoAnne stay outside. "Your adoptive parents' names please."

"Cynthia Jane Greene and Giles Arthur Greene," said Juliette, and although she had spent all but the first few weeks of her life with her adopted parents, was most definitely part of their family, here in this wood-panelled room they felt as unreal, unconnected to her as long-dead movie stars.

"And your place of birth, dear."

"Acton," said Juliette, as confidently as she could manage. The man was perceptive and looked at her, gently inquisitive.

"Or maybe Clacton," she admitted, and as she said it she thought for the thousandth time how strange it would be if it did turn out she'd been born there − after all, that was where JoAnne was from. The man looked puzzled. "I'm afraid I'm not 100% sure," she added lamely.

"Oh. Well, I suppose we can always check Clacton too if

we need to," he said. He coughed. "Erm, I don't suppose you know which Acton?"

"Er, no... *oh no*, is there more than one?"

"I'm afraid so, my dear, there are four or five I think."

Juliette looked crestfallen. "Shall we try the one in London and start from there?" he said. She nodded gratefully.

"And can I see your ID please."

Juliette handed over her passport. The photo was from when she was 13 and she'd had great silver braces on her teeth and a velvet Alice band taming her hideous hair, and she remembered the horror she'd felt when, after what seemed like a lifetime, the machine had spat out the photos, as if in disgust, and Juliette had begged her mother to let her take them again, but Cynthia had just laughed and said they were fine, not in a mean way, but in a way that made Juliette feel unconnected with her mother, not misunderstood exactly, just *un*-understood. She wondered whether her real mother would have acted in that way, and then she thought, well maybe she's dead, or a hopeless alcoholic, or so deadbeat her daughter wouldn't have had a passport at all, would never have gone anywhere. And then she thought she might be about to be one step closer to finding out, and it made her feel lightheaded, faint almost.

"Are you all right, my dear?" said the clerk.

"Oh, yes, I am, thanks," said Juliette. He wrote down some details from her passport and she handed him the money, which was crumpled and ancient-looking now; she didn't know why she hadn't just kept it in her purse until she'd needed it. The man got up from his chair and walked across the room, to where there was a wooden ladder, and she noticed with a start of sympathy that he limped a little. He climbed slowly, seemingly unable to bend his left leg properly, and Juliette thought he looked well past retirement age, was maybe even in his seventies, and she worried he might fall. He reached one arm up, looking ever more precarious, and after running his finger along the length of identical-looking volumes he eventually selected one of the giant leather ledgers, and as he pulled it down he half-caught it, just avoiding dropping it, and then she watched him one-handedly descend the rickety-looking ladder with this heavy over-sized book that maybe contained her mother (not literally obviously, but it almost felt like that, like she was there in the room with them), tucked awkwardly under his left arm – and as he sat down behind the desk again Juliette found that she seemed to have forgotten to breathe. She thought she might literally take off in excitement, flutter away with nerves.

The man opened the ledger about two thirds of the way through, and as he let the pages fall there was a dull thud that vibrated through the table, across to Juliette. He licked his fingers and thumbed backwards a few pages and then stopped, seemingly having found the right one, and then he ran his forefinger down the records, as though his skin itself could read. It was excruciating. Eventually his finger became stationary, and he looked up, over his glasses again, into her frightened eyes.

"Well, you were right the first time," he said with a kind smile. "I've found the record here." Juliette's eyes sprang with tears, almost as though there were comedy squirters secreted in her head somewhere.

"I'll leave you now, to have a look yourself," he said. "Just come out when you're ready." When he got up he appeared to be limping slightly less now, and as he passed her he squeezed her shoulder hard, just for an instant, and she was grateful to him.

53

Dagenham

In a grim little pebble-dashed house in East London, a wheel was spinning frantically. Sid, or was it Vicious, was in need of some exercise, and he ran like his life depended on it, getting nowhere of course, as if he were trying to exorcise the miserable reality of his pathetic little existence – and it was only as Terry Kingston watched him that he realised that that's all he, Terry, did too. He was no better off than a caged white rat with mean pink eyes and a long kinked tail, spinning his own metaphorical wheel – trapped between his faintly grubby detective work, his solitary obsession with painting miniature figures of Prussian fusiliers in their exact colours, and his dispiriting marriage to a woman he had nothing in common with. He sighed, but in truth he did feel a bit better this morning than he had over the previous couple of days. It was Sunday and the sun was shining and, thank God, he had heard nothing more from the police, so maybe it was all going to be OK after all. Surely if there had been a body they'd have found it by now? The whole thing had been humiliating certainly, and he was still worried he might be charged with wasting police time – he could tell they thought he was some kind of pervert, so they'd be bound to try to throw something at him. But surely that was better than a woman being dead and him having done nothing about it? Or worse, a woman being dead and him being accused of *murdering* her. He shuddered.

Terry Kingston was a surprisingly principled man, and in other circumstances might have led a very different life – he'd just taken a couple of wrong turns here and there, and that's all you need to fuck your life up, isn't it? And so Terry was insightful enough to realise that despite his situation, his moral compass was still essentially intact, and that comforted him a little, even made him feel slightly superior to those braying women in the park, who despite their veneer of respectability all seemed to be having affairs from what he could tell, and were so hypocritically selfish they'd been prepared to leave one of their supposed best friends for dead.

The telephone rang downstairs, which was unusual. No-one really called that number anymore, people tended to call their mobiles these days, and Maria had managed somehow to get their number delisted, so they no longer got call-centre workers haranguing them about changing their energy supplier or installing conservatory blinds or saving starving people, thank Christ. As the phone rang and rang insistently Terry knew definitely what it would be about, and he fretted that perhaps something had happened, after all. He chose not to answer it, he couldn't face talking to the police right now, and Maria wouldn't as she was out – at choir as usual, he presumed. But when his mobile went a minute later Terry knew he couldn't delay for any longer, otherwise he'd have them turning up on the doorstep before he knew it. He sighed.

"Hello, Terry Kingston," he said, in his best telephone manner.

"Mr Kingston," said the voice down the line. "My name is Sergeant Hunter. As you may have seen on the news a body has been found in The Serpentine River in Hyde Park. We'd like you to come in for questioning."

Terry said the right things and made the necessary arrangements. As he put down the phone and picked up his paintbrush he felt anxious again, now more than ever, as well as irrationally annoyed at Sergeant Hunter, with his chirpy manner and supercilious air of authority – surely if he'd been down there fishing a body out of it he should have known that The Serpentine wasn't a river, it was a sodding lake.

54

Somerset House

Juliette wondered how just some smudgy old ink, written nearly twenty years earlier, could be so critically important to her, how the old-fashioned curl of those letters could potentially reshape the direction of her entire life. There it was. Proof. Yes, she had had a life before adoption, she had been borne by a flesh and blood woman, the stork hadn't brought her, it had all really actually happened. *Her mother had abandoned her.* Hammersmith Hospital, Acton, 23rd May 1967, given names Amanda Lily. She was shocked to see she'd had a father too – and *my God* what a father: he wasn't "unknown," like they usually were, like she'd been expecting him to be.

Juliette sat for ages trying to make sense of what she saw. She was vaguely aware of JoAnne loitering outside, obviously desperate to come in, but although she felt for her friend she willed her away with just her mind and the set of her back, and it seemed to be working for the time being. This was her moment, her moment of truth. JoAnne could wait.

Potts. The name was familiar but she couldn't think why.

Was she famous or something? Who was Elisabeth Potts? She'd never heard of her, had she? *Pots and pans.* What did it mean?

Juliette sat in the quietness of the room for more long slow minutes, her mind locked in a peculiar state somewhere between racing and blank. Just before she stood up to leave at last she looked again at the two words that had struck her most, despite all the revelations of the morning. *Amanda Lily.* And that's when she cried. The one thing her mother had given her, apart from life of course, and they'd taken that from her too.

55

Fulham

In the end JoAnne got in the car at about quarter to five on Sunday afternoon, an hour after she'd seen the headlines, and drove round to Juliette's – if she wasn't ever going to answer her sodding phone she'd just have to visit her in person. When Juliette finally answered the door she was in track pants and a tuft of her hair was stuck up in the air as if she'd gelled it like that for a joke, and the bags under her eyes were definitely over the luggage limit, metaphorically speaking. She stared hostilely at JoAnne, but JoAnne wasn't in the mood for histrionics, and instead pushed past her friend and stomped into the cavernous kitchen to put the kettle on. Juliette came in and slumped into one of the white Eames chairs at the dining table. She put her head in her hands and avoided eye contact. The atmosphere was poisonous, like methane.

"Where are the kids?" asked JoAnne, meaning Stephen.

"Flo's upstairs doing her homework and Stephen's taken the boys to the park."

They were both relieved.

"Has anyone contacted you yet?" asked JoAnne.

"No," said Juliette.

"What about Stephen? Have you said anything to him?"

"No."

"Have they named her yet?"

"Not that I know of."

"So what do we do now?"

"I don't know," said Juliette, and she looked up at JoAnne, and for a second it was as if time had turned backwards and none of the stuff with Stephen and Juliette's mother had ever happened, they were still two best friends gossiping over a cup of tea in their university flat share. When the moment passed – and it was over in an instant – both of them felt hollow, lonely again, devastated for their dead friend, scared for themselves.

"Is this room bugged?" said JoAnne then, and she sounded panicked.

"What on earth do you mean?"

"Well, what with Stephen's job..." JoAnne's voice fell away, embarrassed.

"Don't be so bloody silly," said Juliette, but for some reason she felt nervous too now, and as it was such a lovely day they both moved without speaking, through the folding sliding doors that ran the width of the kitchen (as big as the windows in a car showroom) and out into the garden, which their gardener George had worked miracles on this year. The scent of the summer roses hung in the air, sickly almost, and they sat together on the bench under the cherry tree at the end of the garden, unspeaking at first, as they silently mourned their lost friend, their lost friendship.

"D'you think anyone else heard?" JoAnne said eventually.

"What do you mean?" said Juliette, speaking into her sweatshirt as she kicked ineffectually at a weed growing through the concrete between the paving stones, hell-bent on living.

JoAnne lowered her voice, although short of Juliette being bugged somewhere about her person, no one else could possibly have heard them.

"Well, you said that we should just leave her, and that if she ended up drowning we'd just say we'd already left, hadn't heard the splash. That's pretty incriminating."

"No I did not," said Juliette.

"Yes you did," said JoAnne. "I heard you. Why are you lying?"

"I'm not lying," said Juliette, and maybe she even believed it herself, perhaps she'd been married to Stephen for too long.

"Well, what if someone heard us talking?" persisted JoAnne. "We can't say we didn't hear anything if someone witnessed that we did."

"I *told* you," said Juliette, and she wasn't cross exactly, more resolute. "I never said we should leave her. I never said anything."

Finally JoAnne got it. Even if someone had overheard them, it had been dark; they wouldn't have been able to tell who said what. But did that make any difference? The fact that *someone* had said it damned them all, didn't it? They had all left her, to die as it turned out. They were all despicable.

"Juliette," said JoAnne, and she was stern now. "We have got to work out what we're going to say to the police. We'll have to speak to them eventually, we were the last people to see her alive. And we'd all just had a bloody big row. It's not looking good." She stared at the ground, at the edge of the lawn where George had uncharacteristically missed a bit with the strimmer, the few stray blades rising sharp and defiant, glaringly green above the paving stones.

"Well, I don't know what you want *me* to do," said Juliette. "Get Stephen to keep it out of the papers or something? Talk to his mates at Scotland Yard?"

"Don't be so fucking ridiculous," said JoAnne. She waited but Juliette said nothing more. "Well, I'll just have to talk to Sissy and the others then, but if it does all come out *I'm* not going to lie about what anyone said."

"Is that a threat?" said Juliette, and she pulled at her belligerently sticking up hair, tried to tame it like she was trying to tame her temper.

"I don't know," said JoAnne. She hesitated, aware that she should probably leave it there, but this was likely to be her only chance.

"D'you think it *was* an accident though?"

"What the hell do you mean?"

"Well, some of the things that were said between us... I mean, some people wouldn't want any of it to get out..."

"Oh, don't talk such utter shit," said Juliette. "If you mean Stephen, he'd have had to push *you* in, not her, you're the one who made all the vile accusations. You are such a total drama queen, a complete raving fantasist. You always have been, look at what you were like about tracing my mother, thinking we'd have some beautiful reunion, become like the fucking Waltons." She couldn't keep the bitterness from her voice.

"No, I'm not!" said JoAnne. "It's not my fault Elisabeth's like she is, I don't know why you've always blamed me." Juliette went quiet, just kept her gaze focused on the ground, so JoAnne tried again.

"Listen, I swear there was someone there the other night, watching us. I could feel it, and then when we were leaving I think I saw someone, crouched behind a tree."

"So now you're saying Stephen just happened to be loitering in a bush in Hyde Park and killed her, as well as killing Nigel. You've got a fucking cheek coming round here, after the things you've said about my husband."

"I'm not saying it was Stephen. I just think there may have been someone else involved."

"Well, it doesn't make any difference then, does it. If it turned out someone did kill her, it doesn't matter whether we heard anything or not. We couldn't have stopped it." There was a long painful, death-throe silence, before Juliette kicked viciously at the weeds again and said, "I think you should go now."

JoAnne knew that was it, there was nothing more to be said. She stood up from the bench and walked resolutely the length of the garden, past the raised vegetable beds, the slide, the trampoline, the goalposts – all screened cleverly with bamboo fencing or evergreen hedging – past the gravelled herb garden with the Rodinesque centre-piece, through the half open sliding doors into the gleamingly chaotic kitchen, across the book-lined Victorian hall, and out the black-painted door into the front garden full of artfully tasteful topiary. It was only when JoAnne reached the street and the safety of her car that the really ominous feeling left her, and she knew that all she could do now was tell the truth, she'd done her best, and if you'd done no wrong and you told the truth what harm could possibly come of you?

56

Dagenham

Terry Kingston couldn't decide whether or not to put in a call to his client prior to his appointment with the Royal Parks Police. He was convinced his only option now would be to tell the police the truth – after all he didn't want to end up being accused of murdering the bloody woman, and he was fairly sure that would be the outcome if he stuck to his line of being in the park because he'd wanted to enjoy the midsummer sunshine, had travelled all the way from Dagenham in East London purely because he fancied a nice little stroll. He pretty much knew where that would end up.

Terry imagined how the conversation with his client (who tended to lose any social niceties in a crisis) might go.

"What the fuck are the papers going to make of that?" he'd probably yell. Terry could almost hear his brother's voice. "This is so totally humiliating for me. Why the hell did you even call 999, you fucking moron?"

No, Terry knew better than to risk it. He'd see what happened with the police first and then decide what to tell his brother – there was no need to involve him now, it would only complicate things. He darted his mouse on its mat back and forth a couple of times, until the computer flickered to life and brought up the painting guide for Franco Prussian War figures. He had just over an hour before he needed to leave for the police station, plenty of time to finish off his last fusilier's hat – that would help settle his nerves, take his mind off things – but he found to his despair that his fingers were shaking so much he uncharacteristically smudged it.

57

Balham

Sissy stopped scraping hopelessly at the wallpaper, which was several layers deep and mostly stuck solid, resistant to home improvement. Dried bits of paper littered the carpet like worn-out confetti as she pulled out her phone from her jeans pocket and, seeing who it was, answered on the sixth ring.

"Hello," she said, pushing her hair out of her eyes as she headed out to the hallway (which was still grimly dark green), where the children wouldn't hear. "Yes, yes, I know, it's just so awful, I just can't believe it... OK, I agree, it's our only option... Yes, I think the three of us should go in together. If the others want to deny it then that's up to them... All right, I'll wait to hear from you then... Yes, I'm OK (sob), I just feel so terrible for her... OK, bye."

"What was that Mummy?" said Conor, looking up from his Thomas puzzle as she re-entered the lounge. The room looked worse than ever. Sissy hadn't known why she'd attacked the wallpaper like that, but it needed to come off some time – and anyway she'd felt like she had to do something, had to keep busy instead of sitting around feeling helpless and distraught, scared out of her mind. She kept replaying events from three evenings before, and it was driving her insane. *If only I'd trusted my instincts, gone home when I'd wanted to, before everyone started arguing, maybe nothing would have been said, maybe she wouldn't have run off. If only we'd gone back when we heard the splash. If only Siobhan wasn't dead.*

"Who was it on the phone, Mummy," Conor repeated, and he sounded fearful now. His little brow was furrowed under his sandy hair, and he reminded her of his father.

"Oh no-one, darling," Sissy replied.

"Was it the hospital? Are you going to die, Mummy?"

"Oh, darling, of course not," said Sissy, horrified.

"Well, who is then?"

"No one darling, no one's going to die," and as she said it she comforted herself that she wasn't actually lying, the dying bit had already happened. "I just have to go out a bit later, there's been a little accident." And as she said the word accident, she kicked herself, wished she'd chosen a different, less emotive word.

"Will Auntie Siobhan look after us?" asked Nell, who'd stopped playing on her 3DS and was stood facing her mother, blocking the kitchen door, her stance taught and unbearably adult.

"No darling," said Sissy, suppressing a sob.

"Who will then?" she persisted.

"I'm not sure darling. Someone nice."

"I don't want someone nice. I want Auntie Siobhan," said Nell.

"I want Daddy," said Conor, and burst into tears.

58

Belgravia, Central London

As soon as Terry arrived at the police station he'd been unceremoniously arrested and bundled off to a cell, like a common criminal. They'd said they weren't ready to interview him yet, despite him being exactly on time for his appointment, and so it seemed they were entitled to lock him up in the meantime, even though he hadn't actually been charged with anything. It was a bloody disgrace in Terry's opinion.

The cell was small and dirty and stank of urine. Terry felt trapped, desperate, as he paced up and down, unable to sit down. He found he couldn't stop thinking of poor Sid and Vicious, caged not as a one-off travesty, because they were falsely under suspicion of something (no, not just of something, *of murder,* quite unbelievably), but caged forever – and he hated the thought and debated how he could set them free. Would they be able to even survive in the wild, he wondered? Would they know how to find food? Is there an organisation that could help him do it, the RSPCA perhaps? He knew he was being ridiculous, he had far more serious things to worry about than his pet rats' well-being, but the more he paced the more concerned he became, about all of his animals now, fretting whether Maria would feed them if he was kept in overnight, God forbid – not because she was cruel or anything, just whether she'd think to, know how to, know who got which food and how much, even if she did remember. He needed to ring her.

Terry hauled his brain back to his own predicament. He tried to work out what was going on, why he was being held here, what might happen next. He needed to be prepared, know what to say.

Terry's mind winds its way around the facts. He is in Hyde Park, near The Serpentine. He has a woman, his half-sister-in-law, under surveillance. He hears an argument. He hears a splash. The others leave, despite hearing it too. He dials 999. The police find nothing, are annoyed with him for wasting their time. Three days later a body is found, by a small boy in a boat apparently. They think it may be murder. It appears that he, Terry, is the prime suspect, even though he's the one who called the police. He's locked in a cell at this very moment, waiting for them to interview him.

Terry fast-forwards, imagines what he will say. He tries to calm down, think clearly, assess his options. He doesn't know what to do. He goes round in circles, getting tangled in the details of the lies he could tell. Sweat breaks out across his smooth top lip, and his tongue feels dead. He worries about his pets again, about whether Maria will give them fresh water at least.

And then finally, eventually, it comes to him.

Yes, that's it.

He'll tell the truth at last. He has no other option. He'll confess that he was being paid to trail a woman, that's why he was there, not for a nice evening stroll at all. He will confess that the woman is Juliette Forsyth, Stephen Forsyth's wife, a woman possibly familiar to the more dedicated readers of Hello magazine. He will confess that he is Stephen Forsyth's half-brother; that he was working for him as a favour because Stephen suspected his wife of having an affair.

What would the police do? Would they believe him? What the heck was going to happen to him? Terry put his head in his hands, to stop it from moving involuntarily from side to side as if in denial, to stop his hands from trembling like an addict's. He wished he had a paintbrush, a figure, some tiny intricate detail to tackle... an insignia perhaps. That always used to help steady his hands, steady his nerves. He looked down at his shoes, his leather soled smart shoes – he'd dressed up for the interview, almost looked quite handsome in fact, although he didn't quite know why he'd bothered. *So I don't look like a creep, a murderer,* he thought now. He wasn't sure if he'd been successful. He didn't know if he'd be believed, telling the truth didn't always pay, not when people like Stephen Forsyth were involved. All he'd done was try to save someone's life, and now here he was, locked up like one of his own pet rats.

Terry stopped pacing, as if admitting defeat. He was tired, felt like giving up – it was hopeless, he knew it. He hesitated, indecisive, shifting his weight from foot to foot, until he finally decided he couldn't stand up any longer, he'd keel over with fatigue and agitation. At the exact moment he sank helplessly onto the bunk he heard a commotion outside, and then there was a stern-looking policewoman, asking him to come with her. Terry felt even more fed up at this turn of events: ten seconds earlier and he'd have still been standing, wouldn't have made contact with that mattress – if he did ever get out of this nightmare he'd have to get his suit dry-cleaned now.

59

Somerset House

JoAnne was hovering outside the door, wondering whether she should go in; but something told her to give Juliette this time alone – the old man with the half-moon glasses had said on his way out that this was often a very big moment for adoptees, the first concrete step on their journey back to their beginnings. It was terribly frustrating though, JoAnne was desperate to find out, although she knew it wasn't her business, not really.

JoAnne picked up a leaflet entitled, "How to register a death," and sat in one of the booths reading it mindlessly, fiddling with a long black strand of her hair, twirling it round and round her forefinger like she was a little girl still. She was glad for Juliette that she'd taken this first step at last. JoAnne had always fancied herself as something of an amateur psychologist, and was sure that Juliette would feel so much better about herself if she knew the truth of where she came from. She almost shivered with excitement – once Juliette had her mother's name she'd be able to go about trying to trace her. She hoped it was a distinctive name, so it would be easier for them – no, *for Juliette*, she reminded herself. Maybe Juliette could even go and visit her one day, and she, JoAnne, would be more than happy to keep her company, offer moral support if she wanted it. JoAnne's finger was hurting for some reason, and when she looked down she realised she'd twisted her hair so tightly she'd cut the blood off.

When Juliette eventually came out of the anteroom her beautiful face was as white as her best friend's finger. JoAnne smiled and went to speak, but Juliette just shook her head and beckoned her to come, so JoAnne got up and followed her, untangling her hair as she walked. They made their way into the open courtyard and the sky was blue and clear, and the building was luxuriating in its own beauty like a gorgeous girl in the bath, but neither of them appreciated it, they just hurried one after the other. Once they were out in the shivery air of the Strand and it was clear that Juliette still wasn't going to slow down, say anything, JoAnne ran to catch up.

"Well?" she said, almost panting.

"Well what?"

"What did you find out?"

"I don't want to talk about it."

"Oh," said JoAnne. She didn't know what to say. "Was it upsetting?"

"Yes," said Juliette, and there was steel in her voice that JoAnne had never heard before. "You could say that."

"In what way?" asked JoAnne, struggling to keep up as they passed the Savoy, where a group of wealthy-looking people swarmed out into the road, expecting the traffic to slow down for them.

Juliette didn't know why she was so upset, not really. Nothing had actually changed, had it? She struggled for an answer that would satisfy her friend.

"Because what is the point in chasing after someone who didn't want me in the first place? There is no point. It's pointless."

"But you don't know that," said JoAnne, breathless still, and not just from having to walk fast. "You don't know that she didn't want you. Maybe she had to give you away."

"I don't think so," Juliette said, and her voice was sad suddenly. "And whatever way you look at it, she didn't want me *enough*. I should just be grateful for having such lovely adoptive parents, and leave it at that." She thought then of Giles and Cynthia, of what good people they were, how hard they'd tried, how they'd sent her to a lovely school, bought her a pony, of how much they'd always loved her, as if she were their own. And then she remembered how she'd always felt slightly inferior to her younger brother Barney, because he wore laughter around his eyes and never seemed to care where he came from. She wished she could have been more like him. She sighed. Life had been good regardless, hadn't it? She'd been happy with her lot, why was she stirring everything up now? (*Because JoAnne forced m–*, and before she'd even finished the thought she buried it, snapped it somewhere dark and inaccessible in her brain.)

JoAnne said nothing more as they made their way down into the tube at Charing Cross, and the atmosphere between the girls was tense, unfamiliar. They'd become so uncannily close, as if they'd known each other forever (although it was in fact less than a term), but right now they were each in their own worlds. Juliette had set her mind to neutral, and was trying not to think at all. JoAnne was thinking of her own mother, across the channel in a tiny flat in Paris with her handsome French boyfriend. *She* knew how it felt not to be wanted too, she thought crossly. But maybe in Juliette's case there would be a happy ending; they just had to find it. They just had to find *her*.

60

Stephen sat behind his desk, sleeves rolled up determinedly, running his daily editorial meeting in the manner of a despot ruling a tin-pot country somewhere far away. His office was a complete mess – papers everywhere, old editions of the newspaper dumped on the floor like in a hoarder's home – but his secretary and the cleaners never dared touch anything, they knew not to risk winding him up, it could get them the sack.

"OK, what have you got?" Stephen said. His deputy editor ran through the list of stories, an uninspiring lot including an A-list couple visiting Harrods with their kids and having a row in the food hall, a man being trapped for 15 hours after his ceiling collapsed under the weight of his porn collection, the threat of another economic meltdown in Europe, a primary school teacher who'd doctored her class's SATs results, a ten vehicle pile-up on the M4 in which a baby had been killed, yet another rumble in the phone-hacking scandal.

"None of this is really front page news," said Stephen, ignoring the last story. "Isn't there anything better?"

"Uh, sorry, Stephen, that's all we've got," said Barry Smiley, his long-time assistant. "What about going with the baby story, we've got a picture – of him *before* obviously," he hastily added, knowing even Stephen wouldn't put a picture of a mangled baby on the front cover of a national newspaper.

"I don't know, pile-ups aren't that interesting these days unless there's at least 20 cars involved," Stephen said. "I think if that's all you've got (accusing look) maybe we could have a bit of fun with the porn mag story, it is silly season after all."

Stephen's favourite reporter, Maddie, poked her head round the office door. Barry scowled at her; she was a right brown-noser, always trying to muscle in on everything. He was convinced she was after his job, and it kept him awake at night.

"Sorry to interrupt, Stephen," she said breathlessly. "Hold the front page – I've always wanted to say that! – but a body has just been fished out of The Serpentine."

"What, The Serpentine in Hyde Park?" asked Stephen, a little prick of adrenaline shooting through his neck.

"Yes, The Serpentine River! It's a woman, she's not been formally identified yet, but they think they've got the bloke too. Apparently he only went and dialled 999."

"Well done, Maddie! Thank God *someone* is doing some work around here." He looked witheringly at Barry, and Barry went puce with anger, above his pink-striped shirt (which as it happened was beautifully ironed and cuff-linked, unlike his boss's), at being up-staged like this. It was a bloody disgrace how Stephen humiliated him in front of this little upstart, after all he'd done for him over the years. He needed a drink.

"Oh well, I'll leave you to it then," Barry said. He stood up, but they didn't seem to have heard him. He walked across the room, en route to his secret drawer, and then hesitated at the door. He needed a punchline.

"And, in the interests of factual accuracy," he said, always his forte. "I think you'll find that The Serpentine is a lake, not a river," but Stephen was still too wrapped up with Maddie to have heard him.

61

Camden

It became clear to JoAnne, once they were back at her aunt's house, that Juliette really wasn't going to talk about anything she'd discovered, or otherwise, at Somerset House – not now or, it seemed, later. It was strange how she'd clammed up like that – what could she possibly have found out that was so traumatic? The thought came to JoAnne then – what if her mother actually had turned out to be famous, joking aside she did look so like that film star? Or what if she'd known who the mother was, maybe she'd found out it was her neighbour or grandmother or something. Or perhaps she'd discovered who her father was too, it wasn't always the case that it was "Father unknown," and it had turned out there was something shocking about him. JoAnne was almost desperate to know.

"How was your day today, girls?" asked Linda as she stood at the stove stirring something comforting-smelling, a blue-striped butcher's apron tied neatly over her seemingly-regulation jeans and white T-shirt. The aroma of paprika mooched through the air.

"It was fine," said JoAnne, carefully.

"What did you get up to?"

"Oh, you know, a bit of shopping around Covent Garden, not much really."

"I think you're forgetting something," said Juliette then, and she sounded uncharacteristically harsh, pent-up. "We went to Somerset House, didn't we JoAnne?" She turned to Linda, whose boyish face was shiny with steam from the cooking. "I don't know if you know, Linda, but I'm adopted. JoAnne for some reason is obsessed with where I came from, so she forced me to go to Somerset House and –"

"I didn't *force* you," JoAnne cut in, horrified. "I thought you were happy to go."

"Well, you were wrong," said Juliette, but her anger had faded now. She knew she was being unfair – she'd only realised that she didn't want to do it once she'd done it, after all.

JoAnne looked unusually close to tears, and Linda reacted quickly. "Right, who'd like a nice cup of tea?" she said.

"I'm *not* obsessed with where you came from," said JoAnne, ignoring her aunt. "I was just trying to help – I thought you said you'd feel better once you'd found out."

Juliette knew JoAnne was right, she had consented, in fact been even keen at one point, but it seemed when it came down to it she wasn't ready to go there, not yet. It was strange how before all this adoption business JoAnne had seemed so in tune with her, seemed to understand her more than anyone else in the world – but then thinking about it, who else would get her? She had no blood relatives after all; there were no genetic connections to help anyone read her moods or wilfulness. She felt embarrassed now at her outburst, especially in front of JoAnne's poor undeserving aunt.

"Don't worry, Jo, I'm sorry I got so emotional. I just don't think I'm ready to do this, after all." She turned to Linda. "I'm so sorry, Linda, I'm not usually such a nightmare, I promise."

"No, no, that's fine," said Linda. "You don't have to apologise to me. Look, it's none of my business, but it's a big deal what you've done. Don't be too hard on yourself."

"Sorry, Jo," said Juliette again, as JoAnne just sat there, hiding under her orange fringe.

"That's OK," said JoAnne, softening towards her friend, and the ever-obliging Linda served them tea and home-made fruit cake, and as snowflakes started to fall gently on the street outside and disappear into tiny shiny pools on reaching the pavement, the crisis passed, for now.

62

Canary Wharf

Stephen was feeling pleased with himself. OK, "The body in the lake" was not the most original of headlines, but it was a cracking story, and he was hoping to get enough extra material for at least a double-page spread inside – plus he'd almost certainly be able to eek it out for the rest of the week too. He'd got Maddie onto the bloke they'd picked up; she was off now seeing what she could dig up on him.

Maybe today was going to turn out well after all. It had certainly started badly. He and Juliette seemed to be getting on more appallingly than ever, she was so bloody uptight these days, always shouting at the kids, presiding over a pig-sty of a house. How on earth could they have so much domestic help and the place still look like that? He felt sorry for the children sometimes, especially Noah – and he was worried about him, he seemed to have become so withdrawn lately. Stephen didn't know what had happened to Juliette, she certainly hadn't turned out to be much of a wife and mother despite her early promise. He'd been so taken in by her beauty, her utter middle-classness, when they'd met at Bristol, and he'd been immediately smitten, had worshipped her like a precious painting – but she'd changed so much over the years, had become so bitter, and it was like she hated him as much as her mother now. Even worse, he was convinced she was having an affair these days, and the thought made him want to retch. He needed to know. He was annoyed Terry still hadn't got back to him with an update from her supposed picnic the other night; he bet he'd lost her, the useless twat.

His phone rang, and it was her. She didn't usually ring him at work. His heart leapt, despite himself.

"Yes," he said, which he knew didn't help marital relations, but hostility was their modus operandi these days.

"I'm at the police station," she said carefully.

"Why?" he said. Was she all right?

"Siobhan's dead."

"*What*? How?"

"She drowned, in The Serpentine."

Stephen felt his breath fall down, away from his chest, as though gravity had just got stronger. He felt a tightness in his throat.

"Weren't you with her the other night?" he said. "In Hyde Park?" He wondered if Terry knew anything about any of this – he bet he did, the sneaky little cunt, no wonder he hadn't been returning his calls.

"Yes," said Juliette. "But the rest of us had left, it must have happened after." The lie came out surprisingly easily.

"She was pissed," she added, as if an after-thought, and gave a little sob.

"This is fucking awkward for me," he said, thinking of the front page he'd been about to push the button on.

"Well, I think it's a bit more awkward for Siobhan, don't you?" his wife said, and put down the phone.

63

Bristol

Juliette stood alone in the phone box around the corner from the flat, a piece of paper propped up on the scratched black ledge in front of her. It was the torn off back of an envelope that she'd received from her bank a couple of weeks earlier, and she had written the phone numbers on the patterned blue side of the paper, not the plain white side, for some reason she couldn't fathom now. The list of digits was hard to decipher, blue writing against a blue security pattern, the ink smudged and messy, almost as if she wanted not to be able to read it. There were only three numbers in W3, and two in W12. She'd copied out the 14 others she'd found in the rest of London, just in case.

Juliette paused before she pressed the last digit of the first number. Should she really be doing this? What would her mum say if she knew? *She'd be devastated, that's what –* especially at Juliette doing it behind her back. Why hadn't she told her at least?

Juliette stood and watched her breath in the dankness of the booth, little puffs of white going nowhere, just fading into nothingness. She took so long deciding whether to punch in the last digit, whether to make the call or not, that eventually the phone must have thought she'd completed her dialling, and the wrong number tone screamed into the thin air like a warning. She clacked the receiver into the cradle, to stop it.

Why on earth was she doing this? It seemed insane to her suddenly. She thought of her own mother in Berkshire, kind and well-meaning, but ultimately unconnected to her. She thought of who her real mother might be.

What harm can it do, Juliette thought in the end. She wouldn't say who she was. She ran the forefinger of her left hand along the length of the number as she dialled it again. Her nail was thick with over-painting, but there were no actual chips in the bright pink colour today, just a steep ridge of varnish that ran across the nail a quarter of the way down from the cuticle, where it had grown out from the last time she'd painted it.

The phone took forever to connect, but eventually those familiar thrum thrums started and Juliette's heart started to beat faster and louder, and she very nearly hung up but her breath had come up into her mouth so she closed it and it made her feel giddy and fluttery, and she was so distracted that she kept the call going until at last her heart settled down and she almost felt ready to speak, if anyone would ever answer it. After 20 or so rings, just as she was about to give up, there was a clatter and a knock and a rustle and a few moments of silence, and then an impatient breathless voice finally said, "Hello?"

Juliette panicked and went to put down the phone, but

instead she froze and held the receiver away from her, in limbo, as if it were contaminated, which it was.

"Hello," said the voice again, sounding far away, disembodied in the glass box. "Who is it?"

"Um, is Elisabeth Potts there?" said Juliette, putting the receiver back to her ear at last. It reeked of stale saliva.

"No, there's no-one of that name here," said the voice, irritated now. "You've got the wrong number."

"Sorry, bye," said Juliette, and as she hung up her ears were red with shame.

64

Berkshire

Two days later Juliette sat opposite her mother in the sitting room of the house she'd grown up in – Cynthia said it would be better in there, although Juliette hadn't been quite sure what her mother had meant by "better." Barney was at school and her father was at work and the house felt only half-inhabited, as if ghosts instead of real people lived there. Juliette hated the formality of this room today, of sitting across from her mother, perched on the edge of the sofa with a cup and saucer on her lap while Cynthia looked thin and sad in Giles' armchair. Why couldn't they sit in the kitchen where the sun streamed in and forced a modicum of jollity into the atmosphere, where the aga gave the room some warmth, some substance? Juliette felt her heart beating fast in her mouth, and despite the wild erratic thuds there was a vacant, empty feeling in there, above her tongue, and it wouldn't go away, even when she sipped her tea.

"What is it Juliette, dear?" said her mother eventually, once it was clear Juliette wasn't going to start the conversation. "Why have you come home like this? Is there something wrong, darling?" She paused. "Is it Stephen?" she asked, although she knew it wasn't.

Juliette looked at her right hand, in its black lace fingerless glove, holding the delicate handle of the teacup, clumsily, like a chimpanzee in one of those tea ads. Why couldn't she just have had a mug? She looked at her mother's hands, which although small were large-palmed and raw with washing, it must be all the cooking she did, she really ought to use hand cream. She looked past her mother to the window-ledge, full of nick-nacks and photos: of Juliette and Barney on the beach at Salcombe; of Juliette with Popcorn (the latter proudly wearing a blue and white rosette, his head at a jaunty angle, as if he knew he had won); of Giles and Cynthia on their wedding day, the looks in their eyes innocent and virginal, from a different era (the only photo of their wedding she'd ever seen, now she came to think of it); of Giles as a boy with his brother and their parents, and this picture was from another even earlier time, another universe – the dour dark clothes, the two boys' ears jutting out of their brutal haircuts, their parents looking old despite surely being still in their thirties, the grimly startled expressions: fear of the camera she supposed. She wondered why that picture was framed at all, it wasn't a good one.

"Juliette," said her mother again. "What are you thinking about, dear?"

The question yanked Juliette out of the distant past, back to more recent events, to the furniture-polish smell of Somerset House, the inky curl of the letters, the thickness of the paper, the words. The phone box.

"You know," said Juliette finally, but she didn't say it accusingly, just in a *let's get on with it* kind of resigned tone.

"You wanted to know where you're from," said Cynthia. "It wasn't for your course, was it, dear?"

Juliette shook her head slowly as tiny tears formed just above her eyelashes, and they sparkled like drizzle in the sunshine.

"What have you done about it, Juliette?" said Cynthia. "Have you done anything?"

Juliette put down her tea on the mahogany coffee table and the clink of the fine bone china, of the cup and saucer chattering with each other sounded loud, explosive to them both, even though it wasn't.

Juliette stared out the window, past the eclectic assortment of photos, towards the house across the street, and she noticed that the neighbours must have got a new car, it was red and shiny and had a new number plate. She would never normally have noticed, she had little interest in cars, but as Cynthia had driven her home after picking her up from the station she'd spotted that the garage on the corner of the main road, right where they'd turned down the lane that eventually led to their house, had sported a large home-made yellow and red banner that said, "C-ing is B-leaving," which at the time she'd acknowledged was clever, and she'd wondered who had thought of it.

Juliette sat silently still. She didn't know how to broach it, even though she'd come home specially, on a Friday – after her abortive phone search she'd felt like she'd explode with the not knowing. Cynthia waited resignedly, looking at Juliette's black-lace hair band and tights and gloves and thinking it all looked a bit over-the-top, how the lace didn't go with the pink flowery skirt and arran knit jumper, but she didn't say anything of course, she didn't want to hurt her daughter's feelings.

"Elisabeth Potts," Juliette said in the end. "Who is Elisabeth Potts?"

Cynthia tried not to react but she did and they both knew it. Her back stiffened.

"Where did you get that name, Juliette?"

"You know," Juliette said. "It's on my birth certificate."

Cynthia looked forlorn then, as if it were game over, although of course really it had only just started. This was the end of the family she'd tried so hard to create. She'd always been aware Juliette would want to know one day, but she felt like she'd failed her somehow. Poor Juliette, she was too young still – she, Cynthia, should have managed it better. It was never meant to be like this.

"Maybe we ought to wait until your father gets home," said Cynthia. "We should all talk about it together, as a family."

"NO," said Juliette. She looked shocked at herself. "I'm sorry, Mum, but I can't wait any longer." And Cynthia saw that she couldn't, she was bursting with hope and fear.

"It's just I know the name," said Juliette. "I know that I know it, but I can't think how, or where."

Elisabeth Potts. A name to remember? Juliette sat across the room from her mother, auburn hair glowing, her mind searching forensically over her past life, searching out the time, the place, she had first heard those two words. Elisabeth Potts.

65

Belgravia

Terry Kingston sat sullenly in the fluorescently bright interview room feeling thoroughly resentful. He'd been being interviewed for over two hours and was fed up with saying the same thing over and over again. He'd known they thought he was dodgy anyway, but at the mention of his client's name, they had reacted first with disbelief and then with outright hostility, and it seemed to have made it all worse, not better. (The duty solicitor had shifted in his seat and wondered what the hell was going on here, this case he'd been randomly allocated suddenly looked like it might get even more interesting – it wasn't just dead girls in lakes and dodgy blokes in bushes, now there was a major newspaper editor involved, it was bloody dynamite.)

"So what you're telling me is that you are a *private investigator* and that Stephen Forsyth is your client? *The* Stephen Forsyth, the newspaper editor?" The policewoman was openly sneering now.

"Yes, that's right," said Terry, and he felt relieved, now it was out.

"And just what were you doing on *his* behalf?"

"I was keeping tabs on his wife. He... he thought she was having an affair."

"And how do you know Mr Forsyth?"

Terry sighed. "I'm his half-brother."

The male police officer looked incredulous.

"You?"

"Yes, that's right." *A loser like me*, Terry said in his head, but of course he didn't say it out loud.

The policeman seemed lost for words at this revelation, so the woman took over again. She was black with one of those faces that was plain until she smiled, and then was transformed by her beautiful white teeth, like the sun coming out. She wasn't smiling now though.

"And so you were in the park *spying* on Mrs Forsyth, and then what happened?"

Terry sighed again.

"I wasn't spying on her, I was being paid to keep her under surveillance."

"Then what happened, Mr Kingston?"

"I told you, I was bored because it was clear to me that this was just a tedious women's night out, with them all going on about school admissions policies and salmon recipes and the like, but I couldn't leave in case Mrs Forsyth was going on to a rendezvous later in the evening, which was possible I suppose. So I was just sat minding my own business..."

"Hardly," said PC Williams, her gleaming teeth firmly under wraps now, and he realised, quite perceptively considering the pressure he was under, that his misogynistic bent wasn't helping him here.

Terry tried again. "I was waiting for Mrs Forsyth to leave, not really listening to the conversation, and once they'd moved from the Diana fountain I couldn't really hear the detail of what they were saying anyway – but then I think they'd all been drinking and everyone started arguing (he chose not to bring up some of the words he'd overheard, particularly the ones like *rape* and *murder*) and there was lots of screaming and shouting, and then one of them just seemed to totally lose it for some reason and ran off hysterically. The others were all packing up anyway, so they started to leave without her – they were really fed up with her I suppose and it was getting late anyway... and... and then... and then there was a splash."

"Who heard the splash?"

"We all did."

"How do you know they did?"

"Because one of them said, 'What was that splash?'" He tried not to sound sarcastic, he knew it would do him no good. "And then they all started discussing it, and they were nearer to me now, although they still couldn't see me, so I heard it all... And one of them said she was sick of her anyway, and... and... and that she could drown for all she cared."

"Who said that?"

"I don't know, they all sounded the same." (*Horsey, posh*, he meant.)

"And then what happened?"

"They started saying they thought it was a bird, but it obviously wasn't, it was much too loud to be a bird – but the weird thing was that after the splash there was no other sound. No splashing, no struggle, nothing. And then one

258

of them said that if her friend really had gone and drowned herself she'd just say she'd already left and hadn't heard it, and that she was going home, she'd had enough of all the melodrama. And once *she* decided to go, they all went, she was obviously the ring-leader... and I was about to follow, to keep up with my target... and then... and then I thought I couldn't just leave... just in case she *had* fallen in... so I ran and looked but I couldn't see anything... but the splash was so loud... I couldn't be sure... and I couldn't just leave her... and so that's when I dialled 999."

PC Williams had been doing this job long enough to know when someone was lying. Up until five minutes ago she'd been convinced this shifty little creep had had something to do with it, the way he couldn't look them in the eye, his evasiveness around their questions. But she'd spotted his resemblance to Stephen Forsyth as soon as his name had been mentioned, knew the part about them being brothers at least might be true – and now the man seemed to have found his voice, become eloquent despite his hesitation, and she just knew that Terry Kingston, pathetic loser, small-time dick, was telling the truth at last.

66

Barnes/Battersea

Early one hot July morning, a week to the day after the picnic, Natasha was jogging effortlessly across Barnes Common trying to get hold of Juliette (she was not only super-fit but the queen of multitasking). She didn't really want to have to speak to her, although she thought she ought to at least try, so she was glad in a way Juliette wouldn't come to the phone – maybe she was having a breakdown, her cleaner had answered and said she was "indisposed." When she couldn't get hold of Camilla either, Natasha tried JoAnne.

JoAnne sounded thoroughly miserable, not herself at all (which undoubtedly wasn't helped by having to talk to Natasha).

"Are you all right Jo?"

"Well, what do you think? This is bloody awful. Poor, poor Siobhan, I still can't believe it." She hesitated. "I feel terrible about lying to the police as well."

"Ssshh," said Natasha, although there was no-one to hear either of them. "That's why I'm ringing. Have the police called you?"

"No," said JoAnne, wary now. "Why should they have? I've given my statement."

"Well, they called me," said Natasha. "And they've said that the bloke who called 999 originally, the one they arrested, they've said he heard us all talking, and he's told them we heard the splash."

"WHAT? Aaaaagggghhhh," screamed JoAnne, and then she started swearing, saying fuck fuck fuck over and over like a mantra, before moving onto panting, virtually hyper-ventilating, down the phone. Her cat jumped off her lap, aggrieved, and then there was a tremendous crash in Natasha's ear.

"JoAnne? Jo? Are you there?"

"Yes, sorry," said JoAnne finally, after loads of clattering. She seemed slightly calmer now. "I dropped the phone. Oh my God, what are we going to do? We'll be arrested. This is horrendous."

"No we won't," said Natasha. I've looked it up on Google – I went to an internet cafe, they'll never be able to trace the search back to me. We haven't committed a crime as such. As long as we say we heard a splash but that we thought it just was a bird, we'll be OK. And even if he did hear us say something about her drowning it was obviously a joke."

"But we've already said the opposite," said JoAnne, sobbing now. "We've given our statements, we told the police we didn't hear anything. We'll get done for perjury."

"I've looked that up too," said Natasha, and she sounded almost pleased with herself. "We haven't perjured ourselves, you can only do that in court. We can just change our police statement, people do it all the time apparently."

"Really? But that makes us look terrible... and surely... even if we don't get done for that... surely it must be a crime to leave someone to drown? Isn't it manslaughter, through negligence or something?"

JoAnne's obviously spent a lot of time agonising over this, Natasha thought. She hoiked her lycra shorts out of her bottom as she jumped across a ditch. She should've been proactive and looked into it, like I have.

"No, we haven't committed any crime," she continued, still not remotely short of breath despite her pace. "We weren't responsible for her in the eyes of the law for a start – that's only the case if she were a dependant, a child or something, not a grown woman. We simply say we didn't go back when we heard the splash *because we thought it wasn't her*. I'm pretty certain the absolute worst that can happen is that we can have a civil action against us, not a criminal one. That's called tort law, I've read up on it. But we can talk to lawyers about that if we need to, once everything's in the open."

JoAnne was too busy thinking about Camilla and her bloody raspberry torte, how the picnic was all her idea, how if they'd never met up in the first place then Siobhan wouldn't be dead, to really take in any more of what Natasha was saying. She'd had quite enough shocks lately. She couldn't believe Natasha could be so matter-of-fact about her friend's death, almost like she was discussing her team's monthly sales performance or what to get for dinner. She knew Natasha hadn't really got on with Siobhan in recent years, even before that final devastating night – they'd been the exact opposite of each other by the end – but even so, it was a bit callous. Natasha seemed to have lost any kind of heart these days,

JoAnne thought, was more driven and ambitious than ever. She imagined her now, head to toe in designer running gear, about the only thing she ever wore when she wasn't in one of her hideous suits, face tight from Botox, sprinting home to set up a spreadsheet about probable outcomes. She was ghastly, really she was, how had she changed so much, how had they ever been friends?

67

Belgravia

Sergeant Hunter looked at the beautiful pale woman sitting across the table from him. Her lawyer looked out of place in the scruffy interview room – in his pin-striped suit and yellow silk handkerchief he would have been more at home in a gentleman's club, he had that air about him, as if this was all beneath him. Sergeant Hunter didn't think he needed to ask any more questions, she was the fifth woman he'd interviewed in the last two days and she was just repeating the same boring account of the evening – they'd obviously all got together and colluded to make sure they got their stories straight, despite the monumental acrimony they'd had towards each other by the time they left the park, according to Terry Kingston.

Now there was an odd bloke, Sergeant Hunter thought. He'd seemed like such a creep at first, but it turned out he'd been the only one who'd tried to save the dead woman, after her so-called friends had all just upped and left her to her fate. And it appeared he'd only lied at first to try to protect his half-brother – it seemed now they were getting to the bottom of exactly what had happened it was Terry Kingston who had more morals than the rest of them put together.

Sergeant Hunter wasn't interested in the interview with this woman. They'd had the pathologist's report back and nothing she was saying added to it. No, it seemed he'd have to let her go. He asked her a few more questions, just for the hell of it. Let her sweat a bit, he'd thought – even if it did turn out she was criminally in the clear (which seemed likely, seeing as the funeral had already been approved to go ahead, what had become of the criminal justice system!), morally she and her friends were definitely guilty in his book. Typical selfish middle-class values, he told himself, somewhat bigotedly – give me my Sandra and the lads at the snooker club any day over these stuck-up cows.

Sergeant Hunter took a final glance through his notes – had he covered everything? He looked up, saw her frightened frigid face next to her lawyer's fleshy smug one, sighed and said, "OK, madam, that's all, you're free to go."

68

Royal Leamington Spa, The Midlands

Juliette drove Sissy and Katie to the funeral in her Range Rover. The others took the train – Natasha and Juliette were no longer talking if they could help it, now Juliette's affair with Natasha's husband was out in the open, and it seemed Juliette would never speak to JoAnne again either, after all the vile things she'd said about Stephen. Anyway it was more practical that way – it would have been far too cramped in the car with everyone. It was a nightmare, but despite everything they had to go: they were some of Siobhan's oldest friends, and they'd been together on the very night she'd died. They couldn't not go.

As Juliette parked up in the narrow car-lined lane she couldn't believe what a huge event it was. The media were there and an outside screen had been erected for all the mourners who wouldn't fit inside the church. Juliette was horrified by the photographers – who immediately recognised her and began taking photos – but more than that she was shocked by how many people were there, for Siobhan. She'd had no idea Siobhan had so many friends. "It must be because it's all over the news," she overheard Natasha whisper, as she sat down in front of her in the church, and Juliette thought there was no need for cattiness at a time like this, but of course she didn't say anything.

The service had an unbearable poignancy that inked through the air and made almost everyone sad. Siobhan's father, an elegant old-fashioned-looking man, stood tall through his grief as he addressed the congregation, dark suit immaculate, tie militarily straight, hand-made shoes polished, as he talked of his love for his funny, eccentric, warm-hearted daughter, who although at times could be a little outspoken perhaps, undiplomatic even, had empathy and generosity that more than made up for it. He spoke of his and his wife's pride at how well Siobhan had done over the years, how she had grown into such a capable young woman who'd achieved so much in her career (it appeared she'd just been made a director at her publishing company, how come she'd never told them that), how much her boyfriend Matt had adored her, although she often didn't seem to realise it. Derek had choked a little at this point, and stopped, seemingly unable to go on, and after a few seconds the vicar had taken his arm and guided him gently back to his seat, where Margaret had grabbed his hand and held it tightly, as though letting go would cause something to break.

Matt's speech was even more devastating, if anything. Juliette thought it odd that only Camilla and Sissy had ever met him before, it seemed he'd been going out with Siobhan for ages, and he was much more handsome than she'd expected. He spoke of Siobhan's lust for life, her success in her career, her courage, her risk-taking, her integrity. He talked of her love of acting that she'd discovered in just the last year or so, when she'd joined a group and even been in a play in a small theatre in Chiswick. Juliette and the others were stunned – *how come she'd never told them?* It was like the service was about a different person from the one they'd known.

But it was when Matt spoke about how Siobhan could never do too much to help someone and was such a wonderful friend, that Natasha felt uncomfortable, and the others succumbed to remorseful tears. Although the service, as these things are wont to, teetered into over-indulgence at times, the odd thing was it felt real, heartfelt, not just false flattery in death. Juliette found herself recalling the time when Nigel had cancer, of Siobhan helping Sissy through the pregnancy, the birth, although Sissy had been so delirious with grief she'd barely noticed. She remembered Nigel's death ten years later, of Siobhan being there for Sissy *every* weekend for months afterwards, of how Sissy's kids had adored her. As the music signalling the end of the service started up ("It's my life," by Talk Talk, which Siobhan had played over and over again in the flat in Bristol and driven them mad with) Juliette finally realised that they'd misjudged Siobhan, not appreciated the person she'd become, and probably always had been.

Juliette felt faint. She had failed her friend in life and *had left her in death*. She was despicable. They were all despicable. As she looked desperately around the church, searching for something, someone to comfort her, she could see the shame on their faces, all their faces except one; the lucky one, the one who'd already left and truly hadn't heard the splash.

69

Three and a half weeks later, Siobhan Benson's parents travelled from their home in Royal Leamington Spa to the coroner's court, for the inquest. They were still in shock. Margaret
hadn't slept for longer than a couple of hours at a time, not
since the police had knocked on their door on that terrible
Sunday afternoon nearly two months earlier, and the exhaus-
tion had changed the shape of her face: it looked skull-like
now, as if the flesh around her eyes had been prematurely
gouged out by maggots. Derek stood tall and stiff, with an
achingly sad air about him, and as they walked from their
Audi past the waiting photographers he put an arm around
his wife's shoulder, but the contact didn't comfort either of
them. There was no comfort to be had.

The coroner felt for the Bensons (the most difficult inquests
were always when it was somebody's child involved) and he
ushered them away from the throng into a private room, and
as they sat down he sent one of his officers to make some
coffee, there was still half an hour to kill. No-one spoke.
Largely to break the silence, the coroner went over what was

about to happen, although the Bensons were already vaguely aware of it. He gently reiterated that they'd only be trying to establish the cause of death today, not who, if anyone, was responsible. He showed them the list of people he was calling as witnesses. Margaret Benson looked at the names, recognising many of them, and felt sad that her daughter had even been out with these women. Siobhan had been so hurt over the years at their various put downs and slights, Margaret had tried on several occasions to suggest that maybe she shouldn't see them so often, maybe even leave some of those relationships in the past – it was no good keep getting upset love, she'd said. But Siobhan hadn't wanted to – they were her friends, she'd insisted, and besides, they all had so much shared history, accumulated like books over the years, and you never got rid of those, did you. Margaret knew that her daughter only really saw Camilla and Sissy by the end, she'd never failed to give Sissy support with those poor children. That was the thing about Siobhan, her mother thought, her throat constricting, she'd always wanted to help people. And now following one of the most innocent activities you could hope to partake in – a picnic in the park with some old college friends – her only child was dead.

The inquest was underway but Margaret could barely follow it. She understood a few things. She understood that her beloved daughter, Siobhan Alice Benson, the most wonderful child she could ever have hoped for, had died, aged forty four, at approximately 10.35pm on Thursday 7th July 2011 at The Serpentine Lake, Hyde Park, London. She understood that she had died through drowning – they were quite unfussy in the way they said that, there seemed to be no fancy medical term for that way of dying. But from this point onwards Margaret struggled to keep up with what was going on. Apparently, the pathologist said, there were marks on the side of the deceased's head consistent with a heavy object, perhaps a polyamide something or other, but not necessarily so. (*What did he say? How did she get the marks? Did someone hit her with the polya-whatever-it-was-called?*) He said Siobhan might have been unconscious when she hit the water. (*Is that why she didn't scream?*) A post-mortem examination revealed she had 164mg of alcohol per 100ml of blood at the time of her death. (*Did that make her drunk? Is that why she drowned?*)

Margaret's head felt thick, as if she had a heavy cold, and the words were finding it hard to punch through to her brain. She was struggling to remember the meaning of quite basic expressions, let alone the technical ones. Eventually the pathologist finished and sat down, looking chipper, self-satisfied. He was small and geeky, and Margaret was dismally reminded of an excited little boy with a bucket of worms, one of those ghoulish types who'd been born to poke over dead rotting flesh, into unexplored cavities, her precious daughter's body nothing but a macabre journey of discovery for him.

Through her bewilderment Margaret still startled — even though she'd been expecting her — as the first of the witnesses took the stand: the shock of flaming hair, pulled back as if in penitence, the exquisite pale face. She listened more intently now, as Juliette explained her relationship with "the deceased," described how the evening had somewhat disintegrated, with "the deceased" running off into the night after what she described as a "bit of an argument." Margaret heard Juliette admit (quietly, her voice choking) that they'd all been drinking, were all rather drunk in fact, and that no-one had known where Siobhan had gone, they'd just assumed home. And so, she said, when they'd heard a splash it hadn't even occurred to them that it might be Siobhan, they'd thought it was just a bird or something – after all, there was no struggling or splashing afterwards – and they'd left without going to look (Juliette looked ashamed at this point, like she might cry). Margaret watched the coroner nod and ask Juliette to take her seat, and apart from the deep screaming red of Juliette's hair the scene felt blank, colourless, unreal to her.

The next bit Margaret couldn't understand. She knew why everyone was gasping and covering their mouths with horror, it was clear Terry had said something dreadful ("'She can bloody drown for all I care,' I heard one of them say, Your Honour,") but she struggled to understand the implications. Did Siobhan's so-called friends know the splash was her all along? *Did they deliberately leave her to die?* No. Surely not. Margaret slumped suddenly in her chair, and as Derek stood up shouting for a doctor the coroner hurriedly adjourned the inquest.

Fortunately it turned out Margaret Benson had only fainted, and a shot of brandy that appeared from somewhere amidst the mayhem appeared to sort her out. Afterwards Derek explained to his wife what she'd failed to comprehend: that Terry had told the inquest the details of the conversation he'd overheard, which was that the women had agreed at the time to say they hadn't heard the splash if it turned out Siobhan really had drowned – and how he, Terry, couldn't be sure exactly which individuals had been involved in the conversation, it had been too dark to see. Derek told his wife how Terry had said he'd seen one of the women stride off into the night half a minute before the others, so she possibly really hadn't heard anything, had left with a clear conscience at least. Amidst the chaos it seemed that no-one knew which woman it was though, and because of the disruption none of the rest of them gave evidence that day.

70

Canary Wharf/Fulham

On the afternoon of the inquest Stephen Forsyth was sent home from work. It was all too awkward. Following the euphoria of his newspaper breaking the original story of the body in the lake (online at least, they even beat Sky News to it), over the following weeks other less convenient facts had kept revealing themselves, like rampaging acne. Facts like the dead woman being a friend of the editor's wife. Like there having been a group of other women present, *including his wife*. Like the fact they'd all been arguing just before the woman died.

As the limo (probably the last one he'd get out of this fucking job) crossed Tower Bridge Stephen didn't bother with the view, he was too busy seething. Those early revelations had been awkward enough, but Stephen had managed to ride out that storm; he had a thick skin, it hadn't been too bad. It had only been a matter of time after that though – he'd known it would almost certainly all come out at the inquest, even though he'd offered Terry so much money to change his story, just a little. It wouldn't have changed the outcome, he'd argued, but Terry wouldn't budge, the cunt – just kept saying he'd already made a statement, he couldn't alter his story now. Stephen had tried his hardest to bully him into it. Deep down he'd known it was madness, but he'd been desperate – and besides he'd got away with worse before.

So now, because of his weaselly half-brother's sudden penchant for integrity, the rest of the facts that would ruin Stephen's hitherto soaring career were out. Facts like despite having heard a splash Siobhan's so-called friends, including his own wife, had left her to die, had said *she could bloody drown for all they cared*. Like all this being known because a small-time private detective hiding in the bushes had seen it all. Like Stephen having hired the detective because he suspected his wife was having an affair. *Like the detective being Stephen's secret half-brother.*

Stephen had known he couldn't hope to have survived putting his own wife under surveillance while all the phone-hacking shit was going on, but it was Juliette's leaving her friend for dead, her apparently saying she didn't care if she drowned, that had caused the most sensational headlines, had finally finished him off. As the car crawled past the dismal sights of the New Kent Road down to the Elephant and Castle (which seemed to Stephen to be lacking both of its namesakes these days, but he was looking in the wrong direction) Stephen let out a groan of humiliated rage, which the chauffeur politely ignored, he'd been doing this job long enough to know when to keep his mouth shut. Stephen was finished, and it was all Juliette's fault, the fucking bitch.

★

Back in Canary Wharf Stephen's assistant Barry Smiley was jumping for joy, totally cock-a-bloody-hoop. He'd been as gob-smacked as everyone else when it all started leaking out, in tantalising dribs and drabs at first, and then building relentlessly to the brilliantly shocking revelations of the inquest. He'd been amazed when everything had turned out to be true too: usually in these situations all manner of fantastical stories get bandied about before the less lurid facts are slowly extracted out of the morass of half-truths – but in this case the more wild the rumour the more accurate it had turned out to be. All it had taken was one emergency meeting less than two hours after the curtailing of the inquest for the publisher to decide to grant Stephen what they were euphemistically calling a "compassionate leave of absence," and had put Barry temporarily in charge.

But no-one was feeling very compassionate. Barry knew his boss had been sidelined just so they could crack on with reporting the story, and although he ought to have felt sorry for his long-time boss for the way his world had come tumbling down, Humpty Dumpty-like, he'd still been smarting from Stephen favouring that upstart reporter Maddie ahead of him, belittling him like that in front of her when she'd come bounding in like a bloody spaniel with her precious sodding lake story. So when Barry had been asked by the publisher to take over the reins, just for a few days initially while they worked out what to do, he had taken tremendous joy in sanctioning every ghastly detail to be printed. He had zero loyalty to his boss now, and why the hell should he after all he'd done for Stephen over the years, and for what? Barry had also delighted in sidelining Maddie to cover Big Brother, which no-one watched any more, and he'd relished having Stephen's office cleaned out – he, Barry, couldn't possibly work in all that mess. It was retribution time. It was bloody brilliant.

71

Sardinia

The bedroom was still so brutally hot Nigel needed to do something, and quickly. He felt frantic, useless, frantically useless. He stared helplessly at the phone his daughter had fetched for him. He didn't know the Italian number for emergency services, and there was no-one to ask. Maybe Sissy didn't need an ambulance anyway, he thought – he shouldn't panic, he just needed to get her cool. What else could he do to cool her down? An idea came to him, and although it wasn't a particularly good one action felt better than inaction. He rushed to the walk-in store cupboard where Stephen and Juliette kept everything that there was no other place for: deck chairs and beach toys, a tool kit, a broken barbecue, spare faded cushions for the outdoor furniture, fishing gear, a battered straw picnic basket. *Yes.* Tucked on a high shelf right at the back was a silver electric fan, still in its box, where he remembered he'd seen it. He clambered over the folded up deck chairs and with his fingertips edged it off the shelf, catching it mid-air as his body bent half backwards into the sun-loungers.

Nigel ran back to the bedroom where his wife was lying with her eyes closed, breathing raggedly, her face obviously badly burnt, and he took the fan out of its box and searched ineffectually for a socket, looking everywhere, seeing nothing. The ones for the bedside table lamps were hidden behind the bed, inaccessible. There must be another one somewhere, surely. He scanned along the skirting boards, and then for maybe the fourth time along the length of the frieze of the tastefully naked couple pastel-painted across the back wall, the one against which the bed was butted up – and finally, there in the corner, amongst the tangled twining grapevines, he found the socket. It was quite a way from the bed, but the cord should be just about long enough to reach her.

Nigel plugged in the fan but it refused to work. He checked its settings, made sure it was definitely meant to be on. He jiggled the plug around. As he wiggled the cord increasingly manically (he wasn't even sure it would do much good, but he didn't know what else to do, he was proving useless in a crisis) the fan leapt into life, and his heart jumped – thank God – and then the whirring stopped, fading out limply, as if it couldn't be bothered, as the electricity cut again. He cursed it. Maybe he should run next door, try to find someone else who could call a doctor, perhaps send Nell; she was sensible. He couldn't think straight – his mind had always been so clear in the face of his own impending death, but at the thought of anything happening to Sissy, he was derailed, a mess. Yes, he'd get Nell to go for help. He'd ask her in a minute, once he'd got this sodding fan going.

Nigel jiggled the plug in its socket yet again, and it seemed to move more freely than it should, as though there was merely space behind it, rather than wall. The fan jittered in and out of life, teasing him. The ads were deafening from the lounge, and there were some groans he didn't like the sound of, this was Italy after all, you never knew what they might put on, even in the middle of the day.

"Turn that TV off now," he yelled, but the children ignored him. He shoved in the cord harder and waggled it angrily, bloody furiously, and at long long last the fan started up its shiny revolutions, rhythmically in synch with the moans from the living room, and at the very same time a blue crack of electricity flew through the air from the socket, and then it flew through Nigel, and the fan stopped again.

72

Fulham

Early on a Wednesday morning in September, not long past midnight, Stephen Forsyth sat in the office in the eaves of his £2 million house with his own newspaper's site open on the 27-inch iMac that graced his vintage Danish desk. His wife lay passed out on the bed in the luxurious guest room below. Although Stephen was ridiculously drunk he could still just about focus on the text. The next day's stories had been published two minutes ago. It was the fourth one, on this, the day after the inquest, which attracted his attention. "Mother who abandoned her son for love," was the headline. "Loner Kingston," ran the copy, enthusiastically endorsed by Barry a couple of hours earlier, "developed a deeply entrenched distrust, verging on hatred, of women after his own mother walked out on him, according to an unnamed source. Terry Kingston, who quite sensationally is the secret half-brother of this paper's editor Stephen Forsyth, who is currently suspended (Barry had that bit put in), was the prime suspect in the initial enquiry into the death of Siobhan Benson, 44. Kingston's mother left the family home when her son was just two years old to move in with her former next door neighbour, a mere half a mile away, and she soon bore a new child, Stephen. According to our source, Terry Kingston never forgave her." Stephen finished reading and put his head in his hands and sobbed snottily, like a toddler.

Ten or so hours later, Juliette and Stephen sat sullenly opposite each other across the solid wood table, which he noticed was badly scratched in one place (had one of the kids been scribbling again, did she ever fucking supervise them?) in their large German-manufactured kitchen. Its white high gloss finish was sparkling, the surfaces unusually clear of the normal detritus associated with a household made up of a (before now) largely-absent father, a sluttish mother and three unruly children. The housekeeper had been so titillatingly embarrassed by the revelations of the Daily Mail when she'd arrived that morning it had given her a rare flare of energy, and she had taken to the kitchen as if to a human catastrophe clear-up – an earthquake perhaps, or maybe a hurricane. She had donned her pale blue housecoat and pink Marigolds and, fuelled by bran flakes and adrenaline, had whipped through the room, emptying the dishwasher, piling all the clean stuff onto the island (making the place look temporarily worse), putting away the cutlery with dangerous efficiency: large knives deftly dispensed to the magnetic rack on the wall, knife-thrower-like; forks and table knives and spoons and teaspoons tossed into the appropriate sections of the cutlery drawer expertly, like quoits at the fair; ladles and serving spoons zealfully attached to hooks like hanging victims.

Mrs Redfern had then turned her attention to all the crap

on the draining board: dinner plates stacked up, still full of leftovers, two wine glasses, one smeared with gash-red lipstick; three (three!) empty wine bottles; an assortment of dirty bone china mugs from Heals and Harrods and various unheard-of stately homes; half-full tumblers of orange juice and water; flattened individual smoothie cartons oozing gunk; a lone squashed pear with a single bite out of it. It's an absolute bloomin' disgrace this house, she'd thought, as she picked bills and colour supplements out of slimy puddles on the counter-tops, shook sticky unidentifiable drips and burnt crumbs off them onto the work surface, scraped the resulting mess off the counter into her rubber-gloved hand to be dispatched into the bin, dunked the dishcloth in hot soapy water and cleaned the Corian (*whatever that is,* she harumphed, *all that money and you're not allowed to use Flash on it, I ask you*) surfaces so they shone. She'd then vacuumed and mopped the floor like a maniac before whirling upstairs, uncharacteristic energy not yet spent, to attend to the children's rooms – on her way stomping noisily past the firmly shut door to the master bedroom in the hope that someone might come out; sneaking a hopeful peek into the spare room, where she tantalisingly saw a pair of bare feet (hers) hanging over the end of the bed; listening fruitlessly at the bottom of the stairs up to the office in the eaves.

Stephen and Juliette were not appreciative of Mrs Redfern's earlier efforts as they sat at the table nursing monumental hangovers – in fact they didn't even notice that the kitchen was tidy for a change. Juliette probably wouldn't have done anyway, even on a good day, and Stephen was too wrapped up in the horror of his apparently unravelling life. It was disastrous. The press was still getting tremendous mileage out of the body in the lake story, especially Stephen Forsyth's involvement, there were just so many angles – his own wife having been under suspicion for a start; the revelation that he'd hired a private detective, and not just any detective, but his hitherto secret seedy little half-brother (who quite unbelievably was also implicated, had been the lead fucking suspect in the initial enquiry into Siobhan's death); the unveiling of Juliette's affair (as it turned out it *was* bloody true, the whore – and not just with anyone, but with that fucking snake Alistair Smart!). Stephen felt sick in his stomach. That wasn't even the half of it, it got way worse than that. Last night with his wife, in their drunken semi-violent shouting match (Juliette had gone for him first, he hadn't meant to catch her eye, he'd just been defending himself, for fuck's sake), she'd told him that Siobhan had claimed *he'd* been to blame for Nigel's death in Sardinia, and that when she'd blurted it out JoAnne had gone nuts and started calling him a murderer. Stephen was terrified – he knew he wasn't guilty of *murdering* Nigel, but he must admit he'd always felt a little bit responsible, and if it got out he definitely could be accused of fraud, or perverting the course of justice or something – or maybe even manslaughter, he didn't know the law on that.

How the fuck would Siobhan have known about the socket though, he thought he'd dealt with all that? Sissy must have known somehow, must have told her. He tried to clear his head, ignore his wife as she sat half-dead across the table from him. OK, he'd known he'd done up the apartment on the cheap, even been aware the electrics were faulty, but he hadn't meant to *kill* anyone, and it's not like he, Stephen, had wired the sodding plugs himself. And he *had* felt terrible for Nigel, killed off by electricity, not cancer, in the end, and after everything he'd been through. But really, Stephen told himself yet again, as if saying it often enough would make it true, Nigel had been lucky to be alive anyway, he'd been read the last rites ten years beforehand, no-one ever thought he was going to pull through. The cancer would probably have come back anyway, it usually did, and Nigel had had ten good bonus years. And at least the kids' screams at discovering Nigel had alerted the neighbours, so they'd managed to get Sissy to hospital in time; they hadn't been left as orphans thank Christ. They could so easily have lost their mother as well, might well have done save for the accident, if all Nigel had been doing for her severe heatstroke was plugging in a fucking fan. Surely it was better for them to have lost their father rather than their mother?

As Stephen sat with his head in his hands he remembered how much he'd panicked when he'd first got the call about Nigel's death, had known he had to do something – you never knew with the Italian authorities, it definitely could have got nasty. So he'd contacted Terry's brother-in-law Gianfranco as soon as he could, just in case the police did end up getting involved, and Gianfranco had sorted it all out, had had the socket repaired by someone who knew what they were doing – Stephen's offer had been far too attractive for him not to.

Stephen had always thought that would be the end of it, but it turned out Sissy had somehow known what he'd done all along. And now, thanks to Siobhan, apparently so did the rest of Juliette's friends. He was fucked, especially as someone had already leaked it – even if the press hadn't actually implicated him yet there'd still been a story about someone dying in his holiday apartment, what if some dogged reporter decided to check it out further? He couldn't go down for murder though, he told himself, he definitely wasn't a murderer... it had been an *accident*. He hadn't wanted Nigel to die, he'd quite liked the bloke. How dare anyone call him a murderer?

As Juliette slumped further into her chair, Stephen thought of all her fucking bombshells last night, all the revelations, the other rumours circling – and he didn't know what the hell he was going to do about any of them, now they were surfacing, rotten and stinking like Siobhan's bloated corpse. He was finished, surely.

Stephen let out a howl, and it sounded villainous, comedic, although in truth it was desperate. (Juliette barely looked up, it was like she'd been drugged or something.) He'd been humiliated, abandoned, well and truly shafted. His life was being picked over as if by vultures on a stinking rubbish dump, and although he tried not to acknowledge it, Stephen realised it was what they call comeuppance, retribution. He thought about Nigel, Juliette, JoAnne, and he felt defeated, ready to succumb, penitent even. He deserved what was coming to him.

As Stephen continued to look across the table at his ghost-like wife, whom he had adored once as an example of what he could become, he thought of the hateful, damning things they had screamed at each other last night, and he wondered whether the children, or worse, the neighbours, had heard — and as he stared at the puffiness around his wife's left eye he wondered where a rope or some kind of lead was, so he could go out to the garage now, before he had to face anyone.

73

Berkshire

"Hello, Giles, it's me, Cynthia... Yes, yes I'm fine. I'm so sorry to ask, but are you able to come home? ... Yes, I know it's the middle of the day, it's just Juliette's here... Yes, yes she is, she got the train, I picked her up from the station... Now, yes please... She wants to know about her mother... Yes, I do mean her... Yes, yes, she has... All right. (Long pause.) Hello, yes I'm still here... You can? Oh, thank you! See you soon dear. Bye bye."

Juliette looked at her mother, at the lines around her eyes that were beginning to belie her approaching middle-age, and she felt sad for Cynthia, could see how hard it was for her too, but it was just too bad. She had to discover the truth at last – it was as if once she'd started this, had found out the name, made the fruitless phone calls, the real story had to come spiralling out, whatever it might prove to be. She'd waited her entire life, and now she couldn't wait any longer. She needed to know *now*.

Cynthia seemed unsure what to do with herself while they waited for Giles, so she made her excuses and went upstairs to put away the clean laundry, blowing her nose as she went, and when she'd finished she came down to the kitchen to make more tea. Juliette had moved from the sitting room and was already there, sat at the table – its blue and white gingham oilcloth and bowl of jaunty yellow tulips made her feel better somehow. Juliette smiled nervously at her mother. Yes, she thought, it was much nicer in here, this was where she wanted to hear her story. She took off her lace gloves and looked at her hands, at the wide palms, the chipped polish, the long snaking lifeline. She studied her fingerprints, unique to her, made by someone. She waited.

74

Barnes

Natasha sat at her dining room table looking out onto the garden, a huge glass of wine and today's newspapers in front of her. As she flicked through the pages she decided she really did have to divorce Alistair now, there was no alternative course of action after all this – the past few weeks had been intolerable, really they had. Her whole carefully constructed world had come tumbling down, her sham marriage revealed, the hardness in her heart right there for all to see, in three glorious double page spreads of a gutter tabloid. All their secrets had been paraded like trophies: the affairs, the feuds, the abandonment of their friend, the role of Stephen's seedy secret brother, even something about Nigel's death – how on earth had they dug that one up? The one thing that hadn't leaked out, thank God, was that she and the others had changed their story – that they'd lied to the police at first, and only admitted later what they'd heard, what they'd said, when called back in for further questioning after Terry Kingston's statement had directly contradicted theirs. Not that it had helped at the inquest, of course – it had still been clear they'd deserted their friend, they'd still come across as callous bitches (*"She can bloody drown for all I care"*), just not lying ones. Their lives would be forever blighted by it.

Natasha wondered for the millionth time what had actually happened that night, how Siobhan had really died. She supposed no-one would ever know for sure. They'd never charged Stephen's brother with anything, and they hadn't managed to turn up any other potential murderer – but neither had they ever been 100% certain what had caused the dent in her head. And of course no-one knew what Siobhan had been thinking at the time, and it was too late to ask her. Maybe she did it deliberately, Natasha thought hopefully, surely that was the best answer of all, if she'd had to end up dead, that she'd intended it. She'd seemed so miserable that night anyway – with her job, her boyfriend – and then she must have regretted some of the things she'd said, they'd been so horrendous; and of course she'd been completely pissed, couldn't possibly have been being rational. Yes, maybe that was it.

Natasha stood up. She was in her office attire: trademark primary-coloured suit, crisp blouse, high heels. Her hair was short – blonde and spiky like it had always been – and her dangly earrings looked incongruous, ridiculous, her pathetic attempt at cheering herself up, moving on. She'd been planning on going back into work this morning, but now it came to it she found she still couldn't face it. No, she'd have to continue to lie low until all the stories had died down – but now Stephen had been suspended that didn't seem very likely any time soon. His own newspaper's coverage seemed to be even more vicious than the others' – he could never go back there after what they'd written about him and his family, and she wondered briefly what would happen to him, not that she gave a shit of course, not after what he'd done.

So, thought Natasha, as proactive as ever, if I'm not going back to work today I need to do something productive, the kids won't be home for hours. She left the warmth of the dining room, with its plate glass windows giving onto the huge slimy-looking pond Alistair had insisted on having dug in their garden, rammed full of monster carp that she vehemently hated but which refused to bloody die.

Yes, that's it. She'd go and sort things out with her husband, start the ball rolling, now was as good a time as ever, now she'd made up her mind at last. As she climbed the stairs she noticed the bare patches on the carpet, a single long loose thread. Maybe she could order some samples, the carpet needed replacing and she never usually had time to sort things like that out, not unless she had a project on. She might as well make an effort to get the house looking nice, she'd be staying in it with the children, obviously.

As Natasha stood on the landing outside the closed door of her husband's office, she was suddenly unsure of herself. It was unlike her to hesitate. She briefly remembered how much she'd loved Alistair once, been mad for him, couldn't get enough of him. She'd believed in him then. In between climbing her own career ladder and shagging his brains out, she'd channelled her endless energy into helping him professionally, launching his book career with her normal invincibility, never taking no for an answer, she'd been so convinced of his talent. He'd have been nothing without her.

Where had it all gone wrong between them? Natasha was

aware he'd started to get fed up with her even before the wedding – maybe looking back she had been a bit dogmatic about it all – and she knew he'd definitely found it difficult when the babies had come. She'd gone back to work after two months each time, and it had been so hard juggling her job, securing her promotions, running the house, she'd ended up exhausted. No wonder she'd gone off the whole sex thing, it was normal, it's just that no-one ever admitted it. She sighed as she remembered Alistair's hurt at her rejections, felt a rare stab of sympathy for him.

And then she remembered he'd screwed one of her oldest friends, and not just Juliette but that little strumpet author too. Possibly even worse, he'd passed off Lucinda Horne's books as his own, was a loafer, a *fraud*. Any remaining nostalgia for her marriage vanished in that moment, was gone forever.

Natasha shifted her weight onto her left side, easing the pain in her bunions, and wondered how to do it. Knock? Barge in? She listened, but it was quiet. She turned the handle. It was time to confront him.

The door didn't open, and she realised it was locked. *She didn't know he had a lock on it*. He's probably wanking in there, she thought with disgust, and it was the most perceptive insight she'd had about her husband in years.

Natasha didn't bother knocking or waiting to see if Alistair had heard her and would come out anyway. She turned around and stomped back downstairs to the dining room, where she took a seat at the table facing the fish and opened her laptop, and demanded the divorce by email instead.

75

Berkshire

Juliette looked younger than her 19 years as she sat opposite her mother in the kitchen of her childhood home. Cynthia couldn't help but notice how beautiful her daughter was, and she was glad she'd taken off the fingerless gloves she'd had on earlier, they were a bit much with the hair band as well, she wasn't too sure about the whole Madonna look. She wouldn't have said anything though, Juliette always seemed too fragile to take any kind of criticism, no matter how well-meaning, and especially not today.

After what seemed like forever they heard the sound of wheels on the gravel, the car door slam, the key in the lock. They waited, unable to look at each other, as they heard shuffling and rustling in the hallway. *Finally* Juliette's father came into the kitchen, looking older, anxious. A cold wind swept in with him, and Juliette shivered.

"Hello Daddy," said Juliette. "Thank you for coming home, I'm so sorry to be such a drama queen." She paused, not sure what else to say.

Cynthia pushed a mug of tea (cups and saucers were

reserved for the front room) across the table at Giles, and it was brown and swampy, stewed.

"You start, Juliette dear," said her father, taking a sip and trying not to grimace, his voice steady and kind.

Still Juliette said nothing. Where did she start?

"It's all right," he said. "You can tell us, love."

"Elisabeth Potts," she said finally. It was all she could think of to say. She took a breath. "She was my real mother." Juliette saw Cynthia flinch. "Sorry, my birth mother." She looked at Cynthia, accusingly. "You know her, don't you?"

"Damn," thought Cynthia. "Damn."

Cynthia looked at Giles. He nodded, almost imperceptibly. She gulped. Her mouth felt dry. The words sounded like they were coming from someone else, someone far away, in another room perhaps.

"Elisabeth's my sister," said Cynthia.

76

Fulham

The weird thing after the grotesque showdown with her husband (who decided, once he'd sobered up, not to hang himself after all), was that all Juliette wanted was her mum, her real mum. She knew better than to call her though, she'd learned her lesson over the years, and she didn't think she could handle Elisabeth Potts' dismissive platitudes, Juliette preferred silence to those. Stephen had been surprisingly compliant since the night she'd confronted him – he was obviously shit scared she'd leak something. She must admit she was tempted, she was so horrified by what he'd done, someone needed to make sure he got his comeuppance – or perhaps she ought to go to the *police* instead of the papers. Why should he keep getting away with everything? She knew she wouldn't do it though, she couldn't do that to the children, they were unsettled enough as it was, particularly Noah. If her friend wasn't going to press charges then she wouldn't stir it up, it wasn't her business, not really. She was only married to Stephen, she hadn't actually been involved, thank goodness.

Juliette lay in the enormous bed with the luxurious

mattress that she'd shared with Stephen for so many years and shuddered. She would never share it with him again, not after this. Their marriage was *over*. She turned her head into her pillow and let out a sob. Poor Cynthia wouldn't do. She wanted her mother.

The phone rang and rang downstairs. Juliette ignored it, her head still buried in the pillow – Mrs Redfern could bloody get it, earn her keep for a change. Eventually the phone stopped and she welcomed back the silence, like an old friend. Then the door opened, just a little, enough for half a curly grey head to make an appearance.

"Juliette, are you awake?" she said. "It's one of your friends, I think. She says it's important."

Juliette groaned and took out her head from under the covers. Her hair was wild in the half-light. Mrs Redfern tiptoed across the carpet and handed her the phone. She slumped it against her shoulder, barely holding it, and it was slippery against the silk of her nightdress.

"Juliette?"

"Yes," she said.

"It's me, Camilla. I was just calling to see how you are. You never return my calls."

"Oh."

"How are you doing?"

"Not bad," said Juliette. She started to cry, silently.

"Why are you blanking me? What have I done in all this, except for maybe be a little bossy over what to make for the picnic? I can't help it, it's my upbringing." Camilla attempted a laugh.

"I'm not blanking you, Camilla," said Juliette. She hesitated. She didn't want to be rude, Camilla of all people didn't deserve it. She decided in the end to be honest for a change, it might do her good.

"It's just that I can't forgive myself over Siobhan's death, for leaving her like that. You don't have to live with the guilt – I know it sounds odd but you're lucky in a way, you'd gone, you didn't hear her." She didn't mention Stephen, she couldn't face referring to what he'd done, although Camilla knew that too of course, everyone had bloody heard the night of the picnic. Juliette wept and had to stop talking for a while as Camilla waited, quietly. "I just prefer not to see anyone from Bristol now, it's all too painful. I'm so sorry," she said, and went to put down the phone.

"Stop, don't go," said Camilla. "You were drunk, you didn't know what you were doing, and anyway you didn't really think it was her, of course you didn't! You're not to blame, really you're not. Look, I'm at Mummy's in Chelsea, shall I pop over? Your cleaner said you're still in bed, and it's the afternoon Juliette. You need your friends at times like these, I should know. Remember how you looked after me when Daddy died?"

Juliette remembered that time, 25 years ago, how they'd all rallied round Camilla after her father's dreadful dressing-up-as-a-baby scandal, how they'd taken her off to a cottage and looked after her, only for him to hang himself the day after they'd got back, deep in the woods on his country estate. Camilla had still managed to stick out university though, and Juliette knew it was because they'd all pulled together, put a cocoon of love and support around their friend, as people who all live together at college tend to do at the time. They'd stuck together through everything back then, even though they'd all been so different – Camilla had been so totally posh in her stripy shirts with the collars turned up and strings of pearls, and Juliette and Siobhan were Madonna wannabes, and JoAnne was punky, and Natasha always looked like she was going for a run, a vision in lycra even then, and Sissy had looked like someone's little brother. But they'd all got through things *together* in Bristol. They'd been real friends back then.

"OK," she said, in the end. What harm could it do? All the harm had been done.

"I'll get a cab, I'll be there in half an hour. So get off your skinny arse and put the kettle on!" And she way she said the word *off* rhymed with *wharf*.

"OK," said Juliette. "Thanks. See you soon, bye."

"Ciao, ciao," said Camilla.

77

Berkshire

Juliette sat quietly opposite the tulips, which seemed to have drooped, lurched downwards under the weight of the revelation, disbelief trickling down her face, as Cynthia recalled exactly how Juliette had recognised her birth mother's name. She could remember every detail of that morning, what, ten or eleven years ago now, when they'd spent Christmas at Cynthia's mother's house, down in the New Forest. Juliette had been such an inquisitive little girl and her nana had loved her so, doted on her, more than poor Barney (as everyone knew but no-one dared acknowledge), and they had shared such a wonderful bond. Juliette had been an absolute poppet, so eager, so helpful – setting the table for Christmas, making glittery name tags for everyone, putting up the Christmas cards her nana had saved for the children to do on lengths of silver ribbon (not that Barney had bothered, he'd just ripped a couple up and been told off), alternating the sizes and shapes, making them look perfect. That morning would have been the 27th or 28th of December, the first day of post after Christmas. Juliette had been sat patiently at the kitchen table, her bowl of Weetabix neatly eaten, waiting for Barney to finish so they could both get down, when the letterbox had clattered and her nana had asked her to run and pick up the post before her badly-behaved dachshund Dexter got to it, he loved chewing it up. There had been only three items – a plain envelope with a cloudy window addressed to Mrs PL Simmons that looked boring to Juliette, a bill perhaps; a thin insubstantial-feeling card for Mrs Penelope Simmons; and another small square card addressed to someone unknown, and then in a different coloured ink, as though written at a later time, a c/o alongside Penelope's address. As she sat in her cosily warm kitchen with not a teacup out of place Cynthia went over that morning in vivid technicoloured detail – how she'd noticed as she buttered her toast that her fuchsia nail varnish had chipped, she must take it off; how she'd nagged Barney to finish his cereal (Golden Nuggets they were, she had scolded her mother for buying such junk, and Penelope had said, "Oh it won't hurt them just this once"); how she'd watched Juliette come back into the kitchen and read out each envelope in turn, showing off what a fantastic reader she'd become; remembering Juliette's nana saying, "Yes, you can open them dear;" hearing Juliette reading, quite innocently in her little girl's voice, "Elisabeth Potts – like pots and pans! – c/o (pronounced "cee oh") 3 Willow Grove, Lyndhurst, Ha-;" she, Cynthia, jumping up from the table and snatching the card off her daughter and saying, more sternly than she ever had, "That one's not for you," leaving poor Juliette looking tearful, violated, and Cynthia knowing she had handled it badly, attracted way more attention than she needed to have, but it had been the shock of course.

Cynthia felt strangely calm, now the secret was out at last, and she wondered whether they should have just told Juliette years before, and to hell with Elisabeth's rights, sod what her sister had wanted – after all she'd been so unfathomably selfish about everything. But it was too late to worry about any of that now, it was what it was, and so she looked across at her trembling daughter (or should she think of her as her *niece* now, what was the etiquette?), and as the colour slowly returned to Juliette's face, Cynthia sat patiently and waited for her to speak.

78

Fulham

The two women sat together on the bench at the bottom of the gently fading garden, where the roses were brown now and only held their shape until the wind blew them into little fluttery petal bombs, flamboyant reminders of the seasons passing. The air had a sharpness to it, as if warning them that there wasn't much of summer left, but the sun felt warm enough on their faces and at least sat side by side Juliette didn't have to look her friend in the eye. They chatted for a while about Camilla's husband and the kids, and it was clear to Juliette that Camilla's married life was so simple, based on real love and mutual respect, on them giving to each other rather than transacting like a business arrangement – and she realised how most of her friends' marriages weren't like that, not at all. Camilla moved on to her favourite subject now, filling time, telling Juliette about a great recipe she'd found for making instant ice cream ("It's so easy, Juliette, you should try it"), and Juliette told Camilla how the kids were doing in school (not great), how little Jack in particular had been unsettled since his father had moved into the spare room, how Flo seemed to be struggling with all the after-school activities and extra tuition and pressure she was under to get into secondary school, and how Noah just ran wild, immune to discipline, so Juliette simply didn't know what to do with him. Finally the conversation had faded out to nothing and they had both just sat there for a while, in silence.

It was the shorter, plainer one who spoke first.

"So what are you going to do, Juliette?"

"About what?"

"You know."

"I don't know."

"About getting better."

"I guess I just have to try to carry on, look after the kids, try to be a better mother, what else can I do?"

"You need to get your head straight, that's what. You owe it to the children, especially now things are so bad between you and Stephen."

Juliette sighed. "I've tried all that. I've read every bloody therapy book under the sun over the years. I've even tried writing it down – that's why I first went to Alistair..." She looked sheepish. "Nothing's worked. I'm officially a nutcase. I yelled at Noah again this morning, just for slopping his drink. I just seem to have so much rage in me... He hates me, and I can't say I blame him."

Juliette's eyes started to fill, and although Camilla had told her that of course he didn't, Juliette had hunched into herself and shaken her head and said, "Yes, he does, he does," and she'd confessed at last to what a hopeless mother she was, and how desperately she loved her children and didn't want to be fucking up their little lives but just didn't seem to know how not to, and she started crying really hard then, and Camilla hugged her until the weeping had stopped and then suggested, ever so gently, that maybe Juliette could get some help with her anger issues, and Juliette nodded, acknowledging it at last.

"You do know why you're so angry, don't you?" said Camilla. "It's not just about the kids – or Stephen – or your affair with Alistair." Juliette coloured again. "It's not even about what happened to poor Siobhan, although of course that's been terribly upsetting. It's all that business with your mother."

"No it's not," said Juliette.

"Yes, it is, Juliette. I told JoAnne at the time not to rush you. We were all so worried about it, once we knew what you were doing. I mean, one minute you hadn't even told us you were adopted and the next you were dashing off to find her. It's a huge deal finding out about your mother, especially before you're ready. You just never had time to come to terms with it."

"No, it wasn't even that." Juliette hesitated. She'd never told any of them the real story, what she'd found out 25 years ago, who Elisabeth Potts really was. It felt humiliating somehow, the rejection even worse than she'd imagined – rejection by a young married couple, not a desperate teenager – and she'd felt ashamed that no-one, not Cynthia, not her grandmother, had told her the truth. She found over time she didn't blame them though. She only blamed Elisabeth. The revelation of what Elisabeth had done, explained to her by her devastated adoptive parents in their sunny kitchen so long ago, had felt too painful, too overwhelming to take in, and so it had seemed easier to leave it all alone for a while. It had been another year before she'd tracked down and confronted her birth mother, met her for the first time, and as Juliette thought back to that day she realised that it hadn't helped at all. In fact it had made it all worse.

Her old friend looked at her in the watery sunshine.

"Tell me what happened, Juliette, you need to talk about it."

And so, for the first time ever, maybe because she'd hit rock bottom and had no-one else to turn to, Juliette did.

79

Berkshire

Juliette sat fiddling with her lace gloves, which she'd put back on, looking at Cynthia like she was mad. The yellow tulips between them were sickly in the sunlight. She finally spoke.

"What d'you mean, your sister? That... that makes you my... my *aunt*." She thought of Cynthia's small square hands, the same shape as hers. "...That makes Nana my *real grandmother*, for God's sake. What on earth do you mean?"

Cynthia picked at one of the tiny pearly buttons on her cardigan. "Well, the thing is darling, Elisabeth didn't feel ready to have a child. She was still so young, hadn't finished college..."

"And who was Alan Potts then? He's on my birth certificate too. It says he was my father. Was that her *husband*?"

Cynthia looked at Giles, and Giles looked desolate for a moment, and then he spoke.

"Yes, Juliette, he was. They'd got married a few months earlier."

"But then why didn't they want me? Why didn't they keep me?" She was shrieking now. "What was wrong with ME?"

"Oh Juliette, nothing was wrong with you. You were so beautiful." Cynthia started to cry, that she was causing her daughter such anguish after having tried to protect her for so many years. She continued, her voice wavering.

"Elisabeth just felt too young to have a baby, darling. They didn't have a house or anything, they were living with Nana..."

"She was 22," said Juliette. "That wasn't that young in those days." Her face was fixed, grim within the halo of hair. No-one spoke.

Pots and pans: Nana's house. That was where she'd heard the name. Of course. Elisabeth Potts was Nana's daughter too.

"So what happened to her? Where did she go?"

"Well, when she said she wouldn't keep the baby, none of us believed it at first. And then she seemed so deadly serious that your father and I discussed it and... and we offered to take you ourselves. You see, we... we had struggled to have our own child, and Nana was so furious with Elisabeth, so desperate not to lose you... it seemed to make sense on so many levels." Cynthia cleared her throat. "So we applied, and... and I'm afraid Elisabeth was so angry that she didn't want to speak to us anymore, and so she didn't. We knew the baby, you I mean, had been born in Acton but we didn't know where Elisabeth went after the adoption. So we lost contact."

Juliette struggled to keep up with what Cynthia was saying. "Why didn't you tell me?" she said finally, and her voice had an edge to it that Cynthia hadn't heard before.

"Oh Juliette, we wanted to, but if you have your baby adopted you have the right to anonymity until the child turns 18. It's only then that you would have been allowed to trace her."

"So why didn't you tell me when I turned 18?"

"We were planning to. But we weren't sure how you would take it... and you never asked, never seemed interested, so we assumed you weren't ready. And then you were going off to university, and we didn't want to unsettle you, it's such a big step. We did our best to get it right, but sometimes we didn't. I'm so sorry, love."

Juliette ignored the apology. She knew she was furious, she wasn't quite sure who with yet.

"And what about Nana? Did she ever see her?"

"I'm not sure. I think sometimes, up in London. We didn't really talk about it."

"So Nana would know where she is now?"

Cynthia looked into the bottom of her mug, where the dregs lay.

"Yes, I suppose she would, Juliette. I suppose she would."

80

Fulham

The sun had gone behind a cloud, one of those flighty ones that keeps changing shape, and the temperature dropped sharply. Both women shivered.

"Bloody hell," said Camilla. "Why would she want to give her own baby away, if she was happily married?"

"Oh, it gets worse," said Juliette. "D'you know what she did then? Got pregnant almost immediately. And then she *kept* that baby, another girl. Now why would she do that? Abandon me and then keep the next one? It's evil."

"Is she still with your father?"

"No, they split up years ago. Apparently it was all her who wanted to get rid of me, he couldn't understand it either. I think he resented it in the end. That's what my grandmother told me anyway."

"So, she had a new husband, you were born in wedlock, she had another child straight after, there must have been something really devastating, it doesn't make sense otherwise."

"Maybe it was my ghastly hair," said Juliette, and as they tried to laugh they looked at each other and it came to them both at the exact same time, and Juliette couldn't believe she hadn't ever thought of it before.

81

Elisabeth

Cynthia was always the more serious daughter in the Simmons household, a typical first born really. Elisabeth was the pretty, fun one, seven years younger, with long wavy hair and laughter streaking through her soul. The sisters had adored each other, despite their different temperaments, the difficult age gap – Penelope had done well on that count, ensuring she handed out her love evenly between her daughters, minimising resentments. They'd even shared a room until Cynthia left home to get married to a nice young engineer called Giles. Elisabeth had been bridesmaid of course, and she had been pretty as a picture, everyone kept saying, but Elisabeth had shushed them, not wanting to upstage the bride.

Elisabeth had missed her sister after Cynthia left home, but she was happy enough – she did well at school, went on to nursing college, had loads of friends, plenty of boyfriends, and then when she was 20 she'd met a lovely boy at a dance, and she'd known he was the one, from the minute he'd asked her to Rock Around the Clock, and she'd been relieved that she'd saved herself, for him.

Marrying Alan turned out to be the happiest day of her life, although the wedding night had been a let-down – she'd been scared stiff and it had been awkward and painful and altogether embarrassing. They'd sat up afterwards, smoking in bed, unable to sleep, both wondering what the fuss was about. But the next day they'd driven to Dorset and they'd stayed in a beautiful little cottage just a short walk up the cliffs from the beach and they'd practised like crazy until they'd really got the hang of it, several times a day for a whole week seemed to sort it. The weather was balmy and the sea was clear and lovely and warm for swimming. Life couldn't get better for Elisabeth. It could only get worse, and it did.

82

Cleveland

While her friends were still out at the bar getting drunk, and Stephen was downstairs waiting to continue where they'd left off, JoAnne stood under the shower watching the grit from her body run red into the tray. The fierce streams of water penetrated through the alcohol and sobered her up a bit, made her heart a little steadier and her legs a little stronger.

JoAnne felt ashamed of her behaviour now, and not only because of Juliette. Although she knew rationally it wasn't her fault, she couldn't stop thinking about the man in his kitchen, couldn't stop blaming herself: "So all I need you to do (giggle) is sign here." (Provocative lean forward – had she been fucking mad, she'd known he was a weirdo; she must have been on auto-pilot, irrefutable proof of the book company's fail-safe training methods.) She'd been unbelievably lucky to have got away, she might even have been *murdered* if she hadn't managed to fight free of him – what man does that in his own home unless he's going to kill you, dump your body, destroy the evidence?

And now here she was, less than two weeks later, drunk,

making out, rolling around in the dirt like a sow on heat. And with *Stephen* of all people.

JoAnne realised as she stood there, water pouring over her like from a bucket, that she wasn't falling for Stephen after all, absolutely not. What had she been thinking? She must simply have been lonely and drunk and depressed – unnerved by bookselling, freaked out by the double dose of trauma on that terrible day a fortnight earlier, what with nearly drowning too. It couldn't have helped her state of mind, and this line of thought comforted her in a way. It really wouldn't do to sleep with Stephen, he was her best friend's boyfriend after all; she had her standards. OK, it was embarrassing, but they hadn't done anything much more than snog thank God, and she knew that Juliette would eventually forgive her if she left it at that – she and Stephen *were* officially on a break, after all. Thank God Stephen had tripped over in the driveway, pulling her down with him like a lassoed calf. Getting all that orange grit over her bare legs and arms and back had brought her to her senses, had bloody hurt for a start. Who knows what would have happened if they'd ended up in the house still all over each other? They wouldn't have fallen into bed though, seeing as there weren't any beds to fall into, maybe they'd have jumped into *floor* together.

JoAnne stopped herself. She knew it wasn't funny. She couldn't bear to lose Juliette's friendship for a start, she was way more important to her than Stephen ever would be, but it was more than that. She was vaguely aware that her attitude to men had been somehow changed since the attack – she needed to be careful, she thought, she mustn't get unhinged by what had happened, as though she were an open door to push against these days. But then again, *what was the point of saying no when no-one listened?*

As she pulled back the shower curtain she was swaying again; it was almost as if the streams of water had created a force field around her, keeping her upright, and now she was standing just in air she found she was still horribly pissed.

I need to go to bed, she thought. No, not bed, *floor*, and she giggled again. *Get a grip JoAnne.* She pulled her towel around herself and unlocked the bathroom door to find Stephen standing outside on the landing, big and bulky, and he had his own towel wrapped around his waist, as if he were waiting for the shower. He took one look at JoAnne, barely covered, and grabbed her and started kissing her again, and although in her head she didn't want to anymore she found herself snogging him back, there was something about the alcohol and the steamy heat and his solid-looking body that made the desire build in her all over again, and he propelled her along the corridor and into the room he shared with James, one of the other (mainly under-tree-dwelling) booksellers – but James wasn't there, he was still getting hammered at the bar. Stephen pushed the door shut behind him and started kissing her even more passionately, and she didn't much like it now, his breathing was heavy and ragged, and anyway her towel was coming down, they should stop, and although she tried to push him away he bent her backwards until she thought she was going to hit the floor, but he managed to get down on one knee and catch her somehow, and before she knew what was happening he was heavy on top of her and she could feel the roughness of the carpet beneath her, and he carried on kissing her like he was trying to eat her, his tongue rigid and choking, and then she realised he was pushing himself into her and although she screamed at him to stop his face was vacant and his eyes were cold, and he started moving backwards and forwards, hard, fast, and each time he thrust into her he hurt her deep inside herself and she beat her fists against his chest and screamed at him to stop, get off her, but he didn't seem to want to hear, he was in his own world, looking down at her as if he owned her, and it was only once he'd finished that he seemed to realise she was even there, and he sank down next to her and muttered something although she couldn't work out what, and then he turned over and went to sleep.

83

Wood Green, North London

Juliette was shocked when her mother opened the door. She looked so old these days, but, Juliette reasoned, she's in her mid sixties now, what did she expect. Elisabeth had that pinched look to her face, of someone who has suffered, and the lines around her mouth, like a hangdog's, were largely thanks to the packet a day habit she still hadn't conquered.

"Oh," said Elisabeth. "Goodness. I wasn't expecting you. Why didn't you ring? Now's not convenient."

"It never is, is it Elisabeth?" said Juliette, but she sounded less hurt, less bitter than usual. Today she just felt sadness to the moon and back for her mother. The hatred had gone elsewhere.

"When can I come back?"

"Well... Oh, you might as well come in now you're here, but you can't stay long, I have to go out. What d'you want to drink?"

"Nothing, thanks," said Juliette. She moved inside the cramped cluttered hallway, and she could smell damp faintly, wet washing perhaps. Elisabeth ushered her through to the kitchen, and it was small and dark, and one of the cupboard doors was hanging at slightly the wrong angle, like it might fall off, and the work surfaces were scratched and stained. There was a gleam of grease covering the once-white walls, and paint was peeling in one corner. The washing up had been done – a single bowl and plate and mug – and the ancient-looking dishcloth was hung over the tap to dry. My God, this place is depressing, thought Juliette.

Juliette sat at the tiny table, which was still wet from wiping. A copy of the Daily Mirror was lying folded next to an unhappy-looking plant, open at the crossword. It was half done.

"What do you want, Juliette?" said Elisabeth. She stood with her back to the sink, arms folded. Her jumper was navy, acrylic, worn out. "Do we have to go over it all again?"

Juliette didn't know what to say. She had literally got in her car, dropped Camilla back in Chelsea and driven straight over to Wood Green, ignoring Camilla's protestations. She hadn't been thinking.

She looked at her mother, at the grief etched into her skin like knife wounds, and she started crying.

"Oh, for God's sake," said Elisabeth.

"I know why you gave me away," said Juliette, snivelling.

"What do you mean? Of course you do, I've told you enough times over the years."

"No, I know the real reason."

"What do you mean?"

"You know," said Juliette.

84

Dorset

On the last day of their honeymoon, the one with no clouds and sky blue as china, Elisabeth was on the beach devouring an Agatha Christie, her second of the holiday. She was smooth peanut brown, the darkest her pale skin would turn in the sun, and she wore a red polka dot swimsuit with a white frilled skirt that kept flapping up in the breeze, revealing the perfect curve of her behind. Alan stood towelling himself after his swim and as he looked down at his young wife lying on her stomach, legs kicking, back arching so that she could read, dark hair loose in the sunshine, he thought again what a total smasher she was, and he felt the desire build in him yet again, was there no end to his ardour.

"Shall we go in a minute," he said. He paused. "We might have time for a quick lie down before dinner."

Elisabeth looked up over her shoulder. "You randy bugger," she laughed. "I need to finish my book, I'm just about to find out whodunnit."

Alan didn't want to sit down and get sand everywhere again, and so he suggested he might go ahead and get cleaned up.

"Shall I see you there then? I'll take everything up."

"Yes, fine, I'll only be ten minutes. D'you mind?"

"Of course I don't." He leaned down and put one hand into the sand as he kissed her, tried to put his tongue in her mouth.

"Stop that," she giggled. "There are children about."

He looked at her green eyes, her flowing hair, her breasts squashed together by her position, and he wanted to reach out and touch her right there, hold her, make love to her, bury himself into her. My God, he had to stand up, before it was obvious.

"OK," he said. He moved reluctantly away from her and packed everything up, the picnic, the thermos, the beach ball, the frisbee, and when it was safe he folded up his towel, put on his shorts and shirt, and left her sundress and sandals neatly beside her.

"I'll see you soon, my darling."

Elisabeth looked up quickly from her book, she'd just found out the murderer was Vera, she needed to know how it ended.

"Bye, love," she said, and blew him a kiss full of promise.

When Elisabeth finished her book just twelve minutes later there were only two family groups left on the beach. The children were still running squealing in and out of the sea, and as it was such a perfect evening none of the adults seemed inclined to move, although it was gone six o'clock. As she put on her dress she noticed one particular little girl, laughing and naked, and she felt a tiny pull of joy that perhaps she might have one of those soon, she wouldn't be surprised if they had a honeymoon baby after the week they'd had. She smiled to herself. Yes, she'd be quite happy with that.

The walk up the cliffs to the cottage was steep, and although it wasn't far it puffed Elisabeth out, she smoked too much even in those days. She stopped for a second, panting, looking back the way she'd come, and she could see the people, small now, still settled in their deck chairs, and a dog cavorting across the sand after a ball, and the green of the sea, reaching out forever, to the end of the world. She shook her head back and shut her eyes and put her face to the sun, and it still felt warm, like it was blessing her. And that's when she felt a hand over her mouth, and something cold and hard against her throat, and that's when she got pulled off the path and into the bushes, down into the thorny bushes that scratched and hurt her, but not as much as he did.

85

Cleveland

JoAnne was on the kitchen floor, Volume Two of Tyler's Educational Handbooks open next to her face, its pages bent at the biology section, the radio blaring the usual dismal news in an inappropriately cheerful tone. The man was heavier than he looked and she couldn't move, was fully pinned down, stripes forming on the undersides of her thighs from the edges of the tiles beneath her.

"Get off me, you bastard," JoAnne screamed as she struggled against him, but that seemed to provoke him, arouse him further, and he brought one hand down from her neck to maul roughly at her top, and then he tried to pull at her shorts, but they were denim and belted and he couldn't get them off.

Even through her panic JoAnne knew this was serious, she could see the madness in his eyes. She'd read something somewhere and it came to her then, so she stopped struggling and went limp as the man humped above her, and at first he didn't know what to do, he had nothing to fight against — and then she started moaning, as if in supplication, and that really confused him, put him right off his stride. So when JoAnne began groaning and writhing beneath him, like she was even *enjoying* herself, he loosened his hold on her throat, just a little, while he undid his belt, and she managed to move enough to get her hand down there and he let her although he didn't much like it, it was all rather odd, he preferred it when they were scared shitless, and soon her hand was free enough for her to take hold of him, and she caressed him, as if he were precious, and he released his grip still further – and then when her hand had just enough freedom she started to twist, hard, until he was screaming in agony, and she twisted further and harder, with both hands now, and once he was in too much pain to be able to stop her she got to her feet and kicked him between the legs, repeatedly, like she was kicking a door in, and then she grabbed her book bag and fled from the house.

86

Wood Green

Elisabeth never broke down, just spoke slowly, mechanically, for the first ever time, of the events on the last day of her honeymoon, and as she spoke she felt like it had happened to a different girl, in a parallel life. She never faltered, even as she described to her daughter how she didn't scream, because of the knife, how much it had hurt, how she had run back to the cottage and locked herself in the bathroom, shouting through the door that she'd just fallen over, that she was fine; how she had scrubbed at herself, had screwed her torn costume into a ball and disposed of it later in the dustbin; how she'd finally come out, smiled, dressed, gone for dinner, but said sorry, she was too tired for anything else tonight, after all. She'd been too tired for anything for weeks, apparently. Elisabeth told her daughter how much she desperately hadn't wanted to be pregnant, had wanted to be sure she wasn't, before she resumed anything like that with her poor bewildered husband. But then when her period had never come she'd been terrified, and she'd told Alan she didn't want to have a baby, and she'd even tried to abort it (abort *me*, Juliette thought), but it hadn't worked, and so she'd suggested they have it adopted, and her husband had gone mad and said no. But he gave in, in the end, Elisabeth had been so insistent, and even though they arranged the adoption she thought secretly she still might keep it, what were the chances of it being the rapist's rather than her husband's after the honeymoon they'd had – but when the baby had been born and she'd seen that unmistakeable curly red hair, even at birth, that had been it. It had destroyed her marriage, she told Juliette.

Juliette tried to process what Elisabeth had told her. She and Camilla had been right, her father was a rapist. She, Juliette, was a *product of rape,* a mistake, the end result of a vile act, an unnatural aberration. As Elisabeth looked desolately, helplessly at her daughter, Juliette felt like she was brittle, might even break.

Juliette thought of her own husband then, with whom she had shared a bed for so many years, raping her best friend long ago in America. She'd known for two months now, since the night of the picnic, when JoAnne had screamed it out through the trees and across the water, that it was *Stephen* who was her rapist, not the stranger she'd always claimed, before collapsing in hysteria. Juliette had been trying to deal with the fact that her husband was a rapist, and now it turned out her father was one too.

Juliette sat for long empty minutes in the kitchen of her mother's grim little council flat. To her astonishment she found that, in a place beyond the horror, she started to feel oddly exhilarated, free even – of guilt that she hadn't ever really loved Stephen, at least not how you should love your husband; of rampant hatred for her mother, whose actions she could finally understand – and although she knew it was the shock (the pain of who her father was, what he had done, the way she'd come into the world not yet able to sink in), she felt in this moment a connectedness at last, an understanding. She felt desperately sorry for Elisabeth then, and for JoAnne too. She spoke gently.

"So that's why you were so against poor Mum having me."

Elisabeth flinched at the word *Mum*, and it surprised Juliette. Usually she didn't react to things.

"Maybe it sounds selfish," said Elisabeth. "But I didn't want any reminders in my life. How could I look at you, and not think of how you were conceived? I tried to get Cynthia to understand, but I couldn't bring myself to tell even her the truth – I felt so ashamed, and besides I couldn't bear poor Alan to know – and when she wouldn't listen, insisted on carrying on with the adoption, I just cut myself off from her and the rest of the family. I'm not proud of it, but it's all I could think to do."

"But why did you have another child so soon afterwards?"

Elisabeth hesitated.

"I don't know, that's what people did I suppose. And it must have been to do with my body as well. It had carried you and then it had nothing. My milk drying up was excruciating."

Elisabeth looked far away, as if deciding what to say next, if anything – and then she continued, but almost like she was talking to a ghost, a phantom daughter, a gorgeous girl from another life, not the one sat opposite her now in her miserable kitchen in North London. She had never said the words out loud before, it was as if they bewitched her.

"Once you were gone I found that I craved you Mandy,

327

and I so wanted to believe you were Alan's, but when I saw you I knew you weren't, I just knew it. So I had another child, another daughter, to... to take your place I suppose."

Juliette said nothing, just stared at her mother. *Amanda Lily.*

"You just called me Mandy," she said.

Elisabeth seemed young again, girlish for an instant, and then it was gone. She looked straight at her daughter.

"You'll always be Mandy to me, Juliette."

And that's when Juliette cried, and instead of scolding her for a change, so did Elisabeth.

87

Cleveland

Late on a putridly hot night in a furniture-less house in mid-west America JoAnne found herself back in the grimy shower, barely ten minutes since she'd last been there. Her party mood had vanished, to be replaced by feelings of helplessness and revulsion. She sobbed drunkenly as she scrubbed and scrubbed at herself, as if willing the fluid out of her, repulsed yet again at what had happened, trying to work out just what it was that had happened, *why* it had happened. As the water grew half-heartedly tepid and then fully cold she was finally able to put a label to it. Rape. That was it! That was the word. *She had been raped*.

JoAnne was shaking as she turned off the shower, unable to stand the onslaught, and she leaned her back against the cold cracked tiles and slumped down to a squat, head between her legs, long hair sodden and straggling in the tainted water that hadn't yet gone down the plughole. She cried and cried and she couldn't seem to stop, the snivels coming in strangled little pants, her heart beating frantically like it was about to stop. It was only when she heard the front door go and

329

realised the others were home, and in drunken high spirits at that, that she pulled herself together. She ran naked from the bathroom up to the room she shared with Sissy, and hauled herself into her sleeping bag although she was still soaking wet. She lay quietly shivering on the horrid green carpet, there was no mattress to comfort her, and although her bones stuck into her at funny angles she didn't mind the pain, she knew she deserved it. She rolled over in the now-sopping bag, onto her side, away from the door, trying to pretend she was asleep in case Sissy came in, although if anyone were to look closely they would see that her body was trembling through the nylon, like a giant brown caterpillar shaking on a leaf in the breeze.

Stephen awoke suddenly and there was a body snoring next to him, and he couldn't work out whose it was. He lay there, uneasy, feeling like he'd been run over, his head especially, but yes, his body too. His knees were sore, the flesh tender, and as he sent his hands down to check on them he could feel the still sticky wounds, on his right knee more than the left. What were they? How had he got them?

And then he realised – *carpet burns*. He didn't need to wonder at where they'd come from. As soon as he worked out what they were his memory of the evening flicked back in, like a channel in his brain had been switched on by remote control. He felt sick, aware of exactly what had happened now, although he refused to put a name to it. *What the fuck had he done?* What would Juliette say? What would JoAnne say? What would the *police* say?

Stephen's body spasmed and his eyes started to prick,

threatening tears of self-interest, so he knew it must be serious. He tried not to think them but the thoughts came anyway. *Why hadn't he stopped, when it was clear that she wanted him to, when he'd heard her screaming the house down for him to get off her?*

Stephen had always been aware of how much he liked to get his own way, right from when he'd been a little boy, but what had happened last night had perhaps taken his inherent sense of entitlement a step too far. She'd seemed so keen though, and then had changed her mind at the very last minute, the fucking prick tease. What did she think men were like? Didn't she know that beyond a certain point there was no turning back? Stephen felt a little better when he took this line of thought – phew, it was her fault, not his – but deep somewhere inside himself, where his heart still resided in those days, he knew it wasn't true.

Stephen lay sprawled on the floor trying to think straight, trying to work out what to do, make sure Juliette never found out – and through the thickness of his headache he realised his first task was to stop JoAnne telling anyone. Who would she tell though? After all it didn't look good on her either – out of her mind on cheap booze, barely dressed, one provocatively short towel loosely fastened. Maybe she wouldn't say anything, it was too damaging for her as well, on so many counts.

He wondered whether he should acknowledge to JoAnne what he'd done, admit it was rape – and before he had time to even get to the end of that thought the voice in his head swooped in and said, "No...," and so he never admitted it again, which was a shame; as a genuine apology then, a confession, even if only to himself, *might* have saved him from his ultimate path of never feeling obliged to tell the truth, of going for what he wanted at any expense, of no moral code being too sacred.

Maybe *this* was the moment that made him.

Stephen knew on that stifling morning in Ohio that there was only one option open to him to save the situation, in the short-term at least: he had to grovel, cry, beg JoAnne to forgive him, explain how he'd completely misread the situation, thought she wanted it too, tell her the last thing he'd wanted to do was hurt her, take advantage of her etcetera etcetera – and he needed to do it fast. It might just work, if he played it right – and after all it was *true*, he did feel terrible about what had happened. He lay next to James, who was snoring and farting in gaping boxers on top of his grubby-looking sleeping bag. He couldn't possibly do it here. Sissy would be in JoAnne's room, he couldn't risk a confrontation in front of her either, she was such a goody-two-shoes, and far too close to Juliette to risk knowing anything. He would just have to camp out outside their bedroom door, wait for one or other of them to come out, so he could get JoAnne alone. Yes, that's what he'd do – the girls' room was at the top of the house so no one else would see him, and Sissy would just think he was being love sick if she came out first. As he lumbered to his feet a crack went through his skull. He bunched his sleeping bag in front of him so the nylon stuck to his weeping knees, and staggered towards the stairs.

After Sissy had got up, assuming her friend was still asleep, JoAnne continued to lie on the thinly carpeted floor of their bedroom, contemplating exactly how she felt, having been raped last night. She found that her feelings kept evolving as the morning sunshine invaded. At first they'd been pretty clear-cut, unequivocal, but it all seemed more complicated now. She kept trying to label her feelings, choose words to explain them, as though that might make it better somehow. She chose carefully: *helplessness, disbelief*, as Stephen pushed her to the floor; *fear, revulsion,* as he forced himself into her; *anger, fury*, as she beat her fists into his chest when he refused to stop; *repugnance, disgust*, as his face contorted and he ejaculated inside her; *shame, revulsion,* as she staggered away from him and into the shower; *guilt, shame*, but not at him, at herself this time, that maybe she'd encouraged him, had even been asking for it; *shame, responsibility*, as she realised it must be her fault, she must give off some kind of signal. It was all she deserved. She was a slag.

JoAnne knew emphatically that if she couldn't respect herself, how could she expect men to respect her – no wonder her father never had, no wonder men came onto her like they did. She hunched into her sleeping bag although the room was too hot for it, ignoring the knocking at the door, as she tried to decide what the overriding emotion was, the single word, above all the others, that she could use to explain her feelings, and she lay there and lay there until in the end – that was it – she decided unequivocally what it was, and the word was *shame*.

Part Three

88

Speke, Liverpool

In a smart end of terrace house not far from the Hale Road – the only one of the row with tidily-blooming petunias in plastic hanging baskets – a small neat woman was preparing to cut up newspapers. Her husband was at the horses and she was taking advantage of some time to herself, about to make a scrapbook about her youngest son.

Irene Forsyth liked making scrapbooks. She had a cupboard-full of them, stuffed with Stephen's achievements. She'd always been so proud of him: of how well he'd done at school, how he'd made it to university, moved to London, got a job at a local newspaper, over time risen through the ranks to become one of the heavyweights of the media world, and even sometimes *on telly* no less. It had been his destiny, she'd felt, she'd always known he was special. She'd spoiled Stephen rotten of course, and she thought that must have helped, turned him into the man he was. And although she never acknowledged it, inside she knew that this deluge of love for him was because she'd left her other, somewhat less appealing son with his father, like a consolation prize, while she buggered off to start a new family. Showering Stephen with enough love for two had seemed the obvious thing to do in the circumstances. It had helped her cope with the guilt.

Today though Irene found herself uncharacteristically hesitant in her crafty pursuits. She'd been armed and ready, scissors poised, glue stick unsheathed, surveying the headlines of the papers spread out in front of her, deciding which one to attack first. But despite it being an incredible story it seemed no-one was coming out in a very good light. Of course Irene had been shocked when it turned out the body in the lake story had involved not one but both her sons. She'd been appalled when the early headlines surfaced: that Terry was under suspicion for murdering the poor woman, that he'd been trailing Juliette, like some kind of pervert, and she'd been glad then that she'd washed her hands of him – she'd been right all along, he was obviously a loser. But as she sat alone at her glass-topped dining table with the lace tablecloth underneath, dressed in smart polyester trousers and a matching cream blouse, a new picture of the saga started to emerge. It opened her eyes to her sons, made her see each of them in different lights, and she hesitated. It was when she saw the story on page five of the Mail, about her abandonment of Terry, that she decided a scrapbook on the body in the lake story most definitely wasn't a good idea after all.

Irene sat quietly pondering the two men, as dispassionately now as if they were fictional. Stephen was ruthless, she'd always known that – even as a small boy he would go to abnormal lengths to get what he wanted (*like her*, came the

338

thought, and she buried it). She didn't know Terry any more, of course, not even what he looked like until she'd seen the pictures in the papers (and she'd recognised him like a shot, he looked so much like Stephen), but from the little she'd heard over the years he hadn't made much of a success of himself – it seemed his most notable achievement was having moved from the lea of one Ford factory to another.

But it was when Irene realised it was *Terry* who had tried to save the drowning woman, the only person who had from what she could tell, that she felt proud of her eldest son somehow. In fact she was perversely more proud of that than anything Stephen had ever done, it being a selfless act rather than a selfish one, and she'd begrudgingly admired it, known that neither she nor Stephen had that kind of thing in them. She'd even thought for a moment of ringing Terry – but she hadn't spoken to him in nearly 40 years, what in heavens would she say?

So after long minutes of vacillation practical-minded Mrs Forsyth (formerly Kingston) finally did the only thing she could think of under the circumstances. She did use her scissors and glue stick to make a scrapbook that day – not one about Stephen after all, but about Terry this time. She kept it, the only evidence of love for her eldest son, hidden away in a cupboard, for it one day to be found by house clearers, and thrown away.

89

Surrey

Gusty rain was hammering at the windows, water streaming downwards as if in a race to the bottom, the sky still black even though it was morning. It was a lousy day for building work, and Darren O'Connell was pissed off that his current job would be delayed even further. He was standing in only a towel in his blandly neutral bedroom (save for the one gaudily-papered wall behind the bed that Katie had insisted on – she wouldn't bloody take no for an answer these days), his muscly body still damp from the shower, wet hair slicked back like a gangster's. He growled as he opened his underwear drawer, rummaged around crossly, found an old pair of underpants that were too small but would have to do, and no clean socks, yet again. Lazy bitch does nothing round here these days, he thought. He yelled down the stairs of the small semi-detached house that had been built for London commuters in the seventies.

"Katie. KATIE. Where are some sodding socks?"

"Mummy can't hear you," said Molly, on her way up, her blonde hair bobbed neatly, just like her mother's. "She's got the kitchen door shut. She's Studying."

"She's always bloody studying," said Darren – but at least she'd admitted it now. He'd never understood why she'd lied about her course, he wasn't that much of a dictator, surely – no wonder he'd become so paranoid when she'd made excuse after excuse to go out every Wednesday.

"Little ears, Daddy," said Molly, riskily, and he hesitated, and then he told her not to be so flippin' cheeky, but not as scarily as he might once have done, and then resignedly he opened the linen basket, which was overflowing as usual, in a bid to find some dirty ones.

90

Charing Cross Road, Central London

Lucinda Horne couldn't believe how many people had turned up to her latest book launch, the third in the Bottersley Dog School series. It seemed extraordinary that everyone had come to see *her*, not Alistair Smart, that they didn't totally hate her after all. It had been excruciating when Alistair's wife had gone to the police about hers and Alistair's "little arrangement," as he'd liked to call it, and it had all come out in the press – yet another weird off-shoot to the long-running story about the woman who drowned in The Serpentine.

The bizarre thing about it all was that Lucinda had felt most betrayed when it turned out that Alistair had been sleeping with Stephen Forsyth's wife at the same time as he'd been seeing her. That's when she'd realised how naive she'd been about it all, but when you're a writer getting nowhere in your bid to be published, who knows what lengths you'd go to – and besides Alistair Smart had been such a hero to her for more than half her life she probably would have done *anything* for him. Maybe she should have taken her parents' advice and got her head out of her books, out of either reading them or writing them, every now and again to see what real life was like. She damned well knew now though, and so far, after a somewhat bumpy start, she found she rather enjoyed it.

Looking back, Lucinda liked to think she'd slept with Alistair for love – he was definitely handsome, if a bit old perhaps – and just so talented of course, and that had been what swayed it for her. What an idiot she'd been! She was so lucky the public had forgiven her, seen *her* as the victim in the scandal, and she'd taken her publicist's advice to tone down her appearance and now firmly kept her wondrous breasts under wraps. ("You don't want the children's fathers lusting after you, dear," her publicist had said. "Not after that Alistair Smart business.") Poor Alistair though, she felt so sorry for him – career washed up, thrown out of the family home, his own children embarrassed of him at school, having to endure the other kids constantly woofing at them. His wife had been an utter bitch from what Lucinda had gathered, the last time she'd rung him, and he'd sounded desolate, even though the fraud charges against them both had been dropped. And when she'd read last week on the internet that he'd checked into The Priory for sex addiction she'd felt awful. She could understand now that he might be an addict – he really had been quite obsessed with sex, rather glassy-eyed about it all in fact – but she'd thought that was quite normal behaviour at the time; after all she'd had nothing much to compare it to.

Lucinda sighed. She did hope he'd get better. Despite his failings he was still Alistair Smart to her, her inspiration. She'd be nothing without him.

The mother of the little girl in front of her coughed self-consciously.

"Oh, sorry, it was Amelia, wasn't it?" The woman and her daughter nodded, matching excited smiles fixed on their faces.

"To dear Amelia," she wrote, "Enjoy Wowser and the gang's latest adventure, love Lucinda."

Her publicist scowled. "You'll have to go faster than that," she whispered. "Look at the queue."

"Oh, sorry," said Lucinda. She sat back, shook her silky blonde hair out of her face, and turned to the little boy waiting expectantly in front of her.

"Hello!" she said, smiling guilelessly. "And what's your name, young man?"

91

Oxfordshire

Samantha Jones lay drowsily in the velvet-swagged four-poster bed, mulling over what an unbelievably fantastic day she'd just had. The grounds of the old abbey sloped down to the Thames, and they'd had the service right there on the grass in the autumn sunshine, a last minute weather-related change of heart. The venue had been super, devoid of that conference feel so many of those places had, completely different to the myriad manor houses and stately homes where she'd sat through countless boring team-building events, drinking gallons of bottled water and sucking Fox's mints all day. She'd loved her dress, it was so flouncy and feminine, just how she'd imagined it as a little girl, and even though she was way too old for it, she'd thought what the hell, we can get married at last, why not. Linda had looked fantastic too, in a white tuxedo, and she knew the pictures would be stunning, with the water glinting behind them, the swans wafting along, the newly-wed (OK, newly civil-partnershipped, but it was close enough) smiles ones of jubilation, of their moment having arrived at last.

The day had been just about as perfect as could be, Sam thought, apart from one hiccup, and really it didn't matter, not in the grand scheme of things. It was just a shame that Linda's niece JoAnne had got so incredibly pissed at the reception, and had had such a horrific go at her mother, that pretty much everyone had heard. Linda's elder sister Simone had come all the way from Paris, she didn't deserve that kind of treatment – they should sort it out in private instead of ruining our day, Sam had fumed at the time, but she hadn't liked to interfere. Linda had smoothed everything over in her usual implacable way, and JoAnne had calmed down eventually, thank God.

Poor JoAnne, thought Sam, she'd never been quite the same since her friend had drowned last summer, although Linda had always said it went way further back than that – certainly to her mother, maybe to her father, definitely to when she'd come back from America all those years ago. She'd just drifted in and out of jobs and relationships, never properly settling down to anything after university. She seemed to have so little self-respect according to Linda, but whatever it was that had fucked her up, she was beginning to show it on her face these days, her looks were becoming quite ravaged. Sam wondered briefly what would become of JoAnne, maybe she should go for counselling or to AA or something – but then she heard Linda give a little snore, and as she turned onto her side to put her arms around her new wife Sam shivered inside with happiness, and then she drifted off to sleep.

92

The sun was weak and wintry as Stephen stood on the ledge of his tiny apartment overlooking the river. It wasn't a balcony as such, but it was just big enough to stand on, get some fresh air. He quite liked living here, the view was amazing and his cleaner kept the apartment spotless, which was a relief after the sluttishness of Fulham.

Stephen was feeling peculiarly optimistic this morning. It had been nearly five months since Siobhan had died, three since Juliette had finally thrown him out (he still found he missed her sometimes, and it annoyed him, that she got to him still), and although he'd lost his job at least he'd had a whacking big pay off. Things had finally calmed down on the PR front too now, thank fuck. Once the media had latched onto the story of how the women had *abandoned* their friend, left her for dead (a prime example of the amorality of our times, according to the Daily Mail) the focus had shifted to them. So although his wife's antics had ultimately got him the sack they'd perversely also let him off the hook in the end. The interest in his own deadbeat secret brother and

347

dysfunctional family, in his penchant for spying on his wife, had disappeared after a while. Chip paper, he thought with a sly smile. And almost unbelievably the rape story had never surfaced, even though there were at least six people who knew now – apart from him – from what he could tell. Juliette had confronted him, the night he'd hit her, and although he'd denied it she'd seen it in his eyes, and anyway she'd said that JoAnne had confessed at last, at the picnic, admitted she'd lied about the other man in Cleveland raping her, although he'd tried to as well, apparently. JoAnne had probably made that whole episode up, he thought, the fucking drama queen. According to Juliette, the only other person JoAnne had ever told before the night of the picnic was Siobhan, years ago, and she was dead and buried, which was probably just as well. So he was almost certainly safe now: JoAnne wouldn't want to go through the ordeal of a trial, especially not with her sexual history, no-one would believe her; and even Juliette wouldn't do that to the father of her own kids, no matter how much she might hate him herself. The others wouldn't do anything either, they'd follow JoAnne or Juliette's lead. Yes, he was off the hook, he was sure of it – and, he reminded himself for the millionth time, it hadn't been *actual* rape, not really, more of a drunken misunderstanding. He'd honestly thought she wanted it too, it wasn't his fault she'd changed her mind too late.

Nothing more had come out about Nigel's death in Sardinia either, although he was much more nervous about that story leaking. He'd been shocked when Juliette had told him how Sissy had known what he'd done all along, how it came out at the picnic that she'd heard through her delirium

Nigel cursing the socket, saying there was something wrong with it, how she'd not trusted using it herself to plug in her hairdryer. But she'd been carted off to hospital and put on a drip while another ambulance had taken Nigel's body away, and the police hadn't even been called. So when the report into Nigel's death had said nothing about the socket being faulty, Sissy must have known then there'd been a cover-up, but had been too scared or distraught to do anything.

Stephen still felt terrible about Nigel dying like that, he hadn't intended it to happen, no way. It had just been an unfortunate accident – he'd been trying to do the guy a favour, for fuck's sake – but he'd panicked, hadn't known what else to do apart from hush it up. Nigel was dead anyway, no investigation would have changed the outcome. It would have wrecked his, Stephen's, life too – and what was the point of that?

Stephen looked down absently at a police boat on the river, cute as a bath toy, cutting through the water. So that's why Sissy had hated him over these past years, they'd always got on all right before that, especially since they'd gone to America together – in fact he'd thought she'd liked him, before.

What got to Stephen the most though, he realised in this rare moment of reflection, was not what Sissy or JoAnne thought of him these days (he didn't give a toss about that), but the fact that Juliette despised him now, after what had been said at that fucking picnic. There'd been no going back after that. They were finished.

Stephen sighed and his eyes glistened in the early sunlight, it was too bright out here. He dabbed at his eyes. Life goes on, he thought, there was no use moping, and besides he was better off without her – she was a lousy housewife, useless mother, unfaithful bitch. He looked at his watch. He'd better think about getting ready in a minute – his meeting to discuss a possible new tabloid launch was at eleven. The hacking scandal had done him a favour in the end – he'd managed somehow to avoid being implicated, and people were dropping like flies these days, which meant there were a couple of very juicy openings in the offing.

Stephen cheered up at this thought. It was a beautiful December day, he might even walk to Soho House, it was an interesting route and the exercise would do him good, make him nice and hungry for his lunch with Maddie later.

93

Lambeth, South London

Terry came out of Elephant and Castle tube station and glanced bewilderedly around – at the semi-subway he found himself in, at the despondent-looking stallholders displaying handbags and scarves and sunglasses that all looked the same, at the seemingly identical roads as he emerged onto the round-about. He'd only ever come out at Lambeth North before and he was disorientated, but he definitely didn't want to be late. He knew he shouldn't stress, it wasn't as though he was on a date or anything, it was just a casual visit to a museum, to indulge a shared interest in military history, that was all. He was pleased though that he'd had his hair cut, he didn't look so insipid with it shorter, and he liked his new Levis and casual jacket, they almost made him look trendy.

It was strange, he'd always found women so hard to talk to before. Maybe that's why he'd married Maria all those years ago, she'd been quiet and sweet and barely spoke English – plus she'd mothered him at first, before she'd got fed up with him. But with this woman it was different. They'd got chatting after the inquest had been adjourned when poor Margaret

Benson passed out – he'd found her distraught outside when he'd popped out to call the vet to check on Hugo, who'd had gastroenteritis and was on a drip. He'd asked her why she was crying – and because she was so overwrought and he seemed kind she'd told him in a timid little voice that she couldn't believe what she'd done, leaving Siobhan to die like that.

"No, I heard you," he'd said. "You wanted to go back to check on her, it was the others who persuaded you it was nothing. You cared, I could tell you did. You have nothing to feel guilty about."

And then he'd taken her back inside and they'd sat together amidst the panic, and somehow or other he'd made her feel better. They'd ended up discussing the Franco Prussian War, she'd done history at Bristol, was passionate about it, especially military history, which was odd for a woman he thought. And then they'd discussed his poor sick spaniel, and she had seemed so concerned about Hugo it was endearing, really it was, not like Maria who'd seemed to almost hope he'd die – although she probably didn't care either way now she'd buggered off with one of the tenors from the Barking and Dagenham Choir. Being splashed across the papers putting out the rubbish in her dressing gown, after her husband had been implicated in *murder*, had given her the perfect excuse.

As Terry walked towards the museum he saw the familiar green dome and the white columns and the two huge guns, and there she was, already there, although he was five minutes early himself, standing between the cannons, in jeans and a puffa jacket and Converse trainers, her hair messily longish, like a teenage boy's: his first ever female friend.

"Hello," he said, and hesitated, unsure how to greet her. He held out his hand, his heart suddenly hammering.

"Hi, Terry," said Sissy, and she shook it, politely.

"Shall we go in? It's freezing out here." She nodded shyly, and they walked together, side by side, towards the entrance.

94

Fulham

The Roman soldiers were lined up smartly, twirling prettily in the faint breeze, the ghost-breath. Light rain was falling half-heartedly past the windows, almost as if it couldn't be bothered. It was quarter past four.

Fiona Pridmore sat back in her chair, relieved, as Noah's parents left the room. That hadn't gone as badly as it could have done, and it was good that they'd discussed it. It was hard being a teacher sometimes – you ended up being responsible for far more than a child's education, you had to be careful not to overstep the line to wanting to become their mother too. But she'd thought about it carefully, discussed with the head beforehand what she was going to say – and anyway she owed it to Noah, he was such a sweet little boy, underneath.

It was odd how Mrs Forsyth seemed to have softened these days, Miss Pridmore thought. She knew it had been hard for her to come into school when she and her husband were still being splashed all over the news all the time, and it must have been particularly awful for her to have been virtually accused of being a murderer like that. Still, Miss Pridmore thought, there was no way *she* would have left a friend in that situation, no matter how drunk she was – sometimes it seemed the more money people had, the less morals they possessed, even if they did just about manage to operate within the confines of the law.

But somehow today Mrs Forsyth had seemed less uptight, less angry than normal, and Noah certainly seemed happier of late too. It was funny sometimes how kids seemed to fare better after the parents had actually split up – Miss Pridmore had seen enough children throughout her career to know that staying together wasn't always the answer. Mrs Forsyth had seemed genuinely interested in what she'd had to say too, as though she was trying desperately hard to support her son. Even the husband had turned up for a change, and although the atmosphere between Mr and Mrs Forsyth had been terribly strained, it was a step forward – he'd never used to come when they were still together.

Miss Pridmore made a note in her diary to book the session for Noah with the school counsellor, and then she shuffled her papers, smoothed back her hair, took a deep breath, and went over to the classroom door where she welcomed in the parents of Rupert Rees-Smith, who, she would be obliged to inform them, was having trouble with his maths.

Part Four

95

Hyde Park

The park was still and moonlit. Clouds seemed to be gathering, as if sensing the danger. A bat flew over silently, but she didn't see it, not even in the reflection on the water. The women's voices were far enough away to be nothing more than low-level bitching now, not in-her-face vitriol, and it was a relief to her.

She knelt at the lake's edge with her head between her knees, oblivious to her surroundings, to the blackness of the water. She was breathing hard, panting almost, trying not to sob. She just couldn't take any more of those women tonight, their feuds, their hatred – Natasha screaming at Juliette that she was shagging her husband, and Juliette not even denying it, and Natasha trying to go for her, pull her hair like they were five year olds; JoAnne sitting there sobbing about being raped, and although she felt desperately sad for her friend, *really*, just blurting out 25 years too late that it was Stephen who'd done it, not the stranger in Cleveland after all, while they were all totally pissed, was not the way to go about it. Siobhan had told JoAnne so many times to go to the police, go to counselling, get help, get closure, but JoAnne wouldn't. She preferred to drink herself senseless and shag other people's husbands, as though she didn't deserve any better.

As Siobhan slumped at the lakeside she knew her behaviour had been far from perfect too tonight. She'd been in a terrible mood by the time she'd got there, she'd had such a lousy day, and they'd all been mean to her, as usual – and then she hadn't helped matters by inflaming everyone over Stephen. She must have been mad to insinuate that Stephen had had something to do with Nigel's death, she'd kept it secret for so long – and although she'd tried to cover it up, pretend she hadn't said anything, she knew it had been her words that had kicked everything else off. Running off screaming had been ridiculously melodramatic too, but she couldn't bear to hear anymore, it was as if her ears had had enough – she'd just had to get away once they'd all got going, screaming at each other like they were in some dreadful soap opera.

Was it really all her fault? It had been years coming, Siobhan realised, and they'd all drunk far too much, even Sissy; and JoAnne had just gone straight in there, given the sniff of an opportunity. She obviously hated Stephen, *despised* him, and Siobhan couldn't blame her, not at all. Even Siobhan had to admit Stephen seemed despicable these days, a serpentine man, but really, JoAnne calling him a murderer, a rapist, in front of everyone, spitting out the words like they were poisoned meat, was too awful. Siobhan actually felt a teeny bit sorry for Stephen, although she knew that she shouldn't. He was the one who had to live with Nigel's death, with what he'd done to JoAnne, even if he hadn't planned either from what she could gather, even if they'd both been accidents in a way.

What was odd though, Siobhan had always thought, was how JoAnne had seemed all right with Stephen when she'd first got back from America, acted almost normal with him still, although it was clear their affair had been very short-lived for some reason, pretty much a one-night stand. At the time Siobhan had just assumed that JoAnne had cooled it with Stephen because she hadn't wanted to upset Juliette, they'd been best friends after all.

When JoAnne had eventually confessed to Siobhan, months later, that it was *Stephen* who'd raped her, she'd broken down as she described how much he'd grovelled to her afterwards, told her he'd thought she wanted it too, and JoAnne had fallen for it, accepted it – at first. She hadn't spoken of it again for years, and now it seemed the impact must have built over time; as if the further away JoAnne had moved from the rape, the more it had affected her – and the more intense her hatred for Stephen had become.

Siobhan gave a great heaving sigh. JoAnne's outburst had been bad enough, but then on top of all the drama little Katie had got stuck in too, she'd obviously been smashed like everyone else – having a go at her, Siobhan, almost seeming to enjoy ganging up on her, like a playground bully, when what she should have been doing was putting her foot down with her pig of a husband. Only Camilla had risen above it all, nothing seemed to enrage her, apart from inappropriate picnic contributions perhaps. No, Camilla and Sissy were the only two Siobhan was going to see from now on – she'd steer clear of the others, even poor Juliette Forsyth, who would never be happy while she stayed with Stephen, especially not now. Imagine finding out, and in such a dreadful way, that your husband is a *rapist*, that people think he's little better than a *murderer!* She never should have gone out with him in the first place, Siobhan thought, through the Prosecco, she was always too good for him. She'd tried to tell her but what can you do, people never listen to the truths that don't suit them – and Juliette had always seemed too vulnerable to be on her own for long.

The clouds moved silently across the moon, and the night became velvety dark. As Siobhan knelt quietly, trying to breathe slowly, ignore the still irate voices from beyond the bushes, she calmed down a little, began to regain some control. And then she thought she heard something near her, and she raised her head and looked up. She felt nervous suddenly, and a feeling of doom drenched through her, as though she were drowning in fear. Words and images tumbled through her head in the darkness, and they were scarier than any movie she'd ever seen. Her heart thudded and seemed to stop. Someone was there, she was sure of it, someone in the bushes. It wasn't one of her friends, definitely not, she could tell it was a man. *Who was it?* As her brain flipped in on itself in panic the clouds passed by and the moon reappeared, as if on cue, to light up her nightmare.

Stephen!

What was he doing here? She was consumed with terror, with what she'd said about him, the secrets she'd unleashed. She knew he was ruthless. Maybe he wanted to silence her. Perhaps he was a murderer after all. Perhaps he was going to murder *her*.

As their eyes made contact she thought she'd pass out with dread and horror and drunkenness. She opened her mouth to scream, but before she had time to, her would-be murderer looked more shocked than her suddenly, and instead of running over and stabbing or strangling her, he turned on his heel and legged it, stifling a sneeze as he went – and as he disappeared along the path she realised it wasn't Stephen at all, he was too slight for a start, her nerves had obviously got the better of her. But then who was he? Why had he been spying on her? Siobhan's head restarted its spinning, sending her thoughts haywire, and she dropped back down onto the hardness of the concrete, trying to quell the nausea.

Her phone rang. She sat up and grappled in her bag, and got to it just before it went to voicemail. Her fears vanished when she saw who it was. She felt giddily drunk, euphoric, relief flooding through her.

"Hello," she said, but even through her joy her voice was slurred and faintly hostile, she couldn't help herself.

"Hi, Shiv," said Matt. He paused. "Are you all right? Are you at your picnic? How's it going?"

"Terrible," said Siobhan, and she started to cry, despite feeling better, or maybe because of it. The man in the bushes seemed to have definitely gone, thank God, she must have imagined he was after her. Maybe she'd even imagined *him,* she was paralytic after all.

"Listen, I'm sorry I haven't called before. It's just that the reception here's rubbish, and I've been a bit distracted lately, you'll understand why soon."

She panicked again, convinced suddenly that he was about

to dump her. "Matt, I'm sorry," she said. "I've had an awful evening. Is it OK if we talk about this another time?"

"Of course, it's just that, well... look, where are you?"

"By the side of The bloody Serpentine," she said. "We all had a row and I ran off like a total drama queen, but you should have heard it, the things that were said, it was poisonous. Then I thought there was someone in the bushes but maybe I was wrong, I don't know, and I'm covered in wine and chocolate and I look like a tramp, a pissed daft tramp." She began to cry harder.

"Someone there? What d'you mean? Are you OK?"

Siobhan listened. Everywhere there was stillness; even the women were quiet now. She tried not to alarm him.

"Oh, I must have imagined it, I'm fine."

"Are you sure, Siobhan? I don't like the sound of it. How are you getting home?"

"I don't know, try to flag down a taxi I guess."

"I wish I could come and get you, make sure you're OK, I wish I wasn't in the bloody Kimberleys."

"It doesn't matter, there's no-one here now, I'm sure of it. I'll be fine. I'll see you after the weekend."

"Come round on Sunday, my flight gets in Sunday morning. Come round then."

"You'll be knackered."

"I'll be OK. I can't wait to see you. Oh, *please* don't cry again. I... look, this isn't quite how I envisioned it, but I hate to hear you so upset... so when I get back... I... Oh, fuck it... (*Deep breath*.) Siobhan, when I get back I've got something to ask you."

Siobhan felt a hot sweet feeling course down her neck,

through her back, like you get when you say hello to a stranger and they respond to you, smile at you unexpectedly. She stopped crying, stopped breathing.

"I've already spoken to your father, don't worry, I've done it all properly. Listen, I've got to go in a minute, the truck's waiting for me."

"OK," she said. "...Matt?"

"Yes?"

"I'm a nutter."

"That's OK, I like it."

"Ma – att?"

"Ye – es?"

"I really really love you."

"I really really love you too Siobhan, I really really love you, always have. See you soon. Look after yourself, OK?"

"I will, don't worry, I'll be fine," she said. "The others are still here, they'd hear me if anything happened. I love you. Bye."

Siobhan shoved her phone into her bag and sat there for a while, stunned, savouring Matt's words, delighted chills still coursing through her spine. Finally she pushed up on her hands and hauled her legs around, resting drunkenly for a moment on her left arm and left thigh, as if she were posing for an old-fashioned swimwear shot. She smiled, hugged the knowledge to herself like a newborn baby. She felt fine about getting home now – the park felt brighter, safer, in fact the whole world felt lovelier, she loved everything about it. There were definitely no more strange men lurking in the bushes, and there was bound to be a cab up on the bridge, she'd be home in no time. She even felt more optimistic about her

365

friends now – she'd be sure to ring everyone in the morning to make up, even Natasha. After all it was her, Siobhan's, lapse in discretion that had kicked everything off – thinking about it maybe it was all her fault really, the least she could do was apologise to everyone. And they *were* all friends still, always had been, always will be, they'd been through so much together. Her mind waltzed a little, full of love and Prosecco. She'd invite them to the wedding of course – in fact maybe they could even be bridesmaids! Yes, she'd sort everything out tomorrow. It would all be all right tomorrow.

Siobhan's head spun as she finally stood up, and she tottered on her ridiculous heels, and she tripped clumsily on the trailing strap of her handbag, and as she fell she gashed her head on the rowlock of the little boat, the one that they'd left there with a hole in it, and as everything went black a splash – was it a bird or a woman – sounded into the night.

Acknowledgements

Again enormous thanks go to my very earliest readers: Val Young, Donna Malone, Claire Smith, Garry Boorman, Gail Walker, Nicole Johnschwager, and especially to my husband and my friends Claire Lusher and Tracy Morrell, who all hated different parts of *A Serpentine Affair* so vehemently I felt compelled to change them – for the better definitely. Continued thanks to Kavita Bhanot and Becky Swift at The Literary Consultancy, who gave the thumbs up on this book as well as on my first novel, along with some vital structural advice. A special mention to my new group of test readers and bloggers that I met through *One Step Too Far* and who have done so much to help me, including but not exclusively: Marion Archer, Christian Anderson, Christine Miller, Betty McBroom, Janet Lambert, Karen Brissette, Cathie Armstrong, Suzanne Rogers, Dianne Bylo, Allison Renner, Teresa Turner, Anne Cater, Sheli Russ, Linda Broderick, Cherra Wammock, Jo Barton, Sue Cowling, Gillian Westall, Karen Rush, Heidi Permann, Helen Painter, Carolina Sanchez, Angela Echanova, Patricia Melo and Liz Wilkins – plus of course those who also read *A Serpentine Affair*, many of whom are quoted at the front of this book. To Paul

Johnson for a fabulous cover and Lyndsey Kilifin for help with the Reading Group notes. To the other professionals who have helped me get to the next stage of my writing journey: Heather O'Connell, Ian Binnie, Debi Letham, Myles Clarke, Penny Faith, Helen Castor, Daniel Cooper, Mel Etches, Rachel Jones, Matt Bates, Sharon Hughes, Emily Cater, Chris Housden, Jo McCrum, Mark McCrum, Becky Beach, Franca Reynolds, Laurel Chilcot Smithson, Louise Weir, Charlotte Metcalf, Geri Hosier and Fiona Webster. To Jane Morgan, Lorelei Loveridge, Alli Campbell, Lakshmi Hewavisenti, Mel Sherratt, Helen Say, James Comer, Rhian Prescott, Jeff Taylor, Bex Davies, Tim Read, Nikki Read and Dee Currid for your help in various ways. To Jackie Parker and Lisa Parsons for undertaking the essential job of vetting the manuscript, and my other friends from university who have shown such understanding and good humour about this novel, and who have supported me for so many years in so many ways. To my husband and son and the rest of my family, and to Connie Bennet, you all know why. To my followers on Twitter, Facebook and Goodreads who have not been otherwise mentioned. And finally to everyone who has read my books and enjoyed them, and who has even written something nice about them, thank you so much.

Book Group Reading Notes

1. What do you think are the key themes in *A Serpentine Affair*?
2. If you had been part of the group leaving after the picnic and you heard the splash, what would you have done?
3. In what ways does the book explore the bonds of friendship?
4. Why do you think the author chose Siobhan as the character to die?
5. Did you enjoy the way the novel switched between the present day and the past? What do you think this structure brought to your experience of the novel?
6. Why do you think the author chose not to give Stephen his comeuppance despite all the bad things he had done?
7. Why did JoAnne keep the true identity of the man who raped her secret for so long? And why did she reveal it at the picnic?
8. Which of the characters (if any) did you empathise with?
9. What role do you think mothers played in the story?
10. What do you think all the main characters had in common, if anything?

11. What significance do you think honesty and deceit had in the relationships in the novel? How did they shape events?

12. Who deserved a happy ending? Did the author get this right?

ONE STEP TOO FAR

by Tina Seskis

An apparently happy marriage. A beautiful son. A lovely home. So what makes identical twin Emily Coleman get up one morning and walk right out of her life to start all over again? How will she survive, and what is the date that looms, threatening to force her to confront her past? No-one has ever guessed her secret. Will you?

ON SALE NOW

COLLISION

by Tina Seskis

A page-turning mystery featuring some of the characters from both *One Step Too Far* and *A Serpentine Affair*.

Worlds collide with alarming consequences, unleashing a torrent of unexpected events in the final instalment of this unconventional trilogy.

"Tina Seskis is proving herself to be master of the twist."
Grazia

Due for release in 2014

Sign up at

tinaseskis.com

to be the first to know the publication date (amongst other things).

Enjoy Tina Seskis's books?
Be sure to leave a review online – thanks.